FOR EVER SERIES BOOK 3

STAYING for EVER

C. M. WYLIE

Dub Press

www.cmwyllie.com

ISBN: 978-1-959583-11-0 (paperback)

ISBN: 978-1-959583-12-7 (ebook)

Playlist

1. Burn It Down, Parker McCollum

2. How Not To, Dan + Shay

3. Beg For Your Love, Kelsea Ballerini

4. Make You Miss Me, Sam Hunt

5. Bad Memory, Nate Smith

6. Dreams, Fleetwood Mac

7. Cut Me Up, Kelsea Ballerini

8. bad guy, Billie Eilish & Justin Bieber

9. One Number Away, Luke Combs

10. Not Good At Not, Morgan Wallen

11. Back To December, Dan + Shay

Contents

Content Warning

This book is meant for mature audiences and contains content that may be triggering for some readers—including sex, alcohol, drugs, profanity, violence, bullying, verbal and physical abuse, domestic and dating violence, pregnancy, pregnancy loss, and references to suicide.

If you or someone you know is contemplating suicide, please call or text the National Suicide Prevention Lifeline at 988 or go online to www.988lifeline.org.

If you're the victim of domestic or dating violence, please reach out to the National Domestic Violence Hotline at 1-800 799-SAFE (7233) or go online to www.thehotline.org.

For those who chose love when it was easier to walk away.
The ones who built family from broken pieces.
For the ones who stayed.

Family isn't always blood. It's the people in your life who want you in theirs; the ones who accept you for who you are. The ones who would do anything to see you smile and who love you no matter what.

~ Dez Del Rio

Staying For Ever

Prologue

EVERLY

"Get the fuck out of here, Everly. You don't belong here." His grip on my biceps cuts off circulation. His face is so close I can see the dark indigo ring around his irises. With a slight shake, he turns, shoves me backwards and releases me.

I stumble back to get my footing and try to reconcile the person before me with the one I think I know. I don't know him. Every line of his face is as familiar as my own, but I don't recognize the man in front of me or the rage oozing off him.

Before I can utter a word, he growls, "Leave. Before I throw you out." His fury scorches, like standing too close to a fire.

I take an involuntary step backwards, the door handle pressing into my spine.

"Don't make me, Everly. I swear I'll do it."

I reach for the handle and unlatch the door without turning around. I track him as I ease it open enough to slip through, my eyes bouncing between his. If I turn my back, I fear he'll pounce—like a wild animal stalking its prey.

As soon as I'm through the door, he slams it shut, rattling it on its hinges. I stare at the woodgrain patterns for a beat, maybe two, willing my brain to kick in, to think, to figure out how to stop him before it's too late. A shot, then a crash from the other side of the door pierces the momentary quiet. *Think, Everly.* I can't think. *Julian!* My knees threaten to buckle.

I reach into my back pocket for my phone and pull up the number I've had *just in case.* I've never used it and wasn't sure I'd ever want to. I tap call. It rings once, twice. On the third ring I hear the voice I remember so well—too well now.

"Hey, Everly."

"I didn't know who else to call."

"What happened?"

"They . . . He . . . I can't stop him."

"Send me your location. I'm on my way."

Chapter 1

Everly

One Month Earlier

"Everly?"

The voice sends adrenaline pulsing through my veins, an electrical shock to every nerve ending. So much for my leisurely stroll through Pepperdine's library before I catch my flight back to Blue Lake. Turning, my hand frozen on the door handle, I fake a smile at a face I haven't seen in months. That she's here in Malibu, on this campus, is strange and frankly unbelievable.

"Taya. Hi. What are you doing here?" I force the smile to stay as I ask. But she asks the same thing at the same time, so my nervous laugh is real.

"What are you doing here?" Laughing, she answers, "I go here. Law school."

"Ah, I didn't know." I nod, still smiling. My face is plastic.

"No, why would you?" Her smile is kind, friendly. "My parents went here, my dad's dad. Not sure I had a choice." Her self-deprecating laugh makes me try harder.

I laugh nervously again, annoyingly. "I, uh, had some content filming here in Malibu and decided to spend my last couple hours here in the library before I fly home. It's my favorite place on campus and why I wanted to come here." She didn't ask, but I'm trying to make conversation. "Ashley—his studio is close by. I motion in the general direction of his house, but I realize too late she may not even know who Ashley is.

"Right. I remember Jay—Julian saying that. How . . . how is he? And you? The business?"

"Great. All good." She's nodding at my answer. *Could this conversation be more awkward?*

"Well, I won't keep you. Good seeing you, Everly. Tell J—Julian hi for me."

"Of course. Take care, Taya. Uh, good luck with . . . law school." *Painful!* That whole exchange was painful. Just as I pull the door open to walk inside, a male voice calls her name. An angry male voice. I'm already through the doors, so I let it close behind me but turn to peer through the reflective privacy glass, knowing I can't be seen.

"What the fuck, Taya? You ghosting me?" The voice fades as the door swings closed. The *voice* belongs to a half frat/half surfer looking guy, tall lumbering build, broad shoulders and sun-streaked tousled hair like he just strolled in from catching a wave. At first glance he gives laid-back, but the way he grabs her bicep and yanks her against him, blonde brows pinched together, prickles the back of my neck. I reach for the door, ready to push through it and intervene. Before I can, Taya shoves him with both hands on his chest, which doesn't budge him an inch.

Whatever she's hissing in his face, I can't hear. It pisses him off further though, because he grabs her other arm and yanks her chest to his and pushes his face into hers, noses touching, and speaks through clenched teeth.

I don't wait or think twice. I burst through the doors. "Hey, Taya," I call jovially and force the plastic smile back into place. That there are no other students around pulling out phones to video is frankly unbelievable and lucky for this frat clown. My head swivels anyway, looking for it, expecting it. Convinced there's no one, I turn my forced cheer on her. "Great, you're here. The study group is waiting. We're the last ones. You ready?" I lean on the door like I'm holding it open for her.

The guy glances at me, drops his hands, then zeros back in on her.

Without looking my way, she arches one brow at him and answers, "Yep. Coming." Shoving off him, she purposely knocks shoulders with him on her way inside. Before she steps over the threshold, she stops, turns and calls out, "Hey, Brody?"

He hasn't moved but clamps his lips together, jaw popping in answer.

"Don't ever fucking call me again. In other words, fuck all the way off." She doesn't wait for a response and stalks inside, hooking her arm in mine and dragging me with her. Once we're through the vestibule, she turns to me. "Thanks, Everly."

"Sure. What the fuck *was* that?"

"Just some rando who thinks he has a claim on me because we hooked up. *Men!*" She huffs and rolls her eyes. That's the only explanation I get. I have more questions, but it's not my place, so I nod instead like I understand perfectly. "Don't tell Jay." That she forgets to use his chosen name, Julian, tells me she's more shaken than she's showing. Since she reappeared *from the dead* she's been trying, out of respect for him or me or both, not to call him Jay, the nickname she gave him when they were kids—teenagers.

"Okay. But if you need help with that douche of a frat boy, I'm sure he'd have no issue with that."

"Oh, Brody isn't a frat boy, or even a student. Just some local surfer on a power trip. He's nobody."

I nod again. "Okay. Will you be okay? I'm kinda ruined for browsing now. Think I'll just head to the airport early."

"Sorry about that."

"No, it's all good. Probably best if I don't dwell too long anyway. Makes me miss what could've been. But it's all good. Remote learning is convenient." I trail off because I realize I'm oversharing with Taya, the ex. We're not friends. Although I do sense in another life we might've been. She acknowledges my comment with a sad smile I don't want to analyze.

"That's two *all goods* in one breath, but I get it."

That she doesn't push makes me like her a little more. And she does get it—what could've been—on a whole other level. After her dad lied to her and Julian, it altered everything.

Then she adds, "Hey, I'll be home for the Lanterns and Lights Festival. Maybe we can . . . Maybe I can help with the setup and stuff."

"Sure, I'll tell Julian. Take care, Taya." I realize I mean it literally. That encounter spiraled my nervous system. I push through the doors again and pull out my phone to text Sean, Ashley's driver, to pick me up sooner than planned. I just want to be inside the car where I can breathe. I look around before I focus on the screen. No blonde unhinged surfer in sight. I hurriedly tap out the message, stuff my phone in the side pocket of my leggings and head toward the guard shack to save Sean a trip up to the library, the fresh salty air helping me breathe. *What the fuck was that?* My phone vibrates at my hip. I slip it back out and see Julian's face filling the screen and slide my finger to answer his FaceTime.

"Hey, pretty girl. How's the library?" As he asks, his brows pinch together when he takes in my outdoor background. "No library?"

"I changed my mind." I decide on the spot not to tell him about Taya and feral Brody until I get home. Does he know she goes here? I know he's checked in on her a few times in the last month or so since she reappeared in his life. He never gives me any reason to feel jealous or doubt his love for me, so I know he's just looking out for her. Honestly, it makes me love him more. His heart is so kind, despite his shitty upbringing. He stays quiet, waiting for me to elaborate. "I'm just anxious to get home. Maybe the pilot can take off earlier if I show up sooner."

"Okay, love. Everything good? Filming go well?"

"Totally. All good. Promise." I ignore my third *all good* and smile into that gorgeous face, those penetrating blue eyes, and wonder for the millionth time how I got so lucky. This beautiful man never fails to make me feel like his world begins and ends with me. Fuck, I love him so much. "Love you, Julie."

"Me too. Miss you, sweet girl. See you soon."

"Kay, bye." Before I tap the end button, I shamelessly blow a kiss to the screen for which I'm rewarded with the little wink that always flips my stomach. My nervous system gives a giant exhale as I reach the guard shack and see Sean approaching. Couple more hours and I'll be kissing my gorgeous man for real. As if he's getting my ESP, my phone vibrates with an incoming text.

Julian: Sleepover at my place tonight? I'm cooking.

Me: Depends. What's on the menu?

I add the wink emoji so he knows I'm teasing.

Julian: Plot twist?

He adds the smiling devil emoji to his response.

Me: Sold.

I shove my phone into my leggings as Sean opens the back door of the Escalade for me.

Chapter 2

Julian

Christmas in California sometimes borders on ridiculous—parts of it anyway. With temperatures only dipping into the upper sixties, it doesn't exactly scream hot cocoa and toasty fires. Still, we bring our own flavor of holiday spirit to Blue Lake, and I've come to love it over the years—well, most of it. Cavern County Christmas is one of my favorite events of the year. Especially the Lanterns and Lights Festival Allie started at Brew that ends with the Blue Lake bonfire. Maybe because it isn't holiday specific and lasts for days. It allows people from all different beliefs and places to come together and celebrate or let go of the past year and welcome the new one.

If you love the commercial side of Christmas, the lights and carnival are perfect. If it's more spiritual for you, the lanterns are a cool tradition for manifesting what you want in the new year, and lastly, there's the bonfire to burn things you want to leave behind. Something for everyone. My least favorite part is probably the cheesy carnival that comes to town on the first day. The rickety rides and shitty food draw the county in droves. Still, I like tradition and seeing everyone in Cavern County come together. For me, it's more about where the carnival sets up in the empty lot next to the Little League fields between here and South Point. Because right next to the clay pits is the shitty trailer park I grew up in, that my equally shitty parents probably still live in. I've never checked or looked them up in any way since I left, except for occasionally perusing the public arrest records and obituary reports to see if either of them is on it, as morbid as that sounds.

That I feel like an integral part of the Cavern County celebrations at all is weird and fulfilling after the life of obscurity I lived in Southy, where I purposely avoided getting involved in anything. The whole event brings people from every town in the county. Brew only started hosting the Lantern and Lights Festival a couple years before I showed up. That's all Allie. I know she has things she doesn't talk about that make her sad, and I think that founding the festival was her way to channel it and help others deal with their grief, too. Ever the helper, leave it to Allie to build something beautiful like that for Blue Lake.

Grief has a funny way of keeping you in a chokehold under the surface though. On the outside you can do all the things—work, play, enjoy life—but underneath, you see the loved one in every single moment. The things they're missing. The things they'll never do. Sometimes it's like a program that runs silently in the background. And sometimes, it takes center stage and cripples you for anything remotely resembling functioning.

For three years, that was my life. I lived in the reality that my high school girlfriend died by suicide. And two months ago she showed up at Brew very much alive. Both of us lied to by her now deceased diabolical and tyrannical father in some misplaced protective act to keep us apart. The huge mental adjustment her existence requires cannot be overstated. The absolute mindfuck is something I'm still reeling from. When the sorrow creeps in, it's immediately followed by the euphoria that she's alive. Then the anger that we were lied to and believed that horror for three years. *She* believed I'd abandoned her, that I'd been scared off by her father and incentivized by a hefty payoff to stay gone. That's another level of anger—for both of us. Then, I rally mine, tuck it away, and find my gratefulness that she's still here and that he's *not*. That I don't have to live in a world with him in it goes a long way to dialing down my rage at the injustice of it all.

"To borrow your line, what's going on in there?" Ever settles onto my lap as the last strip of sunlight fades into the inky glass surface of Blue Lake. "I freaked you out about the Taya stuff, didn't I?"

Wrapping my arms around her and pressing my nose to the spot behind her ear that I love, I kiss her lightly and inhale. "Nooo. No. I promise." I smile into her overcast eyes and peck the tip of her pixie nose. "I do worry though how she's handling it—the new reality of what her father did in the name of fatherly love and his sudden death and that she is essentially the last of her family and alone." My eyes bounce between hers, gauging how my brain dump is registering. I want to be honest with her. She deserves that. I do wonder how Taya's doing and if I should reach out. We care about each other, but we're not friends or in each other's lives. Part of me wants that though. The rescuer in me, I guess. But she's my ex and how does that track with my present relationship? It's all so fucking weird—for all of us. "Maybe I need to reach out." I step back to lock eyes with her, shrug my shoulders, palms out low.

Ever mimics my shrug and nods twice.

"I do worry that she's alone. Not that her dad was a stellar example of a human being, but he was her last living relative that I know of."

Placing her palm on my cheek, one corner of her mouth lifts in a sad smile. God, my girl is sweet. Proving it, she says, "She said to tell you she'd be home for the festival and would help if we want. If you're looking for a reason to reach out. And considering you used the word *worry* twice in two sentences, maybe you should." Ever rustles the hair on the top of my head, then scrapes her fingers deliciously along the back of my scalp as she swipes her thumb along my cheek.

Tipping my forehead to hers, I ask, "How'd I get such a good girlfriend?"

"Just lucky, I guess."

"Yeah, sassy girl, I am." I press my lips to hers.

"So call her, text her. Whatever. I'm gonna dip in the hot tub. Join me when you're done." She kisses me again and scoots off my lap, then rustles the longer hair on top of my head again as she leaves.

In some ways, Ever is an old soul, showing a grounded maturity beyond her years. Sometimes, her inexperience with relationships shows in her reactions to things that feel threatening or uncertain. That she is handling the Taya thing so well blows me away and makes me love her even more—if that's possible. I haven't even explained the extent to which this whole development fucks with my head, but somehow I think she knows. Both of us shy away from the hard talks if we can. We're not exactly afraid to have them. We just like to keep things light and happy as often as possible. Like now.

Before I get too far down my rabbit hole, my phone vibrates on the side table next to me.

Ever: Stop overthinking and text her

Me: ok ☺

Before I type Taya's name into my phone and bring up the text screen, I rub the spot on my chest where Ever's name is now permanently written, in her handwriting, my lips curving up.

Me: Hey, Tay. Ever said you're coming home for the holidays. What dates? We'd love your help and input on the festival.

The three dots pop up immediately, which makes my heart thud a little harder and quicker. I notice too late that I referred to Ever as *Ever* to Taya. I only use that nickname for her ears alone, but I don't want to draw more attention to it by correcting myself.

Taya: I'm on break for almost four weeks. I'll be home the whole time. Gotta make some decisions about the property in Southy. Then I'm all yours. Lmk how I can help.

Me: Cool. It'll be so great to see you. ☺

Taya: ☺

I hate the way my heart is racing for another woman. I can't help that it is, but somehow it feels disrespectful to Ever. There isn't anyone that could be what Ever is to me—never. Maybe that I'm even concerned about it is proof that my heart is in the right place.

I take some deep breaths.

I want to ask her about the douchebag Ever said she called Brody, but I'm not sure it's any of my business. I just want to make sure she knows she has someone she can turn to if she needs it. Again, her being back from the dead is fucking with me. I care about her. I feel protective and somewhat territorial over her. Not like I care for Everly, obviously. Not even close. Still, the thought of some asshole putting his hands on her in any aggressive way makes me see red. But that would very likely be true for any woman being mistreated by a man.

My dad was that kind of man my whole life, but my mom gave as good as she got. At first, I admired how she stuck up for herself, but as I got older, I realized she was part of the problem. He just overpowered her so it was hard to see her as more than a victim. The reality is they abused each other. I don't think their addictions left room for anything else. The alcohol and drugs fed their drama and violence and made perfect sense to them in the moment. The few times I tried to intervene on her behalf turned them both on me and forged their alliance. She'd always come around later making excuses, trying to be motherly.

Fuck! An involuntary shiver rattles my body and snaps me out of the reverie. The darkness surrounds me now that the sun is gone. I stand and stretch, reaching for the twilight. Rolling my neck, I move to the sliders to join Ever and shake off the dark mental turn. She grounds me and calms me. Of course it doesn't take long for everything to turn physical for us. After nine months—*God, it's only been nine months and I can't imagine my life without her*—we still crave each other like it's the first time. To make my point, my body reacts, blood rushing to my groin, my heart rate doubling. I slide the door open intending to find her. Just inside the master bedroom, our room, I hear the shower running. *Damn, missed it!*

"Hey, sorry I missed the hot tub." I peek my head through the open bathroom door. "Can I join you?"

Sluicing water off her hair, she turns her almost opaque eyes on me and smiles. She's gorgeous any day, but Ever dripping wet in the shower is something I'll never get tired of seeing. Long, toned limbs, slender but muscular build now that she's a gym rat and trainer, too. She nods and slides the door open in invitation.

I drop my clothes where I stand and step into the warm spray.

"I was just about done, but I can wash your back." Her ashy eyes turn smoky as she reaches for me.

"You don't have to wait for me. I can be fast."

"Oh, but I like it when you take your time."

"Are we still talking about the shower?"

Her answer is a shrug as she places one dripping foot on the mat and disappears in the steam.

I rush through lathering and am drying off within minutes, my mind already on all the ways I want to make her come. Wrapping the towel around my hips, I step into the bedroom.

Ever stands at the foot of the bed facing the bathroom door. Her hair is twisted into a wet knot on top of her head. A cropped tank covers her breasts and a pair of barely-there cotton shorts hang low on her hips, just skimming the top of her thighs.

When my eyes finally lock on hers, she settles her hands on her hips, her long fingers curving around them like mine are itching to do. I swallow and take the three steps to her. I reach out, intending to pick her up and wrap her body around mine, when she drops to her knees on the fluffy rug and hooks her fingers into the towel and pulls. Never taking her eyes off mine, she takes me in her hand and sinks her lips around me, just the tip, and swirls her tongue, her eyes fluttering closed.

I'm not sure anything has ever looked so hot. I tug on the hair tie coiled in her tawny strands, like I want my hands to be. It doesn't come loose with my efforts. Groaning, I command, "Ugh, Ever, lose the hair tie."

She doesn't stop the suction of her lips on the head of my dick as she reaches up and sets her hair free.

My hands tangle in the wet locks.

Hers wrap around my ass and pull my length into her mouth completely.

"Ugh, fuck," I hiss through my teeth, my head falling back.

She pulls back almost all the way, her cheeks hollowing with the suction, then takes me all the way in again, the tip touching the back of her throat.

My fingers clench in her locks and press her face into my body. My God, nothing has ever felt so good, except maybe sinking into her sweet, tight walls. My chest is heaving at the pace she's set, in, out, so deep. Wrapping her hair around my fist, I pull her back. "Ever, if you don't stop, I'm going to—"

Her moan halts my words. "Mmm-hmm." Her nails grip my ass and pull me to her harder. Increasing her tempo, her lips pucker as they slide up and down my shaft.

I'm yanking her hair, probably painfully, but I can't help myself. I'm trying to stay on my feet as blood throbs in my dick, begging for release.

One tear leaks from the corner of her eye and still she takes all of me. Another on the other side and yet she savors every thrust.

Fuck, she's beautiful.

"Fuck, Ever. Ugh, baby. I'm . . ." Pressing my palm to the back of her neck, I hold her to me as I convulse with an orgasm I feel in my toes.

Her fingernails soften on my ass, and she slides her palms over my skin until she's hugging me. I feel the contractions of her throat as she swallows.

My hand slides up from her neck to caress her head, hugging her to me as well. Empty now, I reach for her, hook my hands under her arms and pull her up to stand in front of me. Her eyes are downcast, her long dark lashes resting on her cheeks. After what she just did, I wonder if this shyness is affected. How can she feel shy after she just owned me completely? I'm an absolute puddle in her hands. She fucking wrecks me.

Bringing her chin up with my index finger, I brush my thumb back and forth across her cheek. "Hi, pretty girl." I swipe the dampness away.

"Hi, boyfriend."

When she tries to drop her gaze again, I bring her lips to mine. Her kiss is shyer than her eyes.

"My turn?" I can't see her blush in the muted room, but I know her smiles—every one of them. And the one she gives me just now is her shy smile and usually accompanies a faint, pretty flush. Hooking my hands under her hips, I lift her. Her legs curl around me as I take the remaining steps to the bed and lay her down, settling myself between her thighs.

Her breath hitches in anticipation.

I keep her waiting because I like watching her ache for me. She doesn't hide her thirst. I see all of her when we're like this and I fucking love it. Crave it like a drug. Her nipples strain against the thin fabric. I graze one with my fingertip.

Her back arches, begging for more, her hips pressing up into me. Her fingers curl around my biceps, pulling on them to give her what she wants.

"I know, sweet girl, you want my hands on you, don't you?"

She nods, panting now. Her hands fall off my arms to slap silently on the bed, pulling a low chuckle from my throat.

I dip my head and nip the jutting bud through the thin fabric. She shoves the fabric up impatiently, exposing her breasts. I suck one gently into my mouth, then the other while she digs her nails into the faded hair at my nape, holding my face to her chest.

"Ugh, yes, Julie. More."

Bringing my lips to her ear, I whisper, "I got you, Ever," then capture her lips and tangle my tongue with hers. Pulsing in and out of her mouth like I want to do with my fingers, with my dick. I'm shaking with my desire to sink into her, but I make us both wait. I want her begging for me, and I'm willing to suffer to get it. Coming up for air, I pull back from her lips and demand, "Tell me what you want."

"I want you to fuck me, Julie, now."

"I know. Not yet. I want you dripping for me first."

"I am. Please, Julie." She grinds her hips into mine, lifting them off the bed.

"Please, what, Ever? What do you want?"

"I wanna come. Make me come."

Before she can finish the sentence, I drive my fingers into her heat. Those little shorts giving me easy access. And she *is* already dripping for me. "Fuck, you're so wet. So good."

Her walls are already clenching around my fingers.

It won't take much to make her come, but I want to taste her first. I pull my fingers out, causing a whimper from my needy girl. When I begin moving down her body, she wraps her hands around my head and pushes me, knowing what she's about to get. Then she remembers the barrier of the shorts and shoves the waistband over her hips and down her legs. I slide them the rest of the way off and sink my face into the vee of her thighs, which part invitingly.

Swiping my tongue up along her opening, I flick over the swollen bud before pursing my lips around it and sucking it into my mouth. The long moan from deep in her throat makes my dick twitch, my hips pressing into the mattress for the friction. I want to bottom out inside her but settle for sinking my fingers all the way in and circling them as I swirl my tongue over her clit.

She's pulling the longer hair on top of my head, her nails raking my scalp. First she's pulling me to her, then trying to yank me away, her thighs pressing in on my ears, quivering. She can't take it, but I make her take it.

"Uh-uh, I can't. Fuck, Julie." Her head swivels from side to side, her eyes squinted shut.

With a sucking kiss on her bundle of nerves, I lift my head and still my fingers.

Slowly her leg muscles relax, her thighs go lax and her hips settle back into the mattress. Her eyelids flutter open, her storm-cloud orbs lock on mine.

My lazy smile contradicts the fire inside me. "Want me to stop?"

"Uh-uh," she repeats. "You know I don't."

Her fingers clench the comforter as I move my fingers in and out, crooking one in just the right way, pressing my thumb down, making tiny circles around her hard bud.

Her back arches, her head tilts back, chin aimed at the ceiling. "Ungh, like that."

"Yeah? You like that, Ever? You gonna come for me?" I press my lips to the tender skin of her inner thigh.

"Mmm-hmm. Don't stop. Yesssss." Her walls contract around my fingers.

I could slow my movements to ease the intensity, but I don't. Her panting turns to sobs, but still I don't stop. When the pulsing of her orgasm slows, so do I. Climbing up her body, I kiss her lips first, then her damp cheeks, then my favorite spot behind her ear until I slowly withdraw my fingers from her tight, slippery walls, stirring a whimpering moan from her.

"Uh-uh."

"Shh, I got you. We're not done." I roll onto my side, feathering my fingers up and down her flat belly.

She rolls toward me, grabbing a fistful of my hair and dragging my lips to hers.

My insatiable beauty is demanding and I'm fucking here for it. Pulling my head sideways to deepen the kiss, she bites down on my bottom lip. I smile, making her bite down a little harder. If my girl ever figures out how to tease me like I tease her, I'm in trouble, but for now, it's exclusively my sweet torture for us both. That I'm mostly in control is only marginally less agonizing for me. I'm as hot and bothered as she is, just a little less frantic about it. That she's so keyed up only incites me more. I pinch her nipple between my thumb and finger, rolling it, puckering it even more.

Her exhale is a pant against my lips. "Don't make me wait, Julie. Don't make me beg."

"What if I want you to beg? Beg me to fuck you, Ever."

Pushing against my shoulders with surprising strength, Ever rolls on top of me as my back flattens against the bed. Taking me in her hand, she guides me to her dripping center and drops her weight down, sinking onto me completely, her mouth forming a perfect little O on a gasp.

I hiss through clenched teeth on a sharp inhale as my hips rise to meet her. Clutching her hips, I pull her forward in a rocking motion as I exhale. "Ughhhh, Ever. So fucking good."

"You like that, Julie?" Her eyes bore into mine as she rises up on her knees and drives back down, rocking as she does. She doesn't need my guidance. She's setting the pace and taking us both higher with each plunge. "Tell me you like it."

"I do," I pant, digging into her soft skin so hard I fear I'll leave marks. I loosen my grip but pull her ass into me with the flat of my palms. "Ugh, you know I do." My words are met with a little giggle bubbling in her throat. "Fuck me, Ever. Make me come, baby. Fuck, so sexy. I love you. So. Much." I'm seconds away from coming, but I want her to come first. I hold her hips down to stop her driving rhythm. My eyes that were squeezed shut find hers.

They're almost charcoal and watch me under thick black lashes. Her lips curve in a half smile as she waits, throbbing around me, to see what I'll do next. She knows me too well. She knows I'm not coming before her. I reach between us and begin slow circles just above where our bodies are joined. Feeling that connection with each swipe only heightens my need to press into her for my release. I'm quaking with my restraint.

"It's okay, Julie. Just come for me. I can feel how much you want to."

My dick twitches in response.

Her thumb drags across my bottom lip before she grips my cheeks and brings her lips to the pulse in my neck, biting and sucking, daring me to let go.

"You first," I pant. That sexy fucking giggle again. Maybe my girl is mastering the teasing game after all.

Swirling her hips and pressing into my thumb, she whispers, "We'll see."

I'm about to fall off the edge without her. With every ounce of will I possess, I lift her off me with a deep groan and toss her onto the mattress on her back. Pushing her knees up and her thighs wide, I slide into her as deep as possible. I pull all the way out and wait till her closed eyes open and find mine. Then I sink again, roughly, bowing her back. A couple more times and I'll be done. I need her to come for me.

I pull out, and it costs me.

Dropping my forehead on hers, I attempt to catch my breath. She's writhing under me. I take her breast in my hand and guide her nipple to my mouth. Sucking hard, I drive my fingers into her and tease her clit with my thumb. Grinding my dick into her thigh, I silently beg her to come again. As soon as I bend my finger, connecting with my thumb on the outside, and apply just the right amount of swirling pressure, she erupts. Her tight, silky skin pulsating around my fingers.

I don't wait. I remove my hand and drive into her mid orgasm and empty myself in two thrusts with an orgasm I feel in my fucking soul.

Collapsing, I roll with her onto my side, still joined. Our hands are roaming all over each other. I'm kissing her damp cheeks, her neck, tangling my fingers in her still-wet hair. Our panting slowly subsides and still we're joined, her leg draped over mine. My nose nuzzles the soft shell of her ear as I whisper, "I love you, beautiful girl, my girl."

"I love you, beautiful boy." Her words are heavy. "So much," she adds, but it's garbled. She's sleepy, spent, and almost nothing feels better.

The rise and fall of her chest against mine lulls me, too. The last thing I remember is her fingers scraping lazily along the faded hair at my nape. *Fuck, I love her.*

Chapter 3

EVERLY

Waking up alone is nothing new. Julian always rises before me and usually falls asleep after me. I'm not sure how he does it, because he doesn't drag or act tired—ever. Blinking against the daylight streaming through the wall of windows and slider, I see him leaning against the doorframe of the sliding glass, back to me. His silhouette highlighted by the morning sun *is* new. His muscled frame is outlined in sparkling detail, like a pop culture vampire. I watch silently, slowly blinking the sleep out of my eyes as he brings a steaming mug of coffee to his lips and sips, his bicep bulging against the white cotton fabric of his shirt. He's barefoot, one leg crossed over the other, the low-slung gray sweats cling to his chiseled legs. He looks snuggly but somber.

"Morning, pretty girl."

My stomach somersaults at the sound of his voice, and my eyes fly back up to his profile. He doesn't turn when he greets me, and I hadn't moved yet except for opening my eyes. That he knows or senses me awake makes my heart thud and my lower region throb. "Morning, beautiful boy." My voice is scratchy, so I clear it before I add, "Why so sad this early in the day?"

He faces me, his lips rolled inward on a tight smile that doesn't reach his eyes. His usually vivid blue eyes are a muted denim as they roam over my features. "How do you read me so well?"

"How do you sense I'm awake without turning around?"

"Fair." He walks to the edge of the bed and sits down, placing his coffee on the nightstand. "Come kiss me, sassy girl."

"Morning breath," I reply, placing my fingertips over my lips before he can lean in.

"Coffee breath, so we're even." He leans in and takes my fingers in his before placing a soft kiss on my lips. "Speaking of . . . Want me to get you some?"

"Sure, but are you gonna tell me what's going on up there? To steal your line."

"Yeah, but first coffee, to steal yours." He tucks a strand of hair behind my ear as he stands to go get me a mug.

"I guess it's true what they say that couples start to sound alike."

"I thought it was look alike," he calls as he walks out and down the stairs.

"God, I hope not," I call back. "I'm not sure I could rock a fade and morning scruff like you can."

The rumble of his baritone laugh floats up the stairs.

I throw the covers off, stretch and shuffle to the bathroom to brush my teeth, wash my face and throw on some sweats. That I get to start my day with Julian and coffee is making me giddy. Then I remember my man is bothered and the logical reason would be a green-eyed girl back from the dead. I sigh at the reflection in the mirror as I twist my feral air-dried waves into a messy bun. Navigating the Taya situation is going to be weird. He'll want to help her, be there for her. It's what I love most about Julian. His heart for others. His protective instincts. I know how much he loves me. He shows me every chance he gets. Every girl should be so lucky. I have nothing to worry about. So why does my nervous system think I'm about to drop into the free fall on a roller coaster?

Stop, Everly. But first, coffee, I mentally chant.

Julian's voice travels up the stairs. He's on the phone.

There goes coffee. As if on cue, I hear the whirr of my phone vibrating on the nightstand. Flopping across the bed on my stomach, I snag my phone and swipe when I see Lilly's face on the screen. "Friend! Miss your face," I shriek.

"Well, you're about to see a lot more of it. We're coming home for winter break, like tomorrow."

"Yee-aah," I screech. My excitement is short lived.

"Yeah, but uh, Seth is coming with us. He can't get home to Hawaii, so he's coming with us so he's not alone for the holidays." She pauses like she's waiting for me to say something. When I don't, she adds, "It's all good, right?"

"Oh, totally." *It's not.* How did the whole holiday season just become a shit show of past trauma, gray areas and bullshit? My conscience revisits coming clean with Julian about my drunken kiss with Seth. How did I become Ross Gellar? I've always been on Rachel's side of *we were on a break.* Now I'd like to invoke Ross's argument to free myself of my guilt. *Fuck my life.*

"And like our houses are full, so can we stay at the apartment?"

Julian's frame fills the doorway. Schooling my features, I look up and arch a brow in question. He nods immediately and puts his hands together like a prayer, his smile taking over his whole face. *God, I love him.* I shove the Seth kiss and my guilt down and focus on the here and now.

"Are you kidding? Julian would love to have me stay here." Setting the coffee mugs down on the nightstand, he snakes his body across the bed next to me and rests his cheek on my lower back, his hand grazing up and down the back of my thigh.

"Oh, hey, J Mac." Lilly greets him now that he's in the FaceTime frame. "Thanks for putting up with Ev so we can use the apartment. Our little sisters wasted no time taking over our rooms at home."

Propping his chin on his hands, eyes dancing, he replies, "I mean, if I have to."

"We're bringing our Hawaiian friend who can't get home for break. Cool?"

"Of course. The more the merrier. Right, babe?" He tilts his head toward me as he asks, his cheek on his folded hands.

My stomach flops. His eyes are crystal blue, perfectly framed by thick dark lashes and smiling at the corners—for me. My beautiful man. I'd agree to anything he wants.

"Of course. Can't wait to see you, Lill."

"Same. Okay, love birds, gotta jet and get my shit together. And Noah's. And Seth's." She rolls her eyes, laughing. "See you tomorrow."

"Bye," I call out as Julian curls his fingers at the screen.

As soon as I disconnect the call, Julian sits up, straddling my back, and begins massaging my shoulders, neck and biceps. It feels so good, I moan, my eyes rolling closed.

"Talk to me," I say before I get distracted by his hands.

He drops a quick kiss on my cheek and rolls off me, reaching for our coffee mugs.

I sit up, crisscrossing my legs under me, and take one from him. When he mirrors my posture, I smile to myself at how flexible this tower of a man is. Facing me, he takes a sip of his coffee. I do, too, and wait, watching him over the rim like he's watching me. Stretching his arm past me, he sets his down again on the nightstand, settles himself again and flattens his palms on my thighs, skimming up and down in short strokes.

"Spit it out, Julie. Who was on the phone? Taya? Did you call her?"

"I texted her. Just to check in." When he doesn't elaborate, my eyebrows raise, my lips curl inward. "Then she called me," he adds.

I blink once, my eyes tracking back and forth between his, and silently wait.

"She's coming home for break, too."

I tilt my head and nod, kinda sassy-like because I already know this and it's starting to piss me off a little that he's pussyfooting around whatever it is he needs to tell me.

He exhales and drops his gaze from mine. "She doesn't want to stay at her house."

"Okay." I drag the word out with an unspoken *and* after it.

"I thought I could offer her the apartment and ask you to stay with me. But . . ."

"Lilly and Noah are using it now." I nod as I say it, and he nods along.

"What should we do?"

"Did you already offer her the apartment?"

"No, I suggested it as a possible option and said I'd talk to you about it."

I'm nodding again and starting to feel like a wind-up doll. "And she doesn't want to stay at her house because of all the shit that went down." I say it out loud, but I'm more saying it to myself. I get the triggers of places. I hate everything about Oak Valley now, the town I grew up in—except for my sister, Olivia, and her husband, Ryan. The rest of it could vaporize for all I care. Okay, maybe not Mrs. Franklin. And I guess Chase is okay now. Fuck, enough with the morbid spiral. "What do we do?" I throw the same question back to him.

"I mean we have two spare bedrooms here. But that would be weird. Would that be too weird?"

"Truth? Yeah. Super fucking weird. But also, our lives are . . . kinda weird." I shrug. "Or at least not typical. The way we met, got together, our pasts. Maybe we need to embrace the shit show for the sake of the greater good."

His bark of laughter is my only response before he takes my mug and sets it on the nightstand next to his and sweeps me onto his lap, kissing me. "God, I love you, sassy girl. Like really fucking love you. Sometimes, I think you must be a dream or a figment of my imagination. How'd a girl as perfect as you end up with a guy like me?" He's nuzzling his nose into my neck and the sensitive spot behind my ear now, making me lose my train of thought.

"Okay, okay. Stop distracting me." I swat at his hands that are beginning to roam and push his shoulders back, wrapping my fingers around his nape. Looking into the endless pools of his hooded gaze, I resist the urge to kiss him. "What are we going to do with all these people? What if Allie and Ashley come?"

Taking one of my hands in his, he kisses my palm. "It's going to get crowded, that's what. Fuck it. We'll feed everyone at Brew and it can be our own winter campout."

If I don't think too much about Taya being his ex, I find I'm excited to host and create a space where people can relax and come together. A space I would've run to when I felt untethered. That calms my system and gives me all the feels. "Fuck it. Let's do it." I grin, showing all my teeth. "Tell Taya. I'll head over to the apartment and pack my shit, clean the place up."

"I'm coming with you. I'll help. We'll go to the store and pick up provisions for all our guests afterwards." He stands, pulling me with him and wraps his arms around me. "I'm weirdly excited we're doing this. Thanks for rolling with it."

"I am, too, weirdly." Resting my cheek against his pec, his heartbeat thudding softly against my ear, I admit, "I actually kinda like Taya, what I know about her so far. I low-key hope we can be friends."

His arms squeeze me tighter. "My sweet Ever girl. I fucking love you."

Tilting my head, I kiss the dimple at the corner of his mouth. "I fucking love you, too. Do you think we say that too much?"

Swatting my ass, he replies, "Do you? Wait, ask me if I care. Never mind. My answer is no. To both."

I giggle. *Perfect answer.*

He adds, "Snagging two protein bars from the kitchen." When I groan, he adds, "I'll treat you to a killer lunch before we hit the store."

"Deal." I link my fingers with his and pull him through the bedroom door toward the stairs.

Chapter 4

JULIAN

"**B**abe, the garlic bread is done. Are they almost here?" I call to Ever from the kitchen loud enough so my voice carries up the stairs. Just as I'm pulling the sourdough loaf from the oven, the doorbell chimes. "Never mind," I call out again, before I set the bread on the stovetop and move toward the door and the voices on the other side.

I'm excited to see Noah and Lilly. It's been too long. Pulling open the door, I reach for Lilly first, scooping her into a hug that lifts her feet and spins her around.

"J Mac," she shrieks as she squeezes my neck. "I see you're not skipping workouts. Good man." She pats me on the pec with her palm as I set her down and shake hands with Noah.

"Hey, man. I've missed you." He claps me on the shoulder with his free hand as we shake.

"Same. Damn, you look good. Surfing agrees with you." I squeeze his shoulder for emphasis. Noah's physique has changed since I last saw him at the end of summer. From Lilly and Ever, I know he's been surfing almost every day. He's ripped, shoulders broader, torso deeply V-shaped.

"Thanks, J Mac. I fucking love it. Speaking of surfing, this is Seth."

"Hey, welcome to Blue Lake, Seth. Glad to have you." Just as I take his hand, Lilly squeals and bounces past me.

"Davis!" She and Ever hug and bounce as the three of us chuckle watching them.

"Come in, guys." I motion them in and close the door. "You get settled okay?"

"You bet. The apartment is perfect. What a view. Thanks for letting us crash." Seth claps me on the back as we step into the living room from the entryway.

"Of course. Hope you guys are hungry. Ever . . . ly made her famous chicken alfredo. The ultimate comfort food."

Unanimous confirmations sound at once.

Ever hugs Noah and grips his shoulders, teasing him about bulking up. Her whole body stiffens when she turns to Seth and gives him what can only be described as an awkward half-hug. "Hey, Seth. Glad you could make it."

"Me too. This place is great." He looks around and seems completely at ease.

Maybe it's the stress and busyness of accommodating everyone, but my girl is for sure giving tense vibes, seemingly out of nowhere.

Ever walks ahead of the group into the kitchen, asking over her shoulder, "Everyone having wine? We have beer, too. But the wine goes well with the dish."

"Wine," Lilly and Noah say in sync.

"Me too," Seth agrees.

As Ever reaches into the cabinet for the wine glasses, I come up behind her and reach over her taking a couple down. With my free hand I lightly squeeze her waist and lean in to kiss her neck. "You good, sweet girl?" She nods and reaches behind her to rub her palm on my face, holding it next to hers for a beat.

"I am. Thanks, Julie." She speaks so low that only I hear her. As she turns to set the glasses on the island bar, I cage her in with my body and tuck a strand of hair behind her ear, tracking her eyes. Yep. Twitchy. Her smile flounders. She pecks me on the lips to back me up and moves to the island, fake smile intact. I don't know what to make of it and can't exactly ask in front of everyone. Instead, I pour the wine and offer everyone a glass.

Through dinner, the conversation flows. Noah and Seth love to talk surfing while Lilly and Ever talk school, classes and campus life. I know Ever sometimes misses not going to college in person, which is why I encourage her to visit Pepperdine whenever we're down south. Tonight, though, she only seems excited listening to Lilly's stories. No one can tell a story like Lilly. I find myself torn between both conversations, trying to listen and engage in both and missing chunks of each. After dinner, in the living room, we open more wine and sit around the L-shaped couch.

When the winter festival topic comes up, Noah pipes up, "Seriously, put us to work," and wags his finger between him and Seth. "I freaking love this tradition. I love that Allie started it."

"Me too," Lilly chimes in. "Way better than that shitty carnival they always bring in."

"Aw, you don't like carnivals?" Seth complains. "We don't get those on Molokai. Gotta go to the bigger islands for that. Maybe that's why I like them."

"Don't worry, bruh, we'll make sure you get to the carnival." Noah salutes him with his glass. Now it's my turn to fidget. I'm with Lilly. I hate that frickin' carnival. Okay, not totally true. It's not the carnival I hate. I hate its proximity to the shitty trailer park. The trailer park I really *do* hate. Fuck that place and the people in it. Except Hal if he's even still there. He was older than dirt when I was young. But everyone else, especially the ones in earshot of the violence and bullshit that went on inside my dumpster fire of a house and never spoke up or gave a shit. I look up from my swirling wine glass to see Ever watching me. That we track each other's moods so well is both a comfort and a curse. I don't want her to worry about me. I force a smile I feel in my cheeks and wink at her. She smiles back, but hers is reserved and a little sad.

I speak up, "My favorite is the bonfire, with the lanterns being a close second. And don't worry, we'll have plenty to keep everyone busy. Right, babe?" I include Ever in my comment, hoping to convey to her that I'm good.

She nods enthusiastically as she sips her wine. "Totally," she says as she sets her glass down and refills it.

My girl doesn't usually drink this much, so her refills are pinging my radar. Self-medicating her nerves maybe? But why? Noah and Lilly being the reason doesn't track. Seth? They barely interact because they don't even really know each other. Right? Ever takes a sip of her newly refilled wine and leans back into the cushions, curling her legs under her. Lilly mimics her and turns her body toward her, resting her cheek on Ever's shoulder. Ever leans her head on top of Lilly's, a buzzy, relaxed smile on her face. Maybe she's just enjoying herself and all of us being together. Maybe I'm projecting my swirling thoughts of the past onto her. I take some silent deep breaths and tell myself to relax.

Chapter 5

EVERLY

Taya takes the freshly poured cup of coffee I pass to her over the center island bar of the kitchen. "I'm serious. I really appreciate this. You have no idea how grateful I am."

"No, Taya, it's fine. We're happy to have you." I'm surprised at how much I mean it. "And I get it. I'd be creeped out, too. Especially after the psycho surfer encounter. I mean, that guy's . . . intense." I shake my head with a low laugh and reach for my own steaming mug. Taya and I drinking coffee together at the kitchen bar alone should feel awkward, but what's weird is how it isn't. Julian is meeting with Pete at Brew to finalize a few things for the Lantern and Lights bonfire.

Taya laughs, too, but doesn't elaborate on the guy she called Brody. "I thought it'd be awkward. I almost didn't ask, but it's been amazing. Relaxing." She sips her mug with one foot propped up on her barstool, the other dangling above the floor. "No wonder you're in love with this place. Both of you. I would be, too." She laughs, almost to herself. "Maybe I already am."

"Do you hate South Point like Julian does?" The more I learn about Taya, the more I like her. She's just real and raw—like she doesn't give a shit what anyone thinks. I envy that.

"I mean, there are things I do love. My horses, the open space to ride them. But most of my memories growing up there are tainted with the absolute shit show of my family. Jay and I bonded on that from the jump. Is it weird to say that to you?"

"What? No. At first, I wasn't sure how this would all work. Not gonna lie. But it's all good, Taya. I like that you're comfortable enough around me to just be your true self. Like calling him Jay. That's who he is to you. Seriously, you're good. We're good."

"I can see why he loves you so much. You're pretty fucking chill. I'm not sure I would be in your shoes." Her lips form a half smile, and she shakes her head a little as she stares into her coffee.

"Don't get me wrong. I'm human. This whole thing is taking some psychology level coping because, let's be honest, it's bizarre."

"Understatement," she interjects.

"Right? We've all had to make our mental adjustments, especially you two."

"Again, understatement. I have to keep reminding myself that Jay isn't the asshole who abandoned me and took a payoff from my dad. I hated him for a long time after I left. Angry fucked a lot of guys because of it, too."

When my eyebrows jump up onto my forehead, she holds one hand up and waves it. "I'm not blaming him. Really! Just saying, I hated him for what I thought he did. It takes me a minute to remember he thought I was dead. God, that still feels weird to say."

"I can't imagine. I know it's fucked with his head, too. Still does I think." I go quiet, unable to keep the pensive mood from taking over. The ghost of Taya, though not a ghost anymore, is more prevalent now than when she was "dead." She's perceptive and picks up on my change in demeanor.

"I can go, Ever. If it's too weird."

I track that she calls me Ever. Julian slips so often now and calls me Ever in front of everyone. Sometimes he corrects himself. Other times he doesn't realize he used the term of endearment instead of my full name. Like it's just my name now. Taya seems to think it is, too. She's the first besides him to call me that. I don't mind it though and even love that it's becoming just my name.

"No. Stop. Not after the weird visitor Mitch had yesterday. I don't want you by yourself in that big house, the sprawling property, alone. Julian is even more adamant than I am. Really. We want you here. And I'm glad you told us about it. That's especially weird out here in this area, right? I mean, you all grew up not even locking your doors."

"That must sound crazy to you, growing up in Oak Valley."

I nod, agreeing with her. Oak Valley may feel small, but it's a city with crime and all the things that go along with it. We lock our doors and don't leave keys in our cars there.

"Again, thank you. Mitch said he's going to stay at the house, just to make sure he doesn't come back and that no one else comes around that doesn't belong." She twirls her mug on the coaster as she talks, so I know the topic is triggering her.

"Did he say what the guy wanted?" I trace my finger around the top of my now-empty mug.

"Nope. 'I need to talk to the girl that lives here. The kid of the man that died, Rusty. I'm looking for someone that used to work here.' He said the guy looked strung out. Maybe he's some ranch hand my dad hired. I don't know. Mitch has been with my dad for three years, so if there were another hand in the last three years, Mitch would've known them. He said there was no one else. Just him since I left for school."

"It has nothing to do with stalker surfers, right?" I look up to gauge her reaction. It feels like it might be borderline intrusive, but I can't help that images of that encounter live rent-free in my head. That guy was unhinged, hostile and scary.

Taya laughs, a genuine laugh. "No way. That guy couldn't find his way off the beach long enough to track down my childhood home—even if he knew my full name."

I file her admission away. She hooked up with this guy and he doesn't know her last name. Her comment about *angry fucking* guys floats into the forefront of my brain to join the image.

"Whoever he was, Mitch just told him I didn't live there anymore. That he managed the place now. Asked for the guy's name and number when he became insistent and wouldn't leave. Then he got weirdly secretive and left."

"That shit doesn't freak you out?" My hand freezes its mug rim rotation, and I raise widened eyes to hers.

"I mean, I'm staying here instead of there, so yeah, I guess it does." She laughs again, but it gives more nerves than humor. "It's why I don't want to go to the carnival. Jay and I share that sentiment. Shitty little town, creepy ass carnival."

"Yeah, I could skip it as well. They don't exactly creep me out like they do you, but if Julian is twitchy about it, I'd rather not go."

"But your guy from Molokai wants to go, right?"

"Not my guy, but yeah. He's pretty stoked to check it out. So I guess we're all going. But you can bail out if you want. It's just that Noah and Lilly are our best friends." I shrug with a closed-lip smile.

"It's all good. I'll suck it up. Least I can do since you're putting up with me for winter break." She slides off the barstool and adds, "Speaking of, should we get going? See what last-minute stuff Jay needs for the bonfire?"

"Yep. If we hurry, maybe we can sweet-talk Pete into some breakfast burritos." I take both of our mugs, rinse them and place them in the dishwasher. "Wanna drive to Brew? Or we can jog if you want?"

"Ugh, no, I'll drive. You and Jay are nuts. Running should only happen if you're being chased."

My giggle is genuine. I know most people don't get running. Even Julian doesn't love it, but he joins me sometimes and does it effortlessly—like everything else fitness related.

Chapter 6

JULIAN

As we make our way into Southy, I tap my fingers on my chest and drive one-handed. I do it subtly so Ever doesn't track it. I want her to enjoy the carnival, not worry about me. That all six of us piled into Allie's 4Runner helps because she's distracted chatting with Lilly, Noah, Seth and Taya. Surprisingly enough, Taya blends right into our group. Even Seth treats her like he's known her forever. But that's the charm of Taya. Always has been. She puts you at ease and sucks you right in.

"Sunset Point has been perfect for learning how, and it's close to campus, so . . . win-win." Taya and Seth are trading surfing stories. That she knows how to surf impresses me and locks me into that conversation instead of my growing unease the closer we get to the vacant lot next to the baseball field.

"Man, you should come to Pismo. Consistent breaks. Perfect for beginners." Seth's passion for surfing oozes from his pores.

Watching the two of them in the rearview mirror, I feel an odd tug on my heart, a warm swirl in my gut. It's clear Seth isn't immune to Taya's thrall, and so far, he seems like a decent guy. Semi-frat guy stereotype aside, he's super chill, go with the flow, kind and genuine. I like him. The dynamic between him, Noah and Lilly is unforced and smooth, like they're a unit. I wonder, fleetingly, if there is a throuple situation happening. Not my business, but their threesome is curiously undefined although natural, effortless. Noah and Lilly are turned toward each other, leaning their arms over the back of the middle seats, joining Seth and Taya's conversation. No territorial jealousy, just openness. I make a note to ask Noah about it when we get a minute alone. He and I have a quiet, honest friendship that I appreciate more than he knows. Not one to become attached to others, I value the bonds I've built with him and Lilly. And Ever. Always Ever. I stop tapping my chest and reach for her hand and lace our fingers.

She squeezes and pulls them to her, settling them against the apex of her abdomen and thighs. Her eyes jump to mine when Seth adds, "Ask Davis. She killed it her first time."

"Ever, you surf, too?" Taya asks, her eyes wide with surprise.

She's taken to using my nickname for her as I've gotten laxer in saying it in front of others. Ever doesn't seem to mind. I personally love it because that's who she is. Just *Ever.* I bring our joined hands to my lips, pressing a kiss to the back of hers. Hearing that she learned when she bailed to Lilly's drops me back into that desperate space of those two days. Combined with the dread of being near the trailer park, I need the contact of her skin to ground me—remind me who I am now.

Lilly pipes up, "She's a little badass, too."

I track her nervousness in my periphery. She's rubbing the palm of her other hand up and down her thigh and tightens her grip on my hand as she answers. "Let's not get carried away. I surfed once. If we're getting technical, I stood up maybe three seconds."

"No, she did," Noah chimes in. To me he says, "It counts." Then he swivels back and adds, "You'd love it, Taya. Especially if you already know how. Nice, consistent breaks, and even some larger stuff if you want a challenge."

"Noted. I'll have to come visit and hit you guys up. When the grind of law school allows."

"Anytime," Seth, Noah and Lilly say in unison, followed by their joint laughter at their timing.

See? Throuple energy, whether it's factual or not.

Pulling into the dirt lot, Lilly squeals, "I'm not riding the Ferris wheel."

"We'll see," Noah retorts.

I turn off the engine and audibly sigh, forgetting to hide my anxiety for a second. Ever releases my hand and grazes her fingertips along the scruff on my cheek. I turn my face into her touch and reluctantly meet her eyes. She reads me too well, and I don't want her to see my apprehension. I smile and kiss her palm. "Let's go win you a ridiculously overpriced stuffed animal at the games."

She rolls her lips inward with a flat smile that doesn't reach her eyes but prompts both dimples to pop out. She's letting me pretend I'm fine, but she sees me, and I love her more for it. I plunk a kiss on the tip of her nose as she nods her agreement.

The air is thick with the aroma of overly sweet funnel cakes, the shrieks of excited kids, the clang of games and the constant hum of overlapping laughter and chatter. Lilly and Noah get accosted by their families almost as soon as we enter the carnival. Between face painting, photo booths and risky rides, I venture we won't see them until it's time to leave. Seth and Taya find the closest beer stand and grab two each, offering one to me and one to Ever. We press our plastic cups together, take a slug of foam and beer and meander toward the rows of games, choosing the ring toss first.

Funny enough, Taya and Ever win more games than Seth and me, but it may have more to do with the mostly male carnies' affinity for their jaw-dropping beauty than their talent for fixed carnival games. The more they win, the sassier they get, lording it over us that they "dominate." Without discussing it, Seth and I unite in sarcastically agreeing with them at every turn that they indeed prevail. We also keep pounding cheap beer until my bladder screams for release.

"Hitting the head," I announce to Seth as we pass the bricked building marked restrooms. To Ever and Taya, I call, "Take it easy on Seth while I'm gone."

"We make no promises," Taya tosses over her shoulder as she steps up to the water guns race.

Washing my hands in the men's room, a voice behind me sends ice through my veins and shoves my heartbeat into my throat.

"Must be my lucky day. Been lookin' for you and here you are."

I turn off the water and roll my weight onto the balls of my feet. As I raise my eyes from the sink basin to the mirror and the reflection behind it, a cold sweat breaks out under my arms and runs down my ribs. A small victory registers that he looks even older than the last time I saw him almost four years ago, the eyes glassier, skin more sallow. He looks strung out. Shocker.

"Ain't ya gonna say hi to your old man?"

"Hadn't planned on it, no. And maybe you couldn't find me because I didn't want to be found." I turn toward the exit, not bothering to look him in the face but clocking him in my periphery as I step to the door. Images of walking the carnival with my parents as a kid and never being able to participate in all the *fun* flash through my mind. *No money for that crap.* Yet they pounded beers all night every night the damn carnival was in town, wandering around, dragging me with them until so late into the night I almost passed out on my feet. Probably their idea of good parenting—taking me to a carnival—and probably why I hate this place so fucking much.

"Well, it seems we have something for you. So you may want to talk to me if you expect to get it."

"Pretty sure you've got nothing I want."

"That's fine. Happy to keep it for ourselves. Just need you to sign it over."

Sign it over? "You're not getting anything from me. So you can forget you saw me."

"Maybe I'll just ask your little girlfriend your new address. Pay you a little visit, deliver it personally."

I stop cold. I don't want him anywhere near me or anyone I care about. I spin on my heel and move to within an inch of his waxy face.

"Did you forget I know where blondie lives?" He continues his cryptic taunting with a sneer that shows yellow teeth to match his skin, the stench of stale cigarettes and alcohol drifting from cracked lips to slither into my nostrils.

Blondie. Taya. He doesn't know about Everly. My relief is short-lived. "I'll catch her at home one of these days."

He's been to her house. The realization draws my shoulders down and drops my chin. He was Mitch's mystery visitor. Exhaling, I close my eyes for a second, maybe two. "Fine, Todd. What do you want?"

His brittle laugh precludes his rebuff. "No way to address your *dad*."

"You're not my dad. You never were."

"Well, your momma says different."

"Takes more than genetics to make someone parents, Todd." I use his given name again in spite. I don't know why I'm standing in the men's room having a pissing contest with this degenerate or even wasting my breath, but I can't seem to help myself. Maybe I'm stalling, trying to figure out how to get out of here without him seeing Everly or Taya, who are surely waiting outside for me by now. "Where's Brandi? She here, too?"

"Show some respect, boy. Your *momma* is at home. She'll be happy to see you."

"First time for everything," I mumble. For his ears, I add, "Look, my friends are probably waiting for me. I'll come by tomorrow?" I hate that it comes out like a question, like I'm asking permission.

"Right. You been MIA for years now. I'm supposed to believe that? Maybe we should invite your friends to join us. But you don't want that, do you? Been ashamed of where you come from since you were born."

Despite being taller and bigger than him now, my throat bobs as sweat trickles down my spine. He's spot on that I don't want Ever, or even Taya, to see Todd—find out who he is, where I come from. Taya's never even seen the house I grew up in. She knows it's in the trailer park—*small towns*. Still, it's more than just not wanting them to know. Todd is dangerous. Way worse than my mom. She at least acted like she cared sometimes. He, on the other hand, never did. Maybe it's just the old tapes playing in my head, muscle memory or whatever, because the man standing in front of me doesn't look like much. He looks thin and strung out and much smaller than I remember. Pretty sure I could take him, but the little kid inside me feels panicky, uncertain. His eyes are still the same—pupils dilated, cold, black and, if you look close enough, dead. Maybe it's the eyes triggering my core memories causing the low-key panic that's tripping my heart rate and making my pits sweat.

"Yeah, well, you two didn't really give me much to work with."

"Still an ungrateful pain in the ass." His laugh sounds like he's gargling gravel. "Shoulda been a stain on the sheets you ask me. But your momma wanted you—convinced me to let her keep you. Eventually she realized I was right. Good for nothin' like I always said." The white globs gathered at the corners of his mouth turn my stomach.

One side of my mouth lifts as my gaze shifts between his beady bloodshot eyes. He always controlled her as far back as I can remember. His hateful words ricochet ineffectively. I've heard it all before, and maybe it's true but I don't care. All I care about is getting him out of here, away from Ever before he sees her. And getting out of here myself without them wondering what the fuck is taking me so long. "Still your favorite bedtime story. Glad to see some things don't change."

"And you're still a smartass. Think you're better than everyone else."

"Look, I said I'd come over and take care of whatever it is and I will. I'll give you whatever you want, okay?" I hate that I sound desperate, scared. "But I can't tonight, while I'm here with a group. You need my help, I'll give it to you."

"That's more like it." He turns toward the door, and my shoulders sink a little in relief. Before he pulls the door open, he adds, "Tomorrow, Jayce, or I'll come looking for you."

Once he's through the door and it clangs shut, metal door against metal frame, I exhale. I wash my hands again, to give myself a minute—regulate my pulse, my breathing.

"There he is," Seth calls. The three of them walk toward me, fresh beers in hand, as I emerge from the bricked structure.

Relief washes over me that they were hopefully off buying beer while Todd exited the bathroom.

"We grabbed another beer since you took so long." Taya's smile is lazy, buzzed.

I look around, my head on a swivel, before I make eye contact with Ever. I don't want to lie to her, but I know I'm going to just the same. "There, uh, was this old drunk guy in there that needed help. Did you guys see him come out?" I look around again, my story making my survey reasonable. I force a smile.

Ever giggles and follows my searching gaze with her own. "No, I think we must've been getting our drinks. Wanna sip?" She's in my space, her gray eyes smiling into mine, her lips parted, showing her teeth.

Still scanning the crowd, I look over her shoulder, both ways. No Todd. I exhale and will my body to relax. "Yeah, sweet girl, I do." Instead of taking her cup, I lean in and kiss her lips, sucking on them a little.

"Ugh, get a room," Taya groans. Her teasing lands as normal, not awkward like I'd expect.

"We've got one," I say low, more for Ever's ears, as my hand slides down to cup her ass, my nose nuzzling that sweet spot behind her ear. Her tinkling laugh is my reward, her head leaning into mine, wanting more. Louder for the group, I ask, "Can we be done with the carnival now? I think I've had enough of Southy's finest." That much is true and plays perfectly into my story of the drunk towny.

"Are you kidding me? We haven't even ridden the Ferris wheel yet," Seth protests, guzzling his beer.

"Ugh," Taya fake groans again. "I'll take surfer boy on the Ferris wheel. You two can . . . stand around and kiss some more." She rolls her eyes, flicking her hand at us with a cheek-splitting grin on her face, belying her indignance.

"Deal." Ever and I say it in unison, then laugh at our timing.

"C'mon, Seth. Let's get this over with." She bumps her shoulder with his.

"Damn. You townies are ruined for the carnival." He slings his arm over her shoulders, shaking his head, as they walk in front of us toward the rides.

I reach for Ever's free hand, lacing our fingers, my eyes still scanning the crowd as we walk. I tell myself he's gone, that I'd feel someone watching me—us. I let go of her hand and wrap my arm around her shoulders, pulling her in close to kiss her temple. *Sunshine.* I can't not hold her close, especially after running into him. If he is watching, he'll know. He'll see it's her, not Taya.

Despite my best efforts, Ever feels my body stiffen. She's so attuned to me. Still, she doesn't get why. It wouldn't occur to her, as it shouldn't.

"You okay, Julie? You really do hate the carnival, don't you?" Her head is turned, studying my profile as we walk.

"Eh, I just don't prefer South Point. Grew up here, remember?" I give her a close-lipped smile, going for a little bit of honesty. She deserves that.

She nods at my answer.

"Okay, one ride for the guest. Then we're outta here." She nods like she's solved all the world's problems.

I kiss her upturned nose and rub mine against hers. We turn and watch the giant wheel begin to rotate, Seth and Taya rising in the air while Seth looks all around like a happy little kid. Taya's laugh filters down to us, the sound so achingly familiar, like this place. It all puts a weird pit in my stomach. So I focus on the one thing that keeps me tethered to the here and now. *Ever.* I drop my chin to the side and press my nose into my favorite spot behind her ear. Her scent is the magic elixir that calms me, grounds me. *Sunshine and Ever.* I can't wait to get her out of this shit hole they call a town. Away from the dumpster fire of memories that assault my brain. An involuntary shiver rolls down my body.

"Cold?" Ever moves to stand in front of me, her back to my chest, so I wrap my arms around her and continue to nuzzle her neck.

"Mmm, maybe a little," I lie.

She reaches her palm up to my neck and pulls my head into her more as she sips her beer.

The smell of it reminds me of Todd and turns my stomach a bit. I breathe through my mouth. "They're almost done." I'm counting the rotations even though I have no idea how many one ride includes. The counting keeps the low-level panic at bay, although I still scan the crowd.

"Ayo, fam," Noah calls out. He and Lilly join us as Taya and Seth whirl past in their cabin, waving exaggeratedly. "Aww, the children are enjoying themselves," Noah mocks.

"Well, Seth is," Ever responds. "I think Taya is tolerating it, aided heavily by beer." Ever's sweet laugh penetrates my nervous haze.

"Yeah, beer definitely raises the allure of this shit show." Lilly taps her plastic cup against Ever's and takes a long sip.

"You and J Mac . . . vibe killers," Noah scoffs, shaking his head.

Ever giggles again, telling me she's feeling her beers.

I just want to get the fuck out of here. I laugh instead, hoping I'm selling *chill* better than I think I am. "Did your families leave already?" I ask them both at once.

"Yeah," Lilly answers first. "The littles had a sleepover to get to."

"Speaking of sleepovers." Taya draws the group's attention as she and Seth emerge from the gated area of the ride. "Can Seth stay with us tonight?" Her fingers are laced with his, her smile lazy with intoxication.

Seth releases her hand to swing his arm around her and pull her cheek to his lips. Ever looks up at me for the answer.

It's weird that it isn't weird for me. Taya with Seth. Other than a familiar protectiveness, I feel nothing.

"Of course. Whatever you need."

Ever's body loosens in my grasp, like an unclenching.

Was she worried I'd be weird? Maybe *I* was worried. It's a strange and soothing relief that Taya being here in my life but not part of my life is okay. Feels good, normal even. She and Ever seem to get along and maybe even like each other, which also makes me happy. "Does that mean we can go now?"

"I second that," Lilly backs me up. Everyone chimes in with assents, so we work our way toward the car.

I continue to scan the throngs of people, the passing cars once we hit the designated parking lot. No sign of Todd. Once we're in the vehicle headed home, I finally truly relax.

***

"**I**s it weird for you that they're in the next room?" Ever traces my tattoo with her fingernail, her head resting on my shoulder.

"You'd think, right? But no. Is it weird for you?"

Her entire body tenses.

I tuck my chin to my chest to gauge her response.

"Why would it be weird for me?"

"I don't know. Because she's my ex, I guess."

"Not really. I thought it would be, but she kinda blends right in."

"I agree." I resume drawing lazy circles on the ball of her shoulder, my post-sex haze drooping my eyelids. "I mean I might be trying a little extra not to picture them having sex, but to be fair, that would be true of anyone."

"Anyone?" Her fingernail draws a line down my abs to the thin trail of hair that dips below my waistband—when I'm wearing clothes, that is. My body responds automatically. "Even me?" My insatiable girl knows exactly what she's doing. Suddenly my sleepy eyes are alert, my body charged instead of tired. When her fingers wrap around me and slide down my length, my eyes roll back and a moan rumbles up my throat to escape my parted lips.

"Never you," I vow.

She slides the leg draped over me higher until it's resting just under her hand that moves up and down on me.

My arm she's not lying on reaches across her, fingertips trailing down her spine, over the swell of her ass until they find her center that is already dripping for me. "My Ever," I breathe into her ear, rolling us until I'm on top of her. "Always ready for me. Fuck, I love you." I claim her mouth as I claim her body, sinking into her completely for round two, sleep forgotten.

Chapter 7

JULIAN

"Thanks, Patrick. Yep, I'll wait for his call. I know, right? No, I totally get it. Appreciate you, man. Okay, sounds good. Bye." I tap the phone screen and set it on the island bar next to my coffee mug and close my laptop as she steps into the kitchen. It's early and our houseguests are still sleeping I assume. "Hi, pretty girl." I turn my gaze on her sleepy rosy face with her storm-cloud eyes and pouty lips. She never fails to trip my heart. So fucking beautiful.

"Hi, pretty Julie." Dropping her chin onto my shoulder, she snakes her arms around my torso, fingers finding and fitting into the grooves of my ab muscles through the thin, soft cotton of my T-shirt. "Whatcha working on so early already?" She smells like sunshine and sleep.

"Just some boring paperwork. In fact, I've gotta get to the post office and check my box for some documents before my session at Fit. Need anything while I'm out?" I hate the frown that forms between her eyebrows. I don't fake anything with Ever. She knows me, knows something's off, but my sweet girl rarely calls me out on my shit. Or more accurately, I don't give her any reason to need to call me out. Until now. Fuck Todd and Brandi Keller—parents of the year. I'm not sure what could've possibly come to their house for me, but Ashley's lawyer, now my lawyer, said he'll ask his associate that handles estate law, have him look into it. Patrick suggesting the estate lawyer got my wheels turning. John Julian McKay, my grandfather, is the only living relative I know of besides my degenerate parents. To my knowledge, Brandi is an only child who told me once that my grandmother, her mom, passed away. I think I was twelve. I didn't really know her or have any memories of her. My grandfather made core memory status, but I only recall snippets. I mostly remember how it felt being around him, that he had a kind face that sometimes looked sad when he talked to me.

"Remember, after your session today, we're off until after the new year." Ever is trying to fix whatever it is she's sensing in me and I love her for it. I try to let her.

"I'm aware." Kissing her noisily on the lips, I wrap my arms around her waist and lean into her as she pins me with her smoky stare.

"Remote access, no clients, no work. So why aren't you more excited?" Or maybe she does call me out. I'm glad she does though, as much as I want to avoid the question—and will.

"I am. Promise." I kiss her again, matching her energy. "Once I take care of this last little to-do list, I'm all here."

She's nodding, still studying me, her eyes bouncing between mine.

"Tell our guests I'll be back as soon as I can."

"I think we'll go raid Brew for some breakfast burritos once everyone's awake."

"Sounds good. I'll check your location before I leave Fit." I smile and tap her upturned nose with my index finger and turn to leave, swiping my phone and water bottle off the counter as I go.

***

"Sorry, Stacey, I've gotta grab this call. Two more sets here, then move over to the press for three sets on number four. You're doing amazing. Already stronger after two weeks. I'll be right back." Stepping away, I swipe to answer the Southern California number, assuming it's the law firm. "This is Julian."

"Mr. McKay, this is Michael Vega from Voss, Vega and Raines. Patrick gave me your info and I did some quick digging and found that your maternal grandfather did pass away almost two months ago. I'm sorry for your loss."

"Thank you, Mr. Vega. I . . . didn't know him very well."

"Michael, please. I just wanted to update you. I'll continue my research and contact the firm handling his estate for further details."

"I appreciate it, Michael. Thank Patrick again for me. I'll wait for your call." I tap the screen and slide it back into my pocket. My grandfather McKay is gone. I guess I'm supposed to feel grief, but I didn't know him. Beyond a basic human take of general sadness, I've got nothing. Even that feels somewhat affected. Does that make me an asshole? Dr. Carver would tell me to own my feelings or feel my feelings or whatever. She'd tell me it's okay that I'm not destroyed over the passing of someone I didn't know, blood or not. My family tree never evoked ties of loyalty in me since I was old enough to know what that meant. Ironically, I feel a closer, pseudo-familial bond to Taya than anyone I share DNA with. That realization hits me square in the chest, and I take a physical step back, as if the impact were literal.

Taya feels like family. Maybe that's why it's so natural to have her staying with us, why her likely hooking up with Seth last night doesn't bother me. Other than caring that she's safe, I don't have feelings for her. This realization puts a calm in my gut, like a key clicking in a lock. *Taya is my family.* Not like Ever, but like Allie. Noah and Lilly. Even Pete and Shelley. I wonder if she feels the same about me. Up until my birthday a couple months ago, she thought I abandoned her. Now that she knows it was a lie, where does she see me in her life? The fact that she asked to stay with us tells me she might feel the same.

As if thinking about her summons her, my phone vibrates and her name flashes across the screen. "Taya? What's up? I'm just wrapping up at the—"

"Jay, Mitch called. Someone broke in last night."

"What? Where?"

"The ranch. Mitch was gone. Found the mess this morning. I need to go. Would you go to the ranch with me? You and Ever? I don't want to go alone."

"Yes, of course. Where's Ever?"

"Shower. She doesn't know. He just called me."

Shit! I fucking know it's Todd. Who else? He's trying to find me. I just fucking know it. And he's not gonna stop. Maybe he thinks I live there now. Never figured him for anything but a drunk and an addict, but he's clearly escalated to petty larceny. Still, what does he hope to gain? Some inheritance? By force? Yeah, clearly not excelling in the common sense department. *You don't know if it even was him.* "I'm on my way." I walk back into the nautilus area, where my client, Stacey, is finishing her rounds. "Stacey, I've gotta cut your session short. There's an urgent issue I need to take care of. I owe you a free one, okay?"

"No worries, Julian. I'm sore enough." She laughs and stands up from the leg press. "Ugh, they feel like Jell-O."

"They look great though," I say automatically. "I'll text you my schedule to book your next one on me." I'm already moving toward the exit.

"Sounds good. Thanks."

I fly into the post office on my way back to Allie's and grab my mail from the box. There are only three envelopes: one credit card promotion, one from my health insurance and one from an unknown law firm. I know now what it's going to say. I toss it on the passenger seat and haul ass home. I'm going to have to come clean with Ever and Taya if Todd is on some warpath for an inheritance, no matter how delusional. Not sure what he hoped to find breaking into her place. He probably doesn't even know. Strung out idiot. Fuck my white trash upbringing. It's been a while since I've identified as that worthless kid. Ever changed that. Seems I can't outrun it, though. No matter how much I grow, heal, achieve, it's still there lurking under the surface, ready to burn it all down. To remind me that I'm Jayce Keller, born to trash and that I don't deserve good things, a good life. Even worse, that the more I grow, heal and achieve, the more I stand to lose when it does come back around. Dr. Carver really would be proud because I'm not going down without a fight. Fuck Todd Keller and his genes. I'm not condemned to the life they brought me into. I'm *not*!

Chapter 8

Everly

Soft knocking meets me when I step out of the shower. "Coming," I call. Pulling the bedroom door open, Taya greets me with a flat-lipped smile, so I swing it wider. I'm in a towel and it doesn't occur to me to feel self-conscious. But for a nanosecond it makes my radar that Taya being in my room, with me in a towel, isn't awkward. Almost as if it were my sister, Via. The expression on Taya's face though pushes the assessment out of mind. "What's wrong?"

"There was a break-in at my house. Mitch, the ranch manager, just called me. I called Jay since you were in the shower. He's on his way home."

"Okay. Umm, okay. Are you okay?" I'm already pulling clothes out of drawers, dropping my towel and throwing them on—no thought of my nakedness. Trauma makes you good at handling other people's crises.

"Yeah. Just kinda freaked out. Shit like that doesn't happen up here." She sits on the edge of the bed and rubs her palms up and down her knees. It's true. The weirdest thing I got used to in Blue Lake is how trusting everybody is. No one locks their doors. It's not talked about. It just is. "He . . . Jay said we'd go check it out. He said he'd go with me. Is that okay? With you?"

"Of course, Taya. I'll go, too." I scoop my towel off the floor and move to hang it up in the bathroom. "I mean, if you want me to. I want to help, if I can."

"Thank you, Ever. Really. Thank you for being so cool with all this. Me. Being here. I know it's fucking weird."

A laugh bubbles out of me before I can stop it. "You know what's fucking weird? That it isn't fucking weird. Like we were friends in another life or something."

"Okay, right? So it's not just me?"

"Nope. Trust me. It's weird, but like . . . not." I tie my kicks, stand and stretch my hand out to her. "Come on, Julie should be pulling up any minute." The door closing downstairs makes my point for me.

Stepping off the bottom step into the living room, Taya a foot behind me, I clock Julian's expression first. I haven't seen it except in glimpses, but he looks furious. "Hey, babe," I try for a reassuring smile. "I threw on some clothes. We're ready. Should we call the sheriff's office to meet us there?" The second thing I track is that his eyes swing away from mine instead of landing on them, no return smile. *Sketchy.* Then he turns to Taya. *More sketchy.*

"Taya, can I speak to Everly for a second? Alone?" He still won't look at me. "Just, uh, wait in the Jeep. I'll be right there."

Taya lets go of my hand that she held all the way down the stairs, sidesteps me and slips silently out the front door, snagging her bag off the entryway table as she goes.

Once the door closes behind her, Julian finally looks at me but doesn't speak.

I already know what's coming and I'm not going to help him say it. I don't move an inch except to raise my eyebrows. I know my resting bitch face is locked in and I don't care. He's gotta know that all things Taya are awkward and his behavior is just making it worse.

"Ever, I don't want you going—in case it's dangerous. Please don't be mad." He takes a step toward me, but I raise my hand up to halt him.

"Fine. Just go. Be careful." I fucking hate Agreeable Everly. That fucking girl is a pushover. Now isn't the time for a walk down therapy lane. I can thank my dad for the military ability to compartmentalize. But, goddammit, sometimes I wish I were a more stereotypical dramatic, nagging female. When Julian has the nerve to look hurt that I held off his affection or whatever he intended, I'm super fucking close to finding her. "I'm fine. I'll go see what Lilly, Noah and Seth are doing."

"I'll be back as soon as possible. Thank you, Ever. I love you."

I think I nod in response. I'm not sure my straight-lipped smile counts as an actual smile, but points for effort in the face of the monumental irritation. I summon my voice.

"I know." And I do know and believe he loves me. So why is he pushing me away, keeping me from this? I don't buy the safety thing. He's gotta know that not including me, especially when it comes to Taya, isn't going to land well. I mean I've heard guys are dumb, but Julian isn't dumb. I turn my back and move toward the stairs. When my foot hits the first step, I hear the door close behind me. I stop the climb and pull my phone out and text Lilly.

Me: Hey wrud

Lilly: making food come over

Me: omw

Chapter 9

Julian

"It's strange that nothing else was touched. Only Rusty's office is ransacked. Like they knew what they were looking for." Mitch summarizes what he found on his arrival this morning as he leads us down the hall into the den that served as Taya's dad's office, concern etched in the fine lines on his face. "It's why I'd like to install cameras, as I've said."

"Yeah, Mitch, I know." Taya walks into the den ahead of us.

Mitch motions me to precede him, so I follow Taya.

She turns a slow circle, taking in the half open drawers and scattered papers, ransacked bookshelves and vandalism. "What the fuck?" She says it more to herself but turns her bottle green eyes on me, askance.

Mitch clears his throat, drawing her attention. "I think they were looking for account information. Would you be able to tell if anything is missing from this drawer? It's where he kept his statements and official documents. Locked, but you can see it's been pried open."

"I don't think I'd know if something were missing. Fuck, I told him he needed a safe. Don't listen to me, you stubborn ass." Taya vacillates between talking to us and herself—or her dead father, I'm not sure.

I'm absently tapping my chest as I look around the room. I know it in my gut as if I'd seen it with my own eyes. *Fucking Todd.* The thought of voicing my suspicions to Taya or Mitch brings a glaze of sweat to my armpits despite the chill in the room. I know I'm going to lie before the words even form in my brain. Snagging my phone out of my pocket, I pretend to get a text. "Guys, I'm sorry, I need to take this. Will you excuse me?" I walk out to the Jeep, retrieve the mail from the console, tear open the envelope from Leva & Goody, Attorneys at Law and read, but I already know what it says.

Leva & Goody, Attorneys at Law
Estate and Probate Division
421 Harbor View Drive, Suite 208
St. Petersburg, FL 33701
Date: March 22, 2025
To: Jayce Keller (Possible Alias: Julian McKay)
P.O. Box 417
Blue Lake, CA 95244
RE: Estate of John Julian McKay, Deceased
Dear Mr. Keller,
Our firm represents the estate of John Julian McKay, deceased, currently under administration through the Circuit Court of Pinellas County, Florida. Court records list you as a potential beneficiary and next of kin.

We are attempting to verify your current contact information in connection with the distribution of Mr. McKay's estate. Please contact our office within thirty (30) days of receipt of this notice to confirm your identity and provide a forwarding address.

If we do not hear from you within that time, the estate may proceed to final distribution under Florida probate law, and any undistributed assets may be held in trust or transferred to the state's unclaimed property division until properly claimed.

This correspondence is not a summons or legal action but an official notice requiring your response regarding an estate matter.

Sincerely,

Renee Goody, Esq.

Leva & Goody, Attorneys at Law

Estate and Probate Division

My grandfather is dead. I guess I'm supposed to feel *something*, but other than some obscure memories, I can't summon a connection to him or any real emotion. Right now, his death is wreaking havoc on my life and the people in it. I quickly dial the number on the bottom of the letterhead. When the receptionist answers, I ask to speak to Renee Goody, the attorney that signed the letter.

"She's in a meeting. Can I take a message?" The chipper voice pauses and waits for my answer.

I leave my name and number and that I received her letter. The chipper receptionist assures me Mrs. Goody will return my call as soon as possible. Now I wait. And hope that fucking degenerate, Todd, doesn't approach anyone I know. In good conscience I should tell them he approached me at the carnival, that my grandfather died and probably left me money, and that my father now wants it. I want to tell them. Or, more accurately, I want to protect them from his lowlife ass. But every fiber of my being wants to *not* claim him or come clean about my past. Todd is right about one thing. I am ashamed of where and who I come from. Who could blame me? Still I plan to solve this without involving anyone else—especially Ever and Taya. That means I've gotta go back to the trailer park.

As I'm shoving the letter back into the console, a sheriff's cruiser rolls to a stop behind my Jeep in the roundabout. Blowing out a breath through puffed cheeks, I unfold myself from the driver's side and turn to greet the deputies. Working my way around to spilling the tea that the break-in may have been my fault, I step toward them as they exit the vehicle.

Chapter 10

Everly

"I don't know why you and Julian hate the carnival so much. It's fun—especially when you can experience it through the lens of a kid." Seth grins like one as he harps on at me.

I take a whopping bite of the funnel cake in my hand and feel the rush of sugar to my veins. I tagged along with him, Noah and Lilly for the last day of the carnival while they chaperone their younger siblings. Seth is ecstatic to get a second day here. My only response is a groan as I swipe powdered sugar off my lips with the back of my hand.

"Oh, no. Don't even act like you're not enjoying this to spite him. I see you, Davis." Lilly tosses her chin toward me in challenge.

"He can go have his sleuthing moment with his ex. I'm fine."

"You seem fine, chowing on a funnel cake that has a year's worth of sugar in one bite."

"Whatever. It's a cheat day. Let it go."

"I was just about to say that to you."

"What? Let it go? I said I'm fine."

"Why didn't you just tell him the Taya thing is delicate and he better tread lightly?"

My only answer is a shrug—and another bite of funnel cake that is starting to make me queasy. "How'd you get roped into bringing the littles again if you hate it so much?"

"Noah doesn't hate it, and his and my littles are a package deal, so . . ." Lilly shrugs now.

I toss my head in Noah and Seth's direction and ask, "How is *that* going, anyway?"

"Next question."

"Wait. Why next question? You guys seem like your old selves, if heavy one surfer."

"Exactly. We're a threesome now I guess. Or a . . . throuple?"

"Seriously?! Say more."

"I really don't have . . . more. It's a bizarre, undefined togetherness. Can we just not?" Lilly dumps her almost full bag of popcorn in the trash bin and dusts her hands together.

I study my friend for a few pregnant moments in silence, and when she won't look at me, I give in. "Sure, Lill. Whatever you need. But you know I'm here for you. No judgment. You've listened to all my bullshit since we met. It goes both ways, okay?" My only answer is her single nod.

"Come on, Lill," Noah calls. "Seth wants us to ride the Ferris wheel with him *again*." Seth is walking backwards ahead of us, motioning at Lilly to join them.

Lilly looks at me, one eyebrow up like they're making her point for her.

Jerking my thumb toward the restrooms, I toss my head at the bricked building to my left. "I'll wait at the ride's exit after I pee."

Checking my phone for Julian's location as I leave the restroom, I collide with a tall, wiry frame standing inside the bricked, half-walled vestibule that encases the bathroom entrance. My brain registers that he's in the wrong restroom right before he puts his face in mine and grips my bicep, dragging me against him.

"Hey, girlie. Don't scream or it might be the last thing you do. We're going for a walk. Nice and calm like." Black pupils take over the blue irises that are nothing but an outline. Leathery cheeks littered with salt-and-pepper scruff frames thin, cracked lips.

The smell of cigarettes and alcohol does nothing to quell my nausea from the funnel cake. The cool metal of the small handgun pressed to my abdomen spikes my adrenaline, giving me an out-of-body hypnotic state—like I'm watching this happen to someone else. *Think, Everly.*

"I . . . you can have my bag. There's money. It's yours."

"I don't want your money, but I'll take it. I want your boyfriend. And I'll just bet he'll come running for you." *Julian.* My brain goes into protective, panic mode.

"Julian's not here."

"Julian." His chuckle sends a shiver down my spine and sweat to my palms. "Yeah, *Julian*." Another chuckle.

Fuck, why did I say his name? Something tells me he already knows it, though.

"Give me your phone." He doesn't wait for me to hand it to him but yanks it out of my grasp. "Let's go before your friends finish their ride."

He was watching us.

Pushing me out in front of him, he presses the fist holding the gun into my back, his grip on my bicep steering me through the carnival games until we reach the back fence that borders the Little League fields. He leads me to the far corner where the chain link is rolled back from the metal pole and shoves me through it and across the infield dirt and outfield grass to another chain link fence that borders a . . . trailer park.

Julian's childhood home. Julian's dad. What the fuck is this? I wonder for a second if I can outrun him, but I can't outrun a bullet. He jerks me to a halt in front of a tan double-wide and veers me toward the four steps that lead to the front door.

Once inside, he shoves me down on a green plaid couch. "Don't move or I'll make you sorry. I'll make Jayce sorry. Or 'Julian.'" He says Julian with finger quotes, using the hand that's not holding the gun.

I catch movement in my periphery.

A woman appears in the doorway that leads to the kitchen. She's thin. Not athletic thin. Unhealthy thin. Her hair hangs in uncombed strands over each shoulder, and while her cheeks are sunken in, her face is unmistakable. The eyes are glassier, bloodshot, but they're Julian's.

"Todd, who's this?" She looks from me to him, notices the gun and adds, "What are you doing?"

His only response is to pull my phone from his pocket and extend it to me. He doesn't look at her or answer her. "Unlock it."

I take the phone, do what he asks and place it back in his palm. Then he addresses her, still not answering her question. "Don't just stand there. Get me a beer. You want one while you wait?" He raises his eyes from my phone to sneer at me.

Is he really offering me a beer right now? I don't speak. I just shake my head.

He starts tapping on my phone one-handed with his thumb, gun in the other. After a few taps, he drops it onto the end table and flops down in the chair next to it. "Brandi," he booms, tossing his head toward the doorway where the woman, *Brandi*, disappeared.

She rushes out, beer in hand, and shoves it at him.

The way he swigs it, wipes the back of his hand across his lips, the house, the woman, *Julian's mom*, strung out and clearly scared of this guy. *His dad?* It's all so ugly. Is this where he grew up, with these people? How could someone so beautiful come from something so ugly? Were they always this way? Pressure builds behind my eyes at the image of little Julian, *or Jayce*, growing up here—with them. It's usurping my fear. I can tell the woman was probably pretty once, like if she were well nourished and groomed she might be again. The guy, Todd, might've been attractive too, but his eyes look hard, mean. They scare me. I don't want him to be Julian's dad, for him to have come from someone so vile. A tear slips down my cheek and I hastily swipe the back of my hand across my face to hide it.

If his snicker isn't proof I didn't succeed, his words are. "Don't worry. He'll be along any minute now." *He texted Julian from my phone. Fuck, why did I say Julian's name? He would've never found 'Jayce' in my phone. Because you're not Olivia Benson and this isn't SVU. You don't know how to get kidnapped, or whatever the fuck this is.* He clearly doesn't know what he's doing either. If he really did summon him, Julian will track me if I don't respond. That much I know. As if on cue, my phone vibrates on the glass surface next to him.

He clanks his beer down next to the coaster (not on it) and reaches for the phone. Rotating it, he reads then sneers, "Like I said."

My heart drops and I swallow the golf ball in my throat. *Think, Everly.* How do I get out of here before Julian gets here? I slowly swivel my head around the tiny room and lock eyes with Brandi. She knows what I'm doing and, just as slowly, shakes her head at me, then side-eyes Todd.

"Stop hovering. Go get a beer and chill the fuck out. I got this. Get her one, too." To me he adds, "I know you like beer. Saw you downing them at the carnival, so don't act too prissy to have one now."

My only answer is to swallow another golf ball, then a swig of beer when Brandi returns with one and Todd insists. I barely get it down without gagging. I may have just lost my taste for beer permanently. I'm not sure how much time has passed while I pretend to drink every time he *insists*.

Brandi sits on the arm of Todd's chair to drink hers. The only other seat would've been next to me on the couch. Todd finishes his beer first, then Brandi. She takes both empty bottles to the kitchen and brings Todd another without being asked. "You gonna finish that sometime today?" He motions his bottle to the beer growing warm in my hand. Right after he asks, the unmistakable sound of tires on gravel pierces the air. "Guess not." He grins, stands and sets his half-empty beer down and picks up my phone and hands it to me. "You can have this back now."

Yep, not very smart.

Brandi is standing in the doorway again, and before I can take it, the front door barges open.

Surging to my feet, I swipe my phone off the coffee table where it dropped and shove it into my back pocket. I turn toward the door and hopefully into Julian's arms.

He grabs me and yanks me to him. "Get the fuck out of here, Everly. You don't belong here." His grip on my biceps cuts off circulation. His face is so close I can see the dark indigo ring around his irises. With a slight shake, he turns, shoves me backwards and releases me.

I stumble back to get my footing and try to reconcile the person before me with the one I think I know. I don't know him. Every line of his face is as familiar as my own, but I don't recognize the man in front of me or the rage pouring off him.

Before I can utter a word, he growls, "Leave. Before I throw you out." Fury oozes from every pore and scorches like standing too close to a fire.

I take an involuntary step backwards, the door handle pressing into my spine.

"Don't make me, Everly. I swear I will."

I reach for the handle and unlatch the door without turning around. I track him as I ease it open enough to slip through, my eyes bouncing between his. If I turn my back, I fear he'll pounce—like a wild animal stalking its prey.

As soon as I'm through the door, he slams it shut, rattling it on its hinges.

I stare at the woodgrain patterns for a beat, maybe two, willing my brain to kick in, to think, to figure out how to stop him before it's too late.

A shot, then a crash from the other side of the door pierces the momentary quiet.

Think, Everly. I can't think. *Julian!* My knees threaten to buckle.

I reach into my back pocket for my phone and pull up the number I've had *just in case*. I've never used it and wasn't sure I'd ever want to. I tap call. It rings once, twice. On the third ring I hear the voice I remember so well—too well now.

"Hey, Everly."

"I didn't know who else to call."

"What happened?"

"They . . . He . . . I can't stop him."

"Send me your location. I'm on my way."

I spin toward the sound of tires crunching gravel.

A sheriff's cruiser rolls to a stop and a young deputy gets out. "Ma'am. Are you okay? We got a call someone may be in danger."

"I can't stop him. He's inside. They're all inside. The gun went off." I clench the fabric of my shirt at my chest, gasping for air. I can't get enough air; my vision closes in on me. "I'm gonna . . . I can't . . ."

"Whoa, whoa. Take it easy. Here, sit down." He pushes me gently onto a flat boulder, one of many that separate the designated parking area from the tiny yards of the trailers. "Are you hurt? Who has a gun?"

I shake my head, hanging it low between my arms resting on my parted thighs.

He starts talking into his radio, requesting an ambulance to 'stage away from the area' as a precaution. There's another crash. This time he—Officer Belson his uniform says—hears it, too. He immediately barks into his radio for backup for an 'audible altercation in progress, possible shots fired.' "Can you tell me who's inside?"

"My boyfriend. Julian McKay. Umm, Jayce. I don't know." I dip my head again. I can't breathe. "Please, get him out of there. He has a gun."

"Your boyfriend has a gun?" He rests his hand on his gun and moves between me and the house.

Behind us another vehicle crunches through the gravel and skids to a stop. I look over my shoulder and stand when I see Taya's truck. She and a blond man hop out of each door and rush to me.

Officer Belson holds up his hand. "Whoa, stop. You need to stay back."

"I called her. Can I . . . Can they . . . Am I allowed to go over to them?"

"Yes. Please stand behind the vehicle, but don't leave." He watches me until I make my way to Taya and the blonde with her. He then goes to the driver's side of his police cruiser and speaks into his PA. "Julian McKay, this is the sheriff's department. If you can hear me, come out slowly with no weapons and your hands where I can see them."

"Everly, what the hell is going on? Are you okay?" Taya grips my shoulders, her eyes searching mine for answers my mouth can't seem to give her.

I'm looking at her, but I don't see her. Behind me, the sheriff's deputy—*Belson*, my mind says—continues to call for Julian. The creak of the trailer door pierces my trance. Jerking out of Taya's grasp, I whip around as Julian walks through the open door, arms above his head. Another patrol car, lights flashing, siren screaming, flies to a halt next to Taya's truck in a cloud of dust. An ambulance stops beyond the graveled parking area.

The deputy in the second cruiser throws his door open and draws his gun, crouching behind his door. Belson approaches Julian and tells him to kneel on the ground, which he does. Once he's on his knees, the deputy cuffs him and asks him who else is inside. I can't hear his words, just the sound of his voice.

"Brandi Keller, come out with your hands in the air."

"Jay's mom." Taya gasps the words beside me, her eyes frozen on the trailer door, hand flying to her gaping lips. "Oh my God, Ever, what the fuck happened?"

"I think we should get back, out of the way. Let's take her to the ambulance to get her checked out." This from the blond guy with her.

"I'm not leaving him." I jerk my arm out of his grasp.

"Mitch, it's okay. Let her . . ." Taya's voice trails off behind me as the door opens and Brandi walks out with her arms lifted above her like Julian did moments ago.

The deputy approaches her, telling her to kneel, and cuffs her, too.

My eyes collide with Julian's. What I see breaks me. He looks over my shoulder. "Mitch, get them out of here."

Chapter 11

JULIAN

With my hands on the thin wooden door, I take a breath and turn to face him. I don't need to look around to see that nothing has changed. Even the smell is the same. Stale cigarettes and beer underneath the overwhelming fake floral scent of a Glade factory. I face him, then take two steps to bring myself within striking distance. I don't speak and neither does he, but as soon as the hand holding the gun lifts a fraction of an inch, instinct takes over.

Dropping all my weight onto my right foot as I pivot, I bury my left foot in the center of his chest with a sidekick. He flies backwards over the chair he vacated when I entered, toppling over, taking the chair and glass end table with him. A gunshot rings my ears as his body thuds to the floor.

I flinch in reflex as a blur of tangled hair and frail limbs swoops from the kitchen doorway to crouch beside him. "Jayce, what did you do? Why did you do that?"

I don't answer her. I can't make words. I just watch, frozen, as the top of her head spins away from me to crouch over his body that's still not moving. His hand feebly shoves hers away. She stumbles back and stands, trying to help him up as he continues to swipe at her efforts. Her hands, slick with blood, wrap around his arm to steady him. He smiles, blood on his teeth and sways as he faces me and says, "That's no way to greet your old man, now, is it?"

Before I can even decide if I'll answer him, his eyes roll back and he plummets to the ground with another crash, disintegrating what's left of the glass and wood end table.

"Julian McKay, this is the sheriff's department. If you can hear me, come out slowly with no weapons and your hands where I can see them." Sirens play in the background of his words.

I back away until my body collides with the door. Reaching behind me, I push the handle to open it.

Brandi doesn't look up and Todd still isn't moving. She's shaking him and calling his name.

As soon as I'm through the opening, I turn and raise my hands above my head and walk toward the deputy. After a few steps, he tells me to turn around and kneel. I comply as he cuffs my wrists behind my back.

"Who else is in there?"

I don't say it's my mom. "Brandi Keller. Todd Keller, but he was unconscious. He fell and the gun went off." The deputy begins calling through the PA for Brandi to come out now.

I hear the door open behind me. I can't turn my head enough to see her, but I hear her footsteps on the metal stairs.

Then she's kneeling on the ground several yards away from me, blood smeared on her hands and arms. Accusation clear on her face before she swings her gaze from mine.

Swirling nausea threatens to climb into my throat.

Angling my neck, I scan the yard—for *her*. She's standing with Taya and Mitch. *Taya, too?* Fuck my life. I lock eyes with Ever's ashen ones. She can't be here. My breathing hitches and grows shallow as I stare at her, my vision closing in on me. *Look away.* I focus behind her and catch Mitch's scrutiny. Will he help me? I have to try. "Mitch, get them out of here," I beg him through gritted teeth.

He understands the assignment. He places his body between me and Ever, blocking her from my view and hers from me.

Deputies are entering the house now as two more patrol cars show up.

One emerges from the house and calls for the EMTs. I don't know if Todd is dead or alive, but he must need medical attention. As the EMTs rush inside, the deputies confer. I can't make out everything they're saying, but they can't find the gun. That much I catch. I glance sideways at Brandi, who won't look at me—my own mother. To be fair, she was never one. Not really. Did she hide the gun? She must've. They would've found it otherwise.

"Got it," one of the deputies calls as his footsteps clunk down the porch steps.

Brandi's eyes swing to mine again as he walks past us, delicately holding a plastic bag with a gun visible inside. Her watery glower tells me she tried. My lips flatten and I turn my head in disgust. Not disgust, resolve. Did I expect anything different? She always backed him up no matter what.

Deputy Belson, his uniform says, helps me stand and takes me to the backseat of his car, ducks my head and places me on the seat sideways, feet on the ground. Another deputy takes Brandi to another car and yet another is talking to Ever at the ambulance across the lot. She gestures wildly, her voice insistent, louder at times, though I can't make out all the words. She's defending me, I've no doubt.

I keep silently pleading with the gods or the universe that Mitch or Taya or someone will take her away from this dumpster fire of a scene. How is it you must pass a test to do basic things like drive a car but any piece of shit can become a parent? I feel dirty that Ever is seeing any of this. That Todd brought her here, possibly at gunpoint. Bile curdles in my stomach and climbs up my esophagus. I swallow thick saliva in fast, quick gulps to keep it down.

EMTs wheel a gurney off the porch toward the ambulance. Todd is still unconscious, head bandaged. So he didn't accidentally shoot himself. Must've hit his head when he fell—when I kicked him.

I hang my head as they pass by. I don't want to look at him. A shadow falling over me brings my head up. Deputy Belson says he needs my statement.

"I . . . my girlfriend texted me *I need your help*. I texted back but she didn't answer, so I checked her location. When I saw it was . . . my old house, I came here."

"Someone reported a gunshot." He doesn't ask a question, so I look up into his face, squinting against the sinking sun but don't respond. "Did you see a gun?"

"Yeah. He . . . Todd pointed it at me. That's when I kicked him. He fell over the chair. Then he stood up but fell again right away. Like passed out."

"Okay, give me a few minutes, Mr. McKay. We should be able to let you go."

"What happens to him? Her?" I toss my head toward the ambulance driving away and the other patrol car holding Brandi. I fucking hate that I care. Do I though? Or am I just making sure they can't come near us again. *Us.* I can't look at her. I feel disgusting and like the shit of my life is tainting the perfection that is her. I've always known she's too good for me, but I kept her anyway. Now my shit is spilling onto her like I always feared it would. I let myself believe for a while that it wouldn't. That it was in the past. That I was Julian McKay now. No longer Jayce Keller. But here I am back in this shitty trailer park, with the shitty humans that made sure I knew every day that I was shit, too.

"That depends on the evidence and the DA." He steps away and talks with the other deputies on scene.

Across the lot, Taya wraps her arm around Ever's shoulders, bringing my focus to them. She's trying to steer her toward their truck, take her away from here. *Thank you, Taya.* She won't leave, though, shrugging off the embrace, pulling away when Taya tries to hold her arm. She walks the three steps to the deputy that questioned her and motions toward me. The pitch of her voice rises, but the ringing in my ears won't let me make out the words. I know she's pleading for them to release me. Of course she is. She loves me. I shake my head to clear the buzz in my ears, in my head.

"Mr. McKay, stand up so I can remove the cuffs. You're free to go. We may contact you for further questioning."

I stand, head hanging, and turn around. As soon as the cuffs are unlocked and I turn back around, Ever throws herself into my arms. I catch her, robotically wrapping my arms around her. The scent of sunshine, *her scent,* combined with the familiar smell of that goddamn trailer swirl the bile in my stomach and force it up into my throat.

Before I can stop it, I shove her off me, hunch sideways and hurl on the ground in the gap of the open cop car door.

"Ever, get out of here. Go with Taya and Mitch. Just get the fuck out of here." The hand resting on my back slides down my spine and off me. She doesn't back away though. Still bent over, I can see her feet behind mine. "Please. Let them take you home." Both of our phones buzz relentlessly in our pockets. Lilly, I'm sure. "Call Lilly. Tell her you're okay. I'll see you there."

Her feet shuffle backwards.

Once she turns to go, I straighten up and wipe my mouth with the back of my hand. I don't turn around until I hear the truck doors open and close, the engine start and the truck pull away. I just hang my head and breathe through the nausea, bracing my arms on the open door and the hood of the cruiser.

Piece of shit had a gun—pulled a gun on Ever. Pressure behind my eyes burns like acid. I keep blinking to relieve the pressure. The dam wants to break. I claw the shirt on my chest, gasping for air. The gulps I suck in aren't enough. My vision closes in, going black around the edges.

From the tunnel, the deputy approaches. His words sound faraway. "Are you okay? Sit down, maybe put your head between your knees for a minute. Catch your breath."

Bending over, I brace my hands on my knees. "I'm fine. I'm fine." I gulp more air. My vision clears. "I just need to get the fuck out of here and I'll be fine."

"You're free to go, Mr. McKay. We'll be in touch if we need anything further."

Chapter 12

EVERLY

"I know. Love you too. See you soon." I end the call with Lilly and can't help the weighted sigh. It's New Year's Eve and everyone is still in shock. Julian is a ghost. I'm not sure what or who I am anymore. Christmas came and went without much fanfare. I'm still staying with Julian at Allie's because Noah, Lilly and Seth are still at the apartment until they go back to San Luis Obispo for spring semester. Thankfully they took Seth to their families' Christmas celebrations. Via and Ryan spent theirs with his family. Mom's off on her latest trip somewhere, and Allie and Luke stayed in Malibu. Taya began staying at her own house after the trailer park incident. It made the local paper as all 911 calls do, but domestic disturbances at the trailer park aren't exactly news around here. Now that we know it was likely Todd who broke in, probably looking for Julian, she's not afraid to stay there. Mitchell agreed to stay with her, just in case. Taya and I talk on the phone and text off and on, but she stays away—for which I'm grateful. Lilly does, too, but she harasses me more blatantly with relentless calls and texts. I keep putting her off. I don't know what else to do. I don't have any answers for her.

While all of this made for an unusually quiet holiday, I'm relieved I don't have to explain the awkwardness between me and Julian—especially since I'm still trying to navigate and understand it myself. Julian's here but he's not. That's probably the simplest way to explain it. He's beyond polite, but he barely touches me—like it physically hurts him to do so. I don't know how much more I can take. We open presents on Christmas morning, just the two of us. Shared a normal dinner that evening. In between, we tiptoe around each other like strangers. It's been a week and not much has changed.

Tonight is the Lanterns and Lights Festival. Julian told me how excited he gets for these events. He and Allie have worked them together since he came here, but this year she's down south and he's . . . I don't know, checked out. He turned all the planning over to Pete and Shelley this year. If he's not working out, here in Allie's home gym because he hasn't left the house since the incident, he's on his laptop "working." We're back to his avoidance routine of rising before me and coming to bed after me.

Aside from his plethora of apologies and asking if I'm okay, we haven't discussed his parents or what happened. I should be more freaked out at being taken at gunpoint, but thanks to the Kyle Davis genes, I'm solid. At least on the surface. *Thanks, Dad.* Julian's stoicism, on the other hand, is messing with my head. The longer he shuts me out, the less patient I become. When I'm ready to flip my shit on him, I remind myself those were his parents that did the heinous shit. When I can't take the confines of the house with him ignoring me, I go for a run. I realize that what once made a perfect pairing of two avoidance souls is now imploding in a communication—or lack thereof—breakdown. After my runs, he's there waiting just inside the door for me—like he needs to assure himself I'm okay. Then he makes some excuse about getting back to work or some other bullshit task.

Our therapists would have a field day with this circus. In fact, I have wanted to suggest maybe he hit up his old therapist, but if I even broach the topic his response is the same. Heavy sigh first, then, like he's talking to a polite stranger, he thanks me and asks if we can *not* talk about it. As the perfect no-drama military daughter, I concede. I'm reaching the end of my tolerance rope, though. My seething lies just below the surface ready to blow. When I think I can't take it anymore, I make myself picture that trailer that was supposed to be a home and those two people who were supposed to be parents. I think about the boy who grew up there and became the man who has been the only person to ever make me feel seen and loved, and I let him pull away from me, ignore me, shut me out. I don't know who or what I'd be if I'd grown up like he did. That he is the sweet and beautiful man he became is either luck or sheer force of will. Either way, he is, despite all he saw and experienced. So I suck it up and go for runs and talk to Lilly as if everything is fine.

Tonight I'll light and release a lantern and make a wish for my haunted man that he can pull himself out of this and let the people who care about him love him again. I've tried so many times over the last five days. Sometimes I just start by rubbing his shoulders when he's sitting at his desk—the desk in the guest room he used before we made this our home. He lets me at first, but if I kiss his neck or give him affection of any kind, he pulls away. Nicely. He takes my hand, kisses my palm, holds it to his cheek, then gives me one of his flimsy excuses about work or whatever. I'm this close to disgracing the memory of my ever-composed father, may he rest in peace, because I'm one more platitude away from flipping my shit on this wounded man. Something's gotta give or we're going to end up in flames like the goddamn bonfire tonight.

"Baby?" He's standing behind me in the mirror.

I didn't realize I'd paused brushing my hair, lost in thought. I didn't see him come up behind me either. That he called me baby gives me hope.

"Hi, Julie. I didn't see you." The smile he gives me is sad and makes my heart ache.

"Are you okay?" He lifts his hands like he's going to touch me, then drops them to his sides like they're weighted.

"Yeah." I smile and try again. "Yeah, totally. How are you?"

He pushes his smile to spread across his face more. "Good. Busy. I was thinking maybe you could go to the bonfire with Lilly and Noah and I could—"

"No." I throw the brush in my hand across the bathroom counter. It bounces on the tile, knocks over a bottle of dry shampoo and clangs into the sink. I spin around to face him and shove him in the chest. "No, Julian." I didn't expect to budge him one inch, but I must catch him off guard because he steps back, momentarily losing his balance and knocks into the shower doors.

True to his training, he recovers quickly and plants his feet, smile wiped from his features. "Ever—"

"Don't 'Ever' me. Stop this, Julian. Fucking talk to me. Touch me. Kiss me." My fist slams against my chest with each plea. "We've never gone five days without you touching me." I clench my shirt in my fist as the first tear spills.

He doesn't reach for me and instead fists his own hands at his sides, his shoulders shrug with a deep sigh. It dumps gasoline on my flames, igniting an inferno.

"Fine." I grab his shirt with both hands. "You don't want to touch me, kiss me, be with me, then fucking end it. Put us both out of our misery." I try to shove him out of the bathroom.

He doesn't budge now, his balance intact.

"You think it was hard believing your girlfriend died? Well try living with a ghost. You're here but you're not. I have to see you walking around all day, every day, but I can't have you. It's breaking me, Julian." I press my forehead to his chest. "I can't do this anymore. You have to fix this." The dam breaks and I sob, wailing inconsolably like I can't recall doing since I was a child.

When his arms fold around me, I cry harder. "Shhh, Ever. Shhh. I got you." He pets my hair and whispers to me, but his body shakes. I don't look up. I don't want to know if he's crying, too. It would undo me more. He sniffles, and that sound quells my crying jag.

Sniffling, I wipe my cheek on his shirt and take a deep shaky breath. Hooking my hands on his shoulders, I tilt my head and peek at his face under my lashes. Wetness glistens on his cheeks, reflecting the bathroom light. I place a light kiss on his jaw.

His lashes flutter closed on a soft moan, and he leans into the kiss, so I kiss him again. His chin this time. He lowers it so it lands on his lips instead. The kiss sears, scorching us both.

Within seconds we're devouring each other. He drops his hands to my hips and scoops me off my feet. Wrapping my legs around his core, I mold my body to his.

The kiss is water in a desert, and we're dying of thirst.

He lays me down on the bed and I don't remember him moving. All I feel is his lips, now his hands, as they move over me, dragging my shirt over my head, peeling my leggings down my hips. He rains kisses down my body, my chest, my abdomen. As he moves lower, I snag a handful of his shirt and yank it up as his body slides down. He breaks his kisses long enough for me to pull the shirt over his head. Like a magnet, they fall back onto my skin, trailing down my body until they find their destination.

The heat of his breath meets the heat of my already hardened bud through the thin fabric of my thong. Pulling it aside, he wraps his lips around me on a low groan.

My moan matches his the second I feel the suction of his mouth. "Ugh." Water in a desert indeed. His touch is a baptism washing over me. "Yes, Julie. Please."

He pauses long enough to answer me. "I know, sweet girl. Me too." With a tug, the string of my thong snaps and his groan sends a rush to my already dripping center. His fingers are sliding into me now, filling me, and I'm not sure anything has ever felt better.

I pull the tufts of hair on his forehead that tease the skin of my belly as his kisses devour me while his fingers drive me higher. He crooks his middle finger and that's all it takes. I erupt and cry his name, holding his lips tight to me, my body throbbing.

As my body comes down from the orgasm, he lays his cheek on the soft skin of my belly and slowly removes his fingers from inside me. I try to move to lie beside him but he clamps his arms around me and just holds on so tight. I find my voice. "Julie." I pet his hair, and he swipes his cheek against my stomach, the dampness unmistakable. I shift my weight and roll till he's flat on his back and I'm draped over him. He's naked. I don't remember him taking off his pants. I slide my body down until I feel his hard-on against the vee of my thighs.

Grabbing my hips, he stops my motion. *Is he not going to make love to me?* That thought extinguishes the afterglow of my orgasm. I reach for his hands, lace our fingers, and flop them onto the bed at the same time as I drop my weight onto his erection, burying him inside me. The swift motion and the sensitivity of my insides from my orgasm rip a cry from my throat and a grunt from his. I squeeze my eyes shut at the intensity. I lift myself and do it again, this time watching him.

His eyes are glassy but they stay on mine.

I set a fast, wicked pace, afraid to give him time to stop me. I don't free his hands and he doesn't try. I'm determined and a little angry. He lets me ride him until I feel him swell inside me, stretching me, and his breaths grow shallow.

The crease on his forehead tells me he's close. Still he watches me. Our skin slaps together with each thrust. Him letting me drive, control our pace, is reigniting the flame in me.

I'm going to come.

"Ugh, fuck, Ever."

His groan and his words send me over the edge. I'm convulsing around him, coming again.

He tugs his hands free of mine and shoves me down on him one more time, holding my hips tight while he empties himself deep inside me. "Ugh, ungh, mmm." He closes his eyes now as he pants through the rest of his orgasm.

I collapse, my cheek resting on his chest, and catch my breath, tracing my fingernails up and down his bicep. I could stay like this all night, but almost right away he's rolling us to our sides, scooting away from me. I reach for him, but he dodges my touch.

"I . . . I'll be right back." He kisses my forehead, gets up, grabs his clothes and walks to the bathroom, closing the door behind him.

Chapter 13

Julian

I'm a piece of shit. My actions are proof I don't deserve her. I couldn't keep my hands off her. That hasn't changed since we met. She's better off without me, but I can't stay away from her. My bullshit life could've gotten her killed. When I thought Taya died, it almost killed me. If anything happened to Ever, I wouldn't survive it. I can't shake that she could've been seriously hurt or worse. That she was taken by gunpoint, threatened, alone, scared. Because of me. Just being with me puts her at risk. I thought I left it all behind, made myself good, but I can't outrun where I come from—what I came from.

Now it's like every time I touch her, I taint her, the perfection of her, with my cursed DNA. She deserves better than some damaged trailer trash like me. At the very least, she deserves to be safe from harm. That only happens if she's not with me. But I'm fucking shameless and don't know how to let her go. We're tiptoeing around each other because I don't have the balls to send her away for good. She needs to be far away from me. Far away from here.

Blue Lake used to mean a fresh start, peace and possibilities. Southy is too close, though. Hell, any place in this tiny county is too close. She deserves to go away to college and live a life of frivolity and fun. Not guns, trailer parks and drugged-out degenerates. I've gotta let her go. I'm a fucking asshole that I just made love to her and now I plan to go out there and tell her to leave. Staring at the pale, sunken face in the mirror, I will myself to do it—push my clenched fists off the edge of the countertop, turn around and walk out of here and end my life as I know it.

I always knew she was too good to be true. I always knew it would come down to losing her. Didn't I? Because that's what Jayce Keller deserves. Nothing and no one. I can change my name, build a career and make more money than I know what to do with, but I can't change who I really am. Todd showed me that, proved beyond a doubt that underneath it all, I'm just like him, *her*. A guy in handcuffs, kneeling in the dirt lot of a trailer park in a nothing town. Knocking my fists against the cool white tiles, I resolve myself to do what I must. What's right. With one last look in the mirror I turn and open the door.

She's sitting on the edge of the bed facing the bathroom, legs dangling, feet bare, toes barely touching the floor. Dressed in a fresh bra and thong, but her eyes are downcast, hands fidgeting with what's left of her thong—the one I tore off her. I ignore the rush of blood to my junk at seeing it and her like this. She's so fucking beautiful—even when she's sad. Maybe more so. I glance over her head at the rumpled bed and yearn to rewind back to that moment, stay in it forever. I blink away the pressure behind my eyes and steel my spine. She's going to hate me. I close my eyes on a long blink.

When I open them, she's watching me, sees the truth in mine before I utter a word. I speak anyway. "I need to catch up on some work, so I'm gonna skip the bonfire."

"Hmph. Sure. Fine." She throws the torn fabric on the floor and stands, locking her hands on her hips. "You know what? Not fine." She rakes her fingers through her hair and begins pacing in front of me. Her long limbs graceful despite her fury.

I brace for the tirade. I deserve it. On some level, I welcome it. The pain of unmet needs and desires feels familiar although I didn't have a name for it most of my life.

Whirling to face me, she points in my face. "Don't fucking lie to me, Julian. At least have the balls to tell me the truth. I think I deserve that." Her hands land back on her hips, her chest and abs rippling as she huffs.

Captivating. She would kill me if she knew the train of my thoughts. I shake my head to stay on track. "Fine. I don't want to go." I hold my hands out to my sides, palms up.

"That's a lie, too. You already told me you love this event. You've planned it with Allie since you came to Blue Lake."

"Things change." I arch my brow in challenge. Why am I provoking her? *Because then she'll do the heavy lifting for you. Because you're a pussy. A coward.*

"Things? Or you?" She arches hers back at me.

"What do you want from me, Ever?"

She jerks her head back like I slapped her. "You know what? Nothing. I'm done with this shit." She stalks to the closet, yanks jeans off a hanger and wrenches them up her legs. Leaving them unzipped, she jerks a hoodie off a hanger next and pulls it over her head, punches her arms through the sleeves and stalks past me out the bedroom door.

I'm getting what I want. Why can't I let her go? *Let her go. Don't do it.* "Ever?" Her footsteps pound down the stairs. By the time I hit the bottom step, she's at the front door pulling on her kicks. "Ever."

She stops her reach for her phone and keys.

"What, Julian? What do you have to say now?" Her eyes are charcoal and swimming with unshed tears. I almost take it all back. One tear falls. She swipes it away. "More lies?"

Find your balls. Let her go. "Just be careful tonight."

"Hmph. Fuck you, Julian." With that, she jerks the door open, marches through it and slams it, shaking the windows. She didn't take the keys to the 4Runner. She'll run to the marina. Running will help. It's her thing.

I head into the home gym. I plan to beat the absolute shit out of the heavy bag until I can't move. I crank my angry playlist, heavy with Eminem, Linkin Park and Muse, and get to work. That I picture beating the shit out of my despicable excuse for a parent while I swing and kick makes me angrier. I shouldn't want to beat the shit out of the people who raised me. I shouldn't want to pummel his face until it's unrecognizable. Tears sting my eyes as I continue to pulverize my knuckles. I purposely left them untaped, relishing that pain to the searing hole in my chest. My grunts turn to sobs but still I strike the bag with fists and feet until I stumble with fatigue and collapse on the padded floor, music and sorrow echoing off the walls. I feel like that powerless little boy in that dirty trailer park, not in control of my own life. *I could be*, a voice whispers in my head. I ignore it. *Let her go.*

Ever doesn't come home tonight. I know this isn't her home any-more, but it has been while Lilly and Noah are here. I figure she's with Lilly—hopefully enjoying herself. I don't check her location, though my fingers itch to. It's New Year's Eve. We should be celebrating together and looking forward to all the incredible things in store for us in the year to come. Instead I'm lying on my bed in the dark staring at the clock wondering what my life looks like without her in it.

It's for the best. She deserves a good life, with a good guy.

My stomach pitches on the image of her with another guy, his hands on her. I snag my phone off the charger and swipe the screen, intending to check her location. The picture on screen is of the two of us squaring off—my favorite. Auz sent it to me after our last content filming weekend. I drag my finger over the image. In it, Ever is strong, confident, fierce. And happy. The memory is enough to make me put the phone back on the charger and stare at the screen again, watching the minutes tick into the new year.

Once it strikes midnight, I roll onto my back and stare up at the ceiling. I can be alone, should be alone. No one else deserves to be dragged into the mess of my bloodline—especially her. She deserves every good thing this life can give her. The one thing I can give her is my absence. And I will. Tapping my chest to ease the rising panic, I force a shaky breath through my pursed lips. A rogue tear slides along my temple and into my ear. I let it fall unchecked. It won't be like it was with Taya. Ever is still alive and well. I'm not sure that mourning the loss of someone who is still on the planet is better or worse for the one who's lost them. I'm about to find out.

Chapter 14

Everly

As I release my floating lantern, I reflect on my wishes and realize they're all for him. I take a second lantern and make myself wish for *my* future, *my* dreams and new beginnings. I visualize what I need to let go of for those wishes and dreams to have space to become beginnings. Swiping at the tears that won't stop, I tell myself that I can't be the only one fighting for us. Fuck, it shouldn't be a fight at all. Isn't that what my dad always said? *Ev, your person—the one you pick to do life with—should be the one who helps you through all the shit life throws at you. It shouldn't* be *one of the things life throws at you. Remember that.* I was twelve, but I remember we were sitting in the garage listening to Guns N' Roses. He would sit and tell me stories or give me advice. It was almost like he knew he wouldn't always be around to do it. I watch the lanterns float away and dissolve in the inky water. *I have to let him go.* My mind stills on that realization.

"Hey, love. Sending off some good wishes?" Lilly plants her butt in the sand next to me.

"Hey, Lill. Yeah. I think so." I side-bump her as she drops her arm across my shoulders. That I'm not freaking out is my proof that I'm on the right path. That's what I'm telling myself anyway. Guilt weighs on me that the last thing I said to him was "fuck you," but under the circumstances that *was* my restraint. I'm not sure I've ever been so angry. Now I'm just contemplative and weirdly calm. As if my psyche is calling me out as a liar, a sob bubbles up my throat and escapes my lips.

"Oh, honey, tell me what's happening"—her embrace tightens—"and who we're burying."

I sniff, and on a watery laugh, I assure her, "No one." I shake my head side to side. "No one. I just . . ." I turn into her as the dam breaks. "I can't save him, Lill. I can't reach him anymore. I have to let him go."

"Shhh, okay." She wraps both arms around me and pets my hair. "It's okay, Ever. I'm here. What can I do?"

What she does is hug me while I cry so hard and so long I feel lethargic after, but also more resolved than ever.

One thing I'm damn sure of is I'm not going to beg him to love me, to be with me. Now that my mind is made up, I'm anxious to get started. After I walk Lilly through the nightmare my *perfect* relationship has become, I feel lighter, determined and maybe a little angry still underneath it all. My exhilaration and resolve are usurping my sadness, at least for the moment. "Any chance you guys are heading back to SLO early?"

"Yeah, maybe. Seth is having ocean withdrawal. Honestly, so am I. It's addictive. You must want your apartment back, right? Considering . . ." She chuckles and bumps shoulders with me like when she first sat down, which feels like a lifetime ago but is mere minutes.

"Actually, I want a ride."

***

Lilly's right. The ocean is addictive. I can't wait to feel the sand under my feet. They dropped me at the Oak Valley airport last night on their way back to San Luis. Lilly pushed back on leaving me in the airport on New Year's Eve (or technically day) heartbroken and alone. Once I assured her I was able to get a flight and wouldn't have to wait long, she gave in. I waited two hours for the next flight to Los Angeles in an almost empty airport. Just as I was about to board my plane, my phone buzzed in my pocket. A text from Julian. Adrenaline courses through my system. I don't want to read it, but I know I will. I tap the screen as I walk down the Jetway.

Julian: I'm so sorry, Ever. I really do love you and want you to be safe.

I resist the urge to hurl my phone onto the ramp and instead tap his name to bring up his contact and hit block, close my phone, slide it into my back pocket and continue to board my flight. I swallow the emotion welling up in my chest and dig deep for the determination that brought me this far. A good therapist might say I'm projecting all my past turmoil onto this one situation, but I don't care. I've taken enough shit from people to know I'm done doing it. Even if some lingering resentment from my past in Oak Valley is seeping into the current bullshit with Julian, so be it. I'm done letting my life be a dumpster fire. I cue up my angriest old-school rock playlist as loud as my ears can take through my earbuds and let myself wallow for the duration of the flight. When I land, I take a few deep breaths and mentally shake off the negative energy swirling around me. My new life starts now.

After the hour-and-a-half flight and waiting until a decent hour to text Sean, it's now creeping into midmorning. I should be dragging from lack of sleep, but revenge goals are better than caffeine. I don't want to think about what I'll tell Allie and Ashley. I'm not going to lie, but I also don't want to trash Julian. I'm not as mad anymore, just sad for what could've been. I'm also not delusional enough to think I'm *over it.* My compartmentalizing tendencies are probably just working overtime to protect my heart, and I'm letting it happen. I'd rather delude myself as long as possible or stay as busy as possible so I don't have time to think, dwell or break down. I turned off my location for him during my wait at the OV airport. If he does check, he won't find me.

"Do they know I'm coming?" I catch Sean's eyes, in the mirror of the town car—Ashley's faithful driver.

"Of course, Miss Davis."

"Sean, I told you to just call me Ever."

His eyes crinkle in the rearview mirror, and he nods but doesn't correct himself.

"What'd they say? Never mind. I hope I didn't put you in a weird spot."

"Not at all, Miss . . . Ever. I'm available whenever you need me. That's my job."

I smile at his reflection for using my first name—the name I want everyone to call me now. It's my name and I like it. I can make it *my* name, not the name I have because of . . . *him.* I push his image from my mind. I frown out the window, but the rushing scenery pulls my lips up. "The weather is crazy beautiful down here." I'm not running away—again—at least that's what I'm telling myself. I'm starting my life. The life I was supposed to live before I moved to Blue Lake. Maybe a life attending Pepperdine. That's what I hope to figure out with Allie and Ashley. My heart thuds faster the closer we get to Malibu. I hope it's okay that I need an adult right now—a real adult. Allie has never made me feel like a burden. Neither has Ashley for that matter. That guy is either a saint or not human. No wonder he captured Allie's heart. I've never seen or heard of her so much as date anyone my whole life. That she utterly fell for him speaks volumes. Though asking for help is foreign to me, asking Allie and Ashley doesn't bring the level of dread it would were it anyone else. Good thing, because we're rolling through the gates now and it's crunch time.

***

"I need a change. That's the simplest way to describe it. I still want to focus on fitness and psychology. I still want to work for ASH . . . if you'll have me."

"That's not even a question." Ashley curves his arm around Allie's shoulders and smiles at me before he looks down at Allie questioningly.

"Of course, Ev. Whatever you need. I've always told you that. What's mine is yours. All the Davis girls. You're my family." Allie wraps her arms around Ashley's waist and squeezes as he kisses her temple.

I ignore the stabbing pain in my chest at seeing the open display of affection. I lower my eyes and focus on my fidgeting hands, take a slow deep breath and look up, bouncing my eyes between them. *I can do this. I'm Kyle Davis's daughter.* I tuck in the hurt, smile and say, "I should have all my Gen Ed out of the way in a few months. Got any sway over Pepperdine?" One cheek lifts and my brows rise on my forehead as I pin Ashley with a calm stare I don't quite feel inside.

"What's the saying? 'It's not what you know, it's who you know.'" He winks as he says it. "We'll see what we can do." His smile reassures me, calms me for real. "Would you want to live here with us? The dorms? We've got an empty cottage we could renovate for you."

"I honestly don't want to be a burden. I'll pay rent. I'll work for you. Whatever I need to do. I just need a change."

"You already said that," they say in unison, then laugh at their timing, gazing at each other.

I stamp down the urge to roll my eyes. Nausea replaces the chest pain. I'm going to need distance from any *lovey-dovey* shit for a while. I force a smile back to my lips. It feels plastic on my face. I hold it long enough to let their moment pass. "The cottage? Just so I'm not in the way," I lie. "But you don't have to renovate it. I'm sure it's perfect the way it is."

"It's actually storage for the content studio. So, yes, we will fix it up for you. It would be our pleasure. Right, babe?" He kisses her on her forehead as she readily agrees.

I turn my back and swallow the rising bile. Blinking, I keep the welling tears at bay. *Please let me hold it together.* "Can I . . . take one of the guest rooms for now? Freshen up, maybe take a quick nap?"

"Of course. Take whichever one you want. Let me help you with your bags."

"Thanks, I got it." That I can fit my whole life into two suitcases almost breaks me. That stops now. I let Allie take one of the bags from my hand. I'm going to build a life for myself. Here. One with roots, where I feel like I belong. Where no one can take it away from me.

Once Allie sets my other bag on the ground, she squeezes my shoulder.

I'm not facing her and I don't turn as the first tear spills. "I just need a minute. I'll be okay."

"Take as much time as you need." She lets go. Her muted footsteps on the carpet turn to soft taps on the hardwood of the hallway.

"Thank you, Allie, for not . . . for just letting me show up here." My response is the door closing softly behind me. I take two steps, fall face down on the soft lavender comforter and bawl my insides out. I sob until my head pounds like a thousand tiny hammers across my forehead. My face feels puffy, my limbs feel weighted, my eyelids almost swollen shut.

Before I pass out from sheer exhaustion, I note the colors of the room. Nothing is blue. It still gives coastal vibes but with lavender, sandy beige and soft yellows. It's a different kind of peaceful. I inhale and exhale deeply, once, twice. I'll be okay. Kyle Davis's daughter is always okay. My dad's image swims into my mind. He wasn't home a lot, but I remember his hugs. Warm. Strong. Safe. A shaky sob escapes my lips, which sends a furious pounding to my temples. I can't cry anymore. My head is screaming at me to the point of making me want to hurl. *I miss you, Dad.* I don't know if that thought that slams into my brain is accurate though. I miss him, sure, but I think I miss how simple things were when he was alive. At least they felt that way to me as a kid. I'm sure there was a lot of stress I never noticed at my age with him being deployed a lot. To me, though, I was loved by a mom and a dad and had a good home and a sister I idolized. Looking back, it felt . . . easy. Easier than this, for sure. I pet the soft velvety duvet, swiping my hands back and forth until the weight of my grief and my pounding post-cry headache pull me under.

Chapter 15

Everly

Six Months Later

"I got in?"

"You got in." Ashley throws his arms around me and hugs me. What's weird is it doesn't feel weird. I've gotten used to his touchy-feely personality. *Physical touch is important for the immune system.* He wore me down over the last six months.

"I'm sure it had nothing to do with your generous donation." I quirk my eyebrow at him, but my smile hurts my cheeks. I'm freakin' stoked Pepperdine accepted me as a transfer student.

"Maybe it had more to do with your kick-ass work ethic and killing your Gen Ed in a year and a half."

My cheeks inch upward at his praise, but I play it cool and brush my shoulders with the backs of my hands, then blow on my curled fingertips.

"We should celebrate," Allie announces as she sails into the kitchen and plants a kiss on Ashley's lips as she passes us and snags the coffee pot, refilling her cup.

"Raincheck? Tatum and Lennon want me to go to this surf thing tonight at Zuma."

"For sure. Just let us know when you can pencil us in." She winks at me as she sips from her steaming mug.

I roll my eyes and giggle.

Ashley sidesteps and snakes his arm around her waist and presses a kiss to her temple.

The pang is so slight it almost doesn't register. Still, I turn my head as my smile falters, and I excuse myself to go get ready for my evening.

In six months, not much has changed except my location. I still take a heavy load of classes. I still work as an online personal trainer and film content for the ASH fitness apps. But now I'm known as Ever Tate, Performance Enhancement Specialist. I still avoid mushy romantic couple-y things like the plague. Thank God for Tatum and Lennon and surfing. They are my proof that coming here to Malibu was the right move. I met Lennon in the Payson Library while studying—a habit of mine since I moved here. Maybe it was my way of manifesting my acceptance into their transfer program. She asked to join me at my table, and her twin sister, Tatum, joined a few minutes later. Tatum is a psych major too, so we'll likely share some classes now that I'm in. Lennon is studying fitness and kinesiology, which overlaps with my goals a little in the sports psychology arena. When they found out I'd just moved to Malibu and planned to transfer as soon as I finished my General Ed., they appointed themselves my official tour guides.

Both prolific surfers, they vowed to turn me into one too once they discovered I'd tried it before. Lilly wasn't exaggerating when she claimed it became their *whole personality*. I'm addicted and getting better every day. The ache in my muscles is different than the ache I get from gym workouts. It's changed my body, too. I look and feel stronger than ever. The weather in Southern California makes it easy to surf year-round. I just got my own board now that I can stand up for more than three seconds.

"Hey, Ev." Ashley stops my hasty retreat. "You taking your board tonight?"

"I might, but I don't think I'll go in. Why?"

"I wanna show you something." He clasps my hand and leads me toward the foyer and the front door. Again, his overly touchy affection no longer alarms me. If I'm being honest, I kinda like it. He gives the-big-brother-I-never-had energy. He doesn't let go of my hand as he sweeps the door open with his other, grand gesture-like. Front and center of the circular driveway just down the stairs waits a brand-new smoky gray Toyota 4Runner.

"Oh my God. That's beautiful."

"It's yours."

"What? No. Luke, it's too much."

Allie speaks behind us. "We traded in my old one and got you this. For getting accepted to Pepperdine."

"But I just got in." I pivot, my hand flying to cover my gaping lips.

"Let's just say we had a hunch." Her hands are folded together in front of her like prayer hands and she's beaming.

I don't want to squash her obvious excitement but . . . this is over the top. "I can't accept this." I tilt my head and lift one corner of my mouth to soften the blow.

"Oh, c'mon. Let us. We don't have any kids to spoil. You're it." She flaps her hands at me like she's shooing me away.

"The board should slide nicely into the back," Ashley chimes in, snugging up to Allie.

I'm speechless and so stunned by the gesture that their cuddly PDA doesn't make my radar for once. The whole scene is giving eighties television family vibes, and I'm letting it suck me in. Tears prick my eyes and I throw my arms around both of them at once.

They squeeze me back while Allie sniffles and Ashley clears his throat.

"Well, I, uh, better hurry and get ready so I'm not late." I haven't cried since the first day I arrived. I've been too busy. I've made certain I'm too busy. That someone had to go back to Blue Lake and get Allie's old 4Runner is not lost on me. I push the thought out of my mind and the image it conjures of a dark-haired, blue-eyed boy I refuse to let haunt me. Maybe I will night surf after all.

Chapter 16

JULIAN

"C'mon, Julian. What the fuck happened? The fans want to know."

"The fans? Or you?" I cock an eyebrow at Callie while Auz snickers behind his camera.

"Same thing." She pops her hip and curls her fingers around it.

"No comment." I let her fuss with my hair for a few more seconds before I reach for her hand, and, smiling to soften the blow, I say, "I think the hair is good," and step back, dropping her hand.

"Looks good through the lens," Auz calls out from across the room, in bro solidarity I'm sure. "Let's roll before the light fades." For sure bro code. I'm grateful.

Callie rolls her eyes and steps back, too.

I lean against the heavy bag and fold my arms over my chest, crossing one ankle over the other.

Auz starts snapping, telling me to tilt my head this way or shift my eyes that way. After about ten clicks, he says, "I think we're good. Wanna go grab a beer, some food?"

"Nah, I've got work, but you guys go ahead. Pete's expecting you. What time do you guys head out tomorrow?"

"Early. Probably won't see you." Auz extends his hand to shake mine.

"Okay, well, thanks for making the trip to me. I've had too much going on to get down south." I smile and grip his hand.

"M-hm," Callie mumbles. "Well, you can't avoid it forever. The ASH anniversary is coming up and you'll have to come to the party."

"Fuck, Callie. Give it a rest," Auz scolds as he packs his camera and equipment.

"Just saying." She shrugs and punches me lightly on the bicep.

"I'm aware." I force myself to look her in the eye, my features schooled into cool composure. The mention of the party sends a cold searing pain to my chest, but I ignore it. This isn't today's problem. "Thanks, again. Safe travels." I turn to gather my towel, bag and water bottle. "If that's everything, I'm going to hit the shower. See you guys soon." I turn on my heel and don't look back. Taking the stairs two at a time, I begin stripping off my clothes once I hit the second-story landing and don't stop until I step into the shower and crank the water. The icy spray jolts me at first, but I welcome the tiny electric shocks. I let the water pelt me until it turns hot, then I duck my head and let the heat pummel my shoulders and neck. I try to clear my mind and find my happy place. I've been working with Dr. Carver on a new one lately—one that doesn't involve cloud-gray eyes and chestnut brown hair.

Speaking of Claire Carver, it's almost time for our video appointment. I rush through lathering up and sit down at my desk just in time to log in to our Zoom call. When her face fills the screen, she smiles, her eyes crinkling at the corners behind her glasses. Her background is different, filled with pines and blue water. "Julian. You look . . . refreshed." She laughs softly, taking in my wet hair.

I smile back politely and change the subject. "Where are you?"

"Oh, we're doing the family thing in Tahoe this weekend."

"Should we reschedule? We can reschedule." She's already shaking her head before I finish.

"Nope, we're good. I would've said if I needed to cancel. But Julian, you deserve to have people show up for you, on time, like they say they will. You're worth someone making time for you."

I nod my head, but she tracks me well. She knows I'm going through the motions, nodding in agreement because that's what I'm supposed to believe. The truth is—

Her voice cuts off my train of thought. "Tell me what you're thinking right now."

"Uh, I guess that not having people show up for me feels better—not better, normal. More normal than when they do."

Her turn to nod. "Recognizing the pattern is the first step to breaking it. Proud of you."

"I know. I mean, thank you."

She smiles. Her smile soothes me. Her porcelain skin and dark eyes, framed by an equally dark bob of silky hair and her pixie features, invite you in and make you want to share your secrets. She curls her finger around her ear, trapping a lock of hair behind it. The simple diamond stud on her earlobe catches the sunlight and winks at me. "Do you want to talk about why you feel more comfortable with people bailing on you?"

"Do I ever wanna *talk* about it?" I use quote marks when I say the word *talk.*

"Yet, you're here. So you must want answers."

I shrug my shoulders with a heavy sigh. "I mean I guess it's my parents never being there for me. It feels familiar to not have anyone to depend on?"

Her smile and slight nod tell me to brace for the analysis that's incoming. "That's the easy answer, yes. Do you ever ask yourself why it feels . . . You said familiar? I'm going to say comfortable. But also, why was that a question? Are you unsure if it still feels familiar or comfortable?"

"I don't know, Doc." I throw my hands out to my sides, palms up. "Can't you just tell me what I feel and we can go from there?"

Her short peal of laughter raises one corner of my mouth.

"Julian." The soft rebuke is evident in her tone.

I hold my hands up in surrender. "Okay, okay. I, uh, guess it's easier to not have anyone around so I don't have to risk losing them or them not . . . loving me back."

She nods and scribbles something on her notepad. "When those first relationships are devoid of basic nurturing and unconditional love, it skews our *love map.*" She uses finger quotes for love map and elaborates. "Or our emotional blueprint for future relationships. Speaking of your parents—"

"What about them? Also, can we not call them that?"

"Children who feel like they must earn their parents' love can grow up with deep-seated feelings of inadequacy. It can create a fear that love is temporary and can be taken away at any moment. It's less about what happened and more about what didn't happen."

"They didn't hold me, therefore I don't like to be held."

"Oversimplifying, but yes. Any updates on your . . . Todd?"

"I guess he could get life in prison. They said twenty-five to life, but it's a process. Could take up to a year before he's sentenced."

"And how do you feel about that?"

A smirk splits my face at her very typical shrink response. I shrug in answer but then add, "He *should* get life for what he did." I can talk about it like it happened to someone else. I don't picture *her* when I do.

Claire is nodding again. "What about your mom?"

More shrugging. "I paid off her trailer. Put the rest of my grandfather's money in a trust for her. She gets a monthly allowance if she stays clean and must submit to drug tests. If she doesn't stay clean, she doesn't get paid, but she can use the money for a treatment program. A trustee handles it all so I don't have to be involved."

"That was nice of you to do that for her." She writes something in her notebook.

I fidget in my chair.

"Have you spoken to her?"

Shaking my head, I profess, "There's nothing to say. The money was her father's. I barely knew him. I don't need the money. And I don't *want* the money that could've caused . . . that made him resort to kidnapping." *Like it happened to someone else. Not her. Because of me.*

"I think that's a reasonable and healthy boundary. I'm proud of you."

"Thanks, Doc." I look down at my hands where my fingers flick my nails in my lap.

"Julian, I'd like to discuss the other side of that boundary. I applaud your ability to draw a line with people who don't deserve to be in your life. I'd like to see you open up to letting people in who do deserve it—who do want to love you and be good to you and be there for you."

I blow a long breath out through puffed cheeks. "What if there's no one around who wants to do that?"

"What if there is but you won't let them?"

"Isn't time up or something?" I really do like her smile. I smile back.

"We can call it good for today. But can you do something for me?"

I nod. "Sure."

"Can you start paying attention to times where someone wants to do something nice for you, be there for you, no matter how small or insignificant it might seem. Then pay attention to your feelings and reactions to those offers, gestures. Can you do that?" More nodding. "Write them down if you can. We can discuss them next time."

"Okay. Sure. Have a nice time in Tahoe."

"Thanks, Julian. See you soon."

Chapter 17
EVERLY

One Month Later

"I'll be fine." My declaration is met with eye rolls and jeers. Standing in the middle of their open floor plan living room, Tatum and Lennon are giving ridicule in stereo. Twin thing, I guess. "Seriously, I'll have you guys—and Lilly promised to show, too."

"We finally get to meet the legendary Lilly. Are her hot boy toys coming with her?"

"I promised them surfing, so yeah, I think they all are. They tend to run as a unit anyway."

Lennon rubs her hands together and arches her brows at her sister.

I deadpan, "You know you can't hit on them, right?"

They hold their right hands up in a mock scout salute at the exact same time.

"Creepy." My comment sends them into a fit of giggles. "You guys really get off on this twin telepathy thing, don't you?"

"It takes more than that to get me off, but maybe Tatum." Lennon sidesteps her sister's shove. Tatum's face turns crimson, the shier of the two and younger by six minutes.

"Lennon, not all of us are ferally thirsty." Tatum rallies from her embarrassment quickly.

Lennon shrugs shamelessly.

I raise my hand. "Can I leave the sister slug match? Thank God Via lives five hours away. Still, we were never as bad as you two.

"Twin thing," they say in unison.

I roll my eyes. "I'm out. Gotta see what last-minute help they still need anyway."

"Wait," Lennon calls as I reach for the door. "We didn't finish the Julian discussion."

Hearing his name doesn't pierce like it used to. Still, I avoid it as much as possible. "Nothing to discuss. It's in the past. We've moved on."

"Uh-huh. Totally. That why you blew off Bronson when he asked you out? Because it's *so* in the past?"

"Fuck, Lennon, is this a roast? I blew off Bronson because he's a fuck boy and I don't want to be his next conquest."

"I think he's a recovering fuck boy," Tatum chimes in but doesn't look up from her fidgeting fingernails.

"Sounds like Tatum wants to be his next conquest," Lennon quips.

"Nah, she wants to shrink him. It's a psych major thing. I get it. And he's a perfect specimen." I toss her a lifeline because I see the way she looks at Bronson. That's another reason I ignore his attention. Girl code. "Girls, I'm out. Gonna have to save the Ever saga for another time. Come early and have a drink with me."

"You mean be your airbags?" Lennon's voice follows me out the door.

I ignore the question—it was rhetorical anyway—and their tinkling laughter that trails me out the door. I stayed over at their house last night because their kickback went late. Now I've gotta book it back to Ashley's to help set up for the ASH anniversary party tomorrow.

With all the windows down and my hair twisted into a messy knot on top of my head, I cruise down PCH to Ashley's as the rising sun glimmers on the ocean. The salty air and the volume of GNR drown out the thoughts, if not the images, in my head. Still, my heart pounds in my chest and my pulse jumps in my wrists. I ignore the white knuckles gripping the steering wheel. *I can do this. God, I miss his face.*

The urge to pull into the beach parking lot and catch a wave is strong. My dad's old-school playlist used to be my foolproof distraction. Now it's surfing. It still requires too much of my concentration to allow for anything else, like worry and stress or blue-eyed boys that shatter your heart.

As I pull through the gates of Ashley's property, I continue around the back of the main house to my private drive that leads to the remodeled cottage I now rent. I insist on paying rent, though it's the same conversation every month. *Just keep it in case you need it for books or something.* I've resorted to dropping it to his Venmo so I don't have to hear about it. He really gives the cutest *dad* vibes though, and I love him for it.

Slamming my foot on the brake, I gasp at the sight of the white Jeep in my spot. *Nooo. Fuck.* I crank the wheel and squeeze my 4Runner in beside the Jeep and the hedge that separates my little driveway from the backyard. Pressing the button to cut my engine floods my world into deafening silence. Slowly the sounds of the property trickle in: birds, the pool sweep, the buzz of a distant hedge trimmer. I want to tiptoe out of my car and into the cottage to hide. Why do I feel like a little kid caught doing something wrong? The adrenaline rush lands like too many espressos. My fingers flounder on the door handle. *Pull it together, Ever.*

Ducking into the cottage, I lean back on the door gulping for air. My phone buzzes in my pocket, startling me.

Allie: Julian's not here. He drove up last night. Luke took him to tour the new gyms. They'll be gone all day.

Me: No worries. Grabbing a quick shower then I'm all yours.

My heart rate slows with the information—a reprieve, for now at least. Before I drop my phone on the entryway table, I text Lilly.

Me: What's your ETA tomorrow?

Lilly: What if we came tonight?

Me: Hell yeah. Hurry up. Just helping Allie all day. Come whenever.

Then I text the twins in our group chat.

Me: New development. He's here. Guess I needed that pep talk after all.

Tatum: Oh. My. Fuck. Are you okay? What'd he say? What'd you say?

Lennon: Yeah. What she said.

Me: Haven't seen him yet. Just his Jeep. Guess he's gone all day with Ashley. Thank God! Lilly's coming tonight though.

Lennon: Okay, tell us the plan, who we hate, how to act, when to show up.

Me: Lol you're the best. I'm good. Just be here tomorrow to distract me.

I'm not sure when I became such a girl. I've never let myself have true girlfriends besides Via, then Lilly. I guess Lilly opened me up to the possibility of real friends—that I don't share DNA with. Lennon and Tatum are like the ocean air though—like a full dose of negative ions. They just make you feel good being around them. Kinda like Lilly but different. I'm so lucky to have such beautiful souls in my life. Twin rows of tears roll down my cheeks before I even realize I'm crying.

Swiping them away, I trek down the short hallway into one of the two master suites the renovated cottage boasts. I asked Allie if I could have the lavender decor from the bedroom I used in the main house. Instead of transferring it all to the cottage, they had it replicated. I bawled when I saw it. The last seven months here have healed me in ways I never even knew I needed healing. From the summer classes Pepperdine approved, to meeting the twins, to settling into my new role with ASH, my nervous system is calmer than it's ever been. Current development notwithstanding, I vow to keep it that way and let the pounding heat of the shower work its magic, despite the climbing heat of the SoCal summer day.

Chapter 18

Julian

"Man, Luke, I can't believe how much ASH has grown since we met. Do you ever stop?"

"You're one to talk. Although, I could stand to have you down here more. Your brand is blowing up. People want to see you in person."

We just finished touring Ashley's newest gym and sit down at the juice bar for a drink before we head to our next stop. He slides me one of the green drinks the young employee sets on the bar in front of us. "I know. I'm just so busy—"

"No, you don't get to play that card with me. I see the numbers. Besides, I'm your friend. You can talk to me—tell me the truth. How are you doing with everything? Real talk. Like being here, for instance. You good?"

I take a long sip of the smoothie to give myself a minute to respond. "I'm mostly good. Real talk though I'm nervous as shit to see her. Like a fucking kid on the first day of school." I shake my head at my declaration. "That honest enough for you?" I laugh and take another drink.

Clapping me on the shoulder, Luke gives me a sympathetic grin. "I can't imagine, buddy. And thank you for showing up. It means a lot to me. To both of us."

I shrug. "It's good for business."

"It is. But seriously. Fuck all that. Thanks for coming. Man to man, friend to friend, I'm glad you're here." He reaches his hand out to shake mine and, when I clasp his, he hugs me with his other.

It's one of those moments Dr. Carver wants me to pay attention to—letting people care about me. Of all the people, Luke is the least awkward for me besides Allie. He's so goddamn genuine and kind, it's hard not to love him. "I appreciate you, Luke. I mean that. You make everything so easy. I can't thank you enough for that. For everything."

"C'mon. One more gym, then we'll head back to Malibu."

We stand to leave and I try to ignore the way my heart races at the thought of going back to the coast, where *she* is. I shove my hands into my shorts pockets to dry the clamminess.

***

Entering through the back of the house, I notice two things: a newer gray 4Runner parked next to my Jeep with a surfboard sticking out of the back window and the sunshine smell that hits my nose as soon as we step into the mudroom/laundry room off the kitchen. I stop as if I smack into a wall and brace myself to see her. I take a deep inhale to calm the adrenaline spike, but I suck in through my nose and forget the room is heavy with her scent. It's like a fucking drug and I'm an addict. I blow it out silently through pursed lips as I trail Ashley into the kitchen.

Allie rushes to throw her arms around Luke and kisses him on the lips while my eyes scan the room. *She's not here.* It's just the three of us, but she must've just left. I don't know if I'm relieved or disappointed.

"How was the tour?"

It takes me a moment to realize Allie is asking me. I focus on her beaming face and lock in. Drug, indeed. My head is spinning. "Good, good. Impressive. You guys don't slow down." I match her smile, glue my gaze to hers.

She reaches for me and hugs me.

I let her and force my arms up and around her slight frame and squeeze.

She lifts herself up on her toes and presses her lips to my ear. "It's just us tonight. Ever is in her cottage." She places a maternal kiss to my cheek and says louder, "So glad you're here, Julian. I've missed you."

She called her Ever. Is that what she goes by now? I don't know how to feel about that. It was *my* name for her. Hearing Allie use it so casually is a little like taking a bullet. I rub the spot on my chest, the one that now holds her name. "Me too." I smile again. "Mind if I head up and shower before dinner? Ash made me do a demo for some new members today, so I'm sweaty."

"Of course. Take your time. Dinner is chicken salad, so it can be served any time."

I nod and cross the kitchen to head upstairs to my room. As soon as my foot touches the first stair, I grab the banister and take a couple deep gulps of air. Air that doesn't smell like her. It's going to be fine. Taking the stairs two at a time, I strip off the T-shirt as I enter the guest room they put me in. Not the same room we stayed in together. This one is across the hall and overlooks the backyard, pool and hot tub.

Off to the right is the cottage and the driveway where my Jeep and the 4Runner are parked. I lean on the window frame and look beyond the yard where the horizon meets the ocean and wonder what it'll be like to see her again for the first time in seven months.

I must summon her with my thoughts because the cottage door opens and there she is, stepping out onto the welcome mat in bare feet. She's in a white gauzy romper that barely skims the top of her thighs. Gaping armholes show off her torso and the sports bra underneath. I drink her in, swallowing like she's water in a desert. Her body has changed. For one, her skin is darker, richly tanned, more prominent in the white fit. The vee of her lats is more defined, her shoulders and arms more sculpted. She's surfing. I'd bet money on it. That's her board in the 4Runner. Part of me is jealous that I don't know anything about her anymore. Part of me is proud she's living her best life. That's the part that has my heart pounding like it wants to escape my chest, my abs clenching at the heat swirling there.

Lilly's old Bronco pulls in behind the 4Runner, and Lilly throws her door open and then hurls herself into Ever's arms. "Ever! My girl." She's throwing her arms around Lilly and she laughs. Nope, *that* was like taking a bullet. That sound pushes me away from the window, silently sliding it closed so I can't hear her voice. The laugh, *her laugh*, almost brings me to my knees. I'm not sure I can do this. Does she miss me at all? For seven months, I've been telling myself I didn't want her to miss me, that I wished her a good, happy life filled with all the things she deserves. And I do. Is it wrong that I hope she misses me a little, too? Mostly, I keep myself running so hard I'm too exhausted to think about how much I miss her. I can't pretend here though, when she's right in front of me. It's why I haven't been down here since she left.

I finish stripping off my clothes and move into the adjoining bathroom. I step under the ceiling-mounted rainfall shower head. The water is chilled but does nothing to douse the flames seeing her ignited. Water sluices over my body and I imagine it's her hands. My body reacts instantly.

It's always the same. She shoves me against the wall, fire in her eyes.

"Fuck you, Julian. Fuck me."

"I got you, Ever." Her skin is silk, her core wet, ready for me, always. I slide into her and capture her moan with my kiss. I can't stop. She doesn't want me to. Her moans urge me on, faster, deeper, harder. I'm panting, about to come. I should wait for her to come. She doesn't want me to.

"Come for me, Julie."

And I do. "Ughhh, yes, Ever. So good. Yes, baby. Mmmm."

I come back to reality with one hand bracing the tiled wall in front of me, the other wrapped firmly around my dick, my head hanging low under the now lukewarm water of the shower. Catching my breath, I soap my hands and scrub them over my body and try to put her out of my mind. That she's within reach makes it harder. I don't have my murderous routine here to drive her out of my head, and I don't have the gift of distance to make seeing her an impossibility. I drag on some cotton shorts and a muscle tee and wonder how I'll get through dinner. I'm not the least bit hungry, but I'll eat for my health and, if for nothing else, to avoid Allie's scrutiny. The way she continues to meet me where I'm at is probably why I stayed when she found me in the first place all those years ago. She doesn't push—at least not in an obvious way.

Putting me in a room that overlooks Everly's cottage might be a subtle nudge to face what haunts me. She's never asked for details. She took my flimsy excuse of staying in Blue Lake at face value. Even Ashley accommodated me, sending Callie and Auz to me whenever they needed footage or content. While they're not pushing for a reunion, time is running out. I'll have to see her tomorrow at the party. Will she talk to me? The last thing she said to me lives rent-free in my head. *"Fuck you, Julian."* I tried texting her on her birthday in February, but it didn't go through. She blocked me. *As she should.* I sent lavender roses to her here, no card, and never got a response. Not that I expected one, but I couldn't let her birthday pass without . . . something. She still owns every piece of my heart. I'm just trying to figure out how to let her have it, if she even wants it anymore.

Chapter 19
Everly

I've been tracking Lilly for the last twenty minutes, so I see when she arrives outside my door. I ignore the pull of the main house and who's inside and focus all my energy on seeing my friends. It's been too long—since New Year's Eve. We talk and FaceTime regularly. I've been sending them surfing videos Tatum and Lennon capture. I think Seth might be the most fired up about that. If I stamp down the utter thrall of the tall, dark, blue-eyed piece of my heart just footsteps from where I stand, I find I'm beyond giddy to see her. All of them. That they still function as a unit intrigues and puzzles me.

Lilly always evades any deep dives into the details, and because I don't want deep dives into mine, I respect it. But it's rare they are not all together.

Lilly throws open the door of her Bronco and hurls herself into my arms. We're dancing in circles hugging each other, laughing when Seth and Noah pull us apart and pretend to fight over who gets to hug me next. God, I've missed them, and now we can talk surfing and even go together before they leave. I'm fucking stoked to show them my skills.

It almost usurps the weight of the other guest I've yet to see. His Jeep being parked here next to mine is enough to keep him in the forefront though.

Once the hugs are done, Lilly wastes no time noticing it, too. She tosses her head toward it and asks cooly, "So . . .?"

I just shrug in response.

Seth, quite the closet empath, drops his arm over my shoulders and pivots toward the door. "So," he says pointedly and swings his gaze to Lilly. "Give us the tour. This place is next level."

"Well, this is my cottage," I reply, grateful for the intervention.

Lilly and Noah grab the bags from the car and follow us inside.

"Don't worry, Seth. We got the bags," Noah deadpans from the rear of the car. To Lilly he says, "I miss J-man." Though he says it for her ears only, I hear him. So does Seth because he tightens his grip on me and presses a kiss to my cheek.

His sweet gesture has tears pressing on the backs of my eyes. I blink rapidly to check them.

As we walk inside, I look up and over my shoulder, the pull undeniable. The second-story window is empty but I felt it—him. Did Allie put him in that room on purpose? *Not tonight.* I wipe his face from my mind and focus my attention on Seth. "What are we drinking? But we're not getting fucked up. We have a party tomorrow."

"Don't worry, I'm a professional."

"Well, I am not. So be cool."

"I'm aware." He knocks me softly on the chin with his fist, pinches it between his thumb and forefinger and pulls me to him. Planting a peck on the tip of my nose, he smiles and says, "We got you, Ever."

My heart pierces on his choice of words. That he says *we* instead of *I* is a small lifeline I cling to with both hands. "I know. I'm glad you're all here. Let's get to the reunion already." Steering him into the kitchen, I swing my hand wide, showcasing the display on the counter. "I've got pizza, popcorn and brownies. Regular brownies before you even go there."

He chuckles and curls his arm around my neck in a faux chokehold and kisses my temple.

"Where should we put our crap?" Lilly calls from behind us.

"Second door on the left." I point toward the hallway.

"Okay, this setup, Ever. They went all out for you. No wonder you don't want to go home." Noah leans on the kitchen counter as Seth elbows him over his comment.

Ignoring the *home* reference, I zero in on the first part. "Yeah, they're too good to me. Ashley even pulled strings to get me into Pepperdine. He swears he didn't, but I suspect he did. It's not the easiest school to get into." I shrug.

"Dude, let him." Lilly slides next to Noah as they sit on the barstools at the counter. "Take all the help you can get. Besides, SoCal looks good on you. And you surf now. So fire."

"Speaking of . . . when do we get to meet the new friends?"

"Tomorrow. They're coming to the party. You'll love them."

"I've always wanted to date twins. Are they single?" Seth still has his arm over my shoulders.

"Dude," Lilly and Noah blurt in sync.

"Yeah, *dude.* No hitting on my friends." I bump shoulders with him as we stand across the bar from Lilly and Noah.

"Kidding." He rolls his eyes. "Let's eat. I'm starving."

"Same," Lilly agrees.

"Waves decent here?" Noah asks, stuffing his mouth with half a slice of pizza.

"I think so. Tatum and Lennon like it. I'm new, so I'm not sure I'm a solid judge. But you guys'll see. We should go before you head back. I gotta show you my skills." I fling my hair over my shoulder. "Not to flex, but I actually surf now."

"Hey, can we check out Ashley's beach right now?" Lilly shoves the last of her crust in her mouth as she asks.

"Totally. It's beautiful. And"—I pull my phone out to check the time—"we're just in time for the sunset."

"Hell yeah." Seth grabs my hand as Lilly and Noah slide off the stools, and we all move toward the door, taking our beers with us.

Chapter 20

JULIAN

Ashley's home gym is next level, but this—standing in the waning sun, feet in the wet warm sand while the foaming waves tease my ankles—is helping me breathe, regulating my nervous system. The roar of the waves crashing on the shore mirrors my insides and drowns my swirling thoughts. The anticipation of seeing her again is like standing at the top of the Blue Lake cliffs, waiting for the free fall. I came out here hoping to find enough calm and peace to get some sleep tonight—to be ready to see her tomorrow. I'm not sure sleep is in the cards.

Before I resort to beating the shit out of a bag to exhaustion and risk injuring my hands, I'm giving Mother Nature a chance first. Beach sunsets rival those of Blue Lake, and the salty air takes it to another level. I inhale deeply and exhale, stretching my hands over my head and begin with some slow tai chi moves.

Her laughter hits me first. It's mixed with other voices and laughter, but hers drives straight through me. I could isolate it in a crowd. I drop my hands and sink them into the pockets of my shorts. It's almost dark but I make out the silhouettes. She's on Lilly's back. They're both giggling as Seth hops on Noah's back and they begin a "chicken fight." I feel like an intruder even though it's a public beach and I was here first. This is her world now. Still, I can't look away. She's ten yards out but doesn't see me. I step back out of the surf, the urge to retreat and leave the beach to her driving me. That movement draws her attention, their attention.

"J-man," Noah calls out as Everly slides from Lilly's back and Noah releases Seth's legs. Noah rushes toward me and grasps me in a solid hug, clapping me loudly on the back. "Too long, brother." He's all smiles as I hug him back, grateful for his golden retriever energy.

My eyes find hers in the dusk, barely visible, but I know she's looking at me. Seth and Lilly flank her, protecting her. I love that she has that, truly. It breaks me a little that they feel the need to protect her from me, but still, I'm glad she has people like that in her life. It drives home that I couldn't protect her when she needed it the most.

No matter how much work I do on letting people love me, the simple fact is if she'd never loved me, she'd never been taken at gunpoint. She deserves better than that. Better than me. "I was just heading back up." I shake Noah's hand, tracking the others moving closer to us. "Good to see you, Noah. I'll . . . we'll catch up more tomorrow." They're here now. I extend my hand to Seth. "Hey, Seth. Long time. Lill." I nod once to Lilly, unsure if she's neutral or not.

She silently hugs me, then steps back to Ever's side.

"Hi, Everly."

"Hi, Julian."

My eyes rake over her features, soaking them in, absorbing them like water after a drought. I think she's doing the same. Everything else falls away. Our friends, the crashing waves, until Seth says, "We're going to head back. We'll see you up there." He takes Lilly's hand and Noah takes her other. They steer her toward the stairs. She looks over her shoulder, not sure if she should leave her friend, but ultimately lets them propel her back the way they came.

Seth's voice breaks the spell, and Ever pivots to watch them for a few seconds before she responds. "I'm right behind you. Save me a brownie." She smiles at their backs, but the only answer is Seth waving his hand over his head.

"You can go. I don't want to interrupt—"

"I know," she snaps. "And you didn't." Her sass is alive and well.

My lips twitch. I stamp down the urge to smile.

Her features soften, and she opens her mouth to speak, then closes it abruptly.

"How are you?" we ask at the same time. "Good," again, in unison.

"Hmph." She gives a half smile with her chuckle.

"Do you want to join your friends?" I ask instead of telling, hoping to avoid her sass even though I secretly love it. I just don't want to piss her off.

"No. I . . ." She waves her hands, palms out, then clasps them together and drops them in front of her. "I'm glad we ran into each other before tomorrow." She smiles, but it looks sad. "Julian, I'm sorry for how I left. For what I said."

I shake my head. "I didn't leave you much choice."

She nods at this. "Still . . ." She shrugs and her eyes trail down my body.

I feel them on me like a searing laser and drop mine to my hands that fidget with my nails. "You've changed," she rasps and pulls at my gut.

I don't look up when she speaks. "You too." I raise my eyes in time to see her swallow and lick her bottom lip. "Surfing?"

"Yeah." She smiles shyly.

Now it's my turn to swallow, my mouth like dry sand.

"How'd you . . . Can you tell?" Her eyebrows crunch together in curiosity.

"Yeah. Plus I saw the board sticking out of your car."

She's nodding again, the warm ocean breeze dragging a lock of hair across her face. It catches between her lips. My fingers itch to tuck it behind her ear. I stuff them in my pockets.

"I love it." Her shy smile again.

"I'm glad, Ever." I bite down on my bottom lip to keep from blurting out that I miss her.

"You . . . got bigger." She laughs at her assertion, more exhale than laugh.

I don't know why her words make me feel self-conscious. I cross my arms and grasp my biceps, then unclasp them and let my arms drop. Why am I so goddamn nervous? The wind gives me my answer when it kicks up for a few seconds and sends her scent swirling around me. It coils in my stomach and lower. I close my eyes and inhale deeply. When I open them, they lock onto her stormy grays. I take a step toward her without realizing it.

Her hand flies up and presses flat to my chest. One touch. That's all it takes. Like a jolt of lightning adhering us to each other.

My hand covers hers. I take it and bring her palm to my lips.

"Julie." She tugs it back, but I don't release it right away.

Instead I turn my cheek into her palm, close my eyes and relish the feel of her skin on mine.

Her fingers curl into my jaw, her nails scraping the scruff there.

"I miss you," I whisper, not sure if she hears me over the crashing waves.

She pulls her hand free and steps back.

My arm falls heavily to my side. It wants to reach out, to make her stay. *Please don't go, Ever.*

"I can't. I have to go." She turns and runs toward the stairs leading back to Ashley's.

I watch her until the night swallows her shadow, and still I stare at the spot until I regain my composure. Until I walk back up to the house with no one the wiser that I'm disintegrating into a million pieces.

Chapter 21

Everly

I can't go back into the cottage and I don't want to chance running into someone in the main house. I just need a minute to compose myself. The motion sensor lights kick on the moment I step into the yard. Glancing around the pool, I spot one lounge chair at the far end that sits just beyond the reach of the glow and collapse on it before the dam breaks. Seeing him, touching him, breaks my heart all over again. I cry for everything we were, everything we lost and everything we never got to be.

Pulling my knees to my chest, I weep quietly into my arms, except for the heaving breaths I take. I don't hear him approach, but I feel his presence like a physical touch.

"Ever." He crouches near the chair and touches my hair.

I lean into it automatically.

His fingers graze my cheek, then his hand cups the side of my face, searing my skin.

God, I miss him. I turn into the contact; my lips kiss the soft skin in the center of his palm. He hisses a breath like the touch burns him, too. I don't fight him when he scoops me up like I weigh nothing and takes my place with me in his arms. Maybe I knew he'd come. Maybe I wanted him to. I should stand up, walk away, keep my boundaries. I know this. I study this. But nothing and no one will ever feel as good as he does. With his arms around me I feel loved. Cherished. Safe. I curl into him and press my face into the crook of his neck, my body shaking with the force of my sobs.

"Shhh, sweet girl. Please don't cry. I've got you." His words penetrate my sorrow, my tears.

I've got you. I press my lips to his neck, feel his pulse jump at the touch.

He blows an exhale through pursed lips. "Ever." He says it like a plea, dragging out the end.

I suck on the pulse that thuds under my lips, scrape my teeth across his skin.

"Ugh." The moan that rumbles in his chest sends a pool of liquid to my center. "Baby, we can't do this."

He called me baby. I ignore his words except that one and twist my body until I'm straddling him. Pressing against him, I feel how much he misses me. My lips move from his neck to his ear, my teeth nipping his earlobe. *Seven months. Seven months without this and now it's right here.* He's *right here.* "Kiss me, Julie." I capture his cheeks in my hands and pull his lips to mine.

His shaky exhale kisses my lips instead. He doesn't pull away but lets his lips rest on mine, our breaths mingling.

I ignore the thoughts screaming through my brain that this is wrong, desperate and a betrayal to all the growth I've made over the last seven months. But his words echo, driving them home.

"Ever, it's been seven months." His hands rest loosely on my hips. And then, "I'm not sure I have the willpower to resist you."

His fingers dig into my hips through the lightweight romper I'm wearing. My breath hitches. *He won't resist me.* I tilt my head and press my smiling lips to his.

He pulls his head back, but it meets the lounger. With barely an inch between us, he groans and tilts his head the opposite way and plunges his tongue into my mouth.

So sweet. He tastes so sweet.

His fingers dig in almost painfully, then slide around to grip my ass and pull me tight to his lap. Another guttural groan.

Yes! I want this. I want him. Logic be damned. *Stupid smart girl,* my mind tries again. I ignore it like a woman possessed. I don't care if it's irresponsible. I don't care if we haven't talked or seen each other in seven months. I don't care if nothing's changed. My hands fly to the waistband of his athletic shorts and free him from the constraints of the fabric.

He hisses when my fingers wrap around him and squeeze. "Fuck, Ever. We can't." He drags his lips across my jaw to my ear and breathes his half-hearted warning before he kisses my neck, his actions betraying his words. He tries again. "What if someone comes?"

I don't care. I won't be denied. I don't answer him with words and instead, with my free hand, I pull the leg of my romper and thong aside and guide him to my slippery opening. *Don't think. Just feel.* Dropping all my weight on him, I let gravity take over and bury him inside me.

His head jerks back, eyes squeezed shut toward the sooty sky. "Ugh." His long resounding groan is followed by an inhaled hiss.

"Fuck. So tight. So wet." He grunts between each word like it hurts to say them.

Don't think. Just feel. But one thought sears itself in my brain. *Don't give him time to stop.* Panting, I move fast and hard. "Fuck I miss this. Ughng. I'm gonna . . . mmm." I can tell the moment he gives in to the gravitational pull of our bodies, his fingers curling into my hips almost painfully—deliciously so.

One hand releases me to reach between us as he presses his thumb to the bundle of nerves above our joined bodies, drawing tiny circles that send me over the edge, convulsing around him, panting audibly. He holds me down tight to him, stills my movement as his own spasms join mine shortly after.

Wrapping his arms around my back, he presses his face to the center of my chest and regulates his breathing. His slow exhales heat my skin.

I regulate my own, running my fingers through the longer tufts of hair on top of his head, cradling him to me. Now that it's over, reality comes crashing back. We're on the patio for anyone to see. We haven't talked in seven months. I blocked him from my phone. The last words I said to him were *fuck you*. One thing hasn't changed. What he does to me. How much I want him. *Will it always be this way?* No other guy has even turned my attention.

Sliding off him, I adjust my clothing and stand up.

He snags my hand before I can walk away. "Don't go. I'm sorry. I should've stopped."

"I'm not." I exhale on the lie and don't meet his eyes. I feel reckless and immature, like I haven't made any strides at all. When I do finally look at him, his eyes say it all. He sees the truth in mine.

"Don't hate me, Ever. I'm sorry I didn't stop. Please don't go." He laces our fingers, squeezing.

"I'm not sure I gave you a choice." One corner of his mouth inches up, but the crease between his brows deepens. "And I won't. Just need to . . . clean up." I toss my chin and point to the poolroom that includes a bathroom.

His eyes follow where I point and he nods and releases my hand.

I return three minutes later to find him sitting on the edge of the lounger, elbows on his knees, head in his hands. I walk up and run my fingers through his hair, scraping my nails along his scalp. I know he likes that. *He used to like that.*

Taking my hand, he brings my palm to his lips and closes his eyes as he kisses it.

I slide it to his cheek and curl my fingers around his ear.

He lifts his face to look at me. "Thank you, Ever."

I'm not sure what I expected him to say, but that wasn't it. Probably not even top ten.

"For what?" *Is he thanking me for sex? He can't be thanking me for sex.* You know how when you're not pissed off but you're pre-pissed, like you glimpse the pissed off that's on its way?

"For loving me. I know it wasn't easy. That I didn't make it easy."
Good save.

"I think I just proved that's not true."

His bark of laughter makes my eyes crinkle and cheeks lift. He snakes his arm out and sweeps me onto his lap, wrapping his arms tight around me.

I curl my legs under me and snuggle into him just as tightly. When we're like this I can almost pretend the last seven months never happened. But it did. I let myself pretend a little longer because it feels so fucking good to be in his arms again.

Chapter 22

Julian

With her in my lap and her scent swirling around me, my eyes droop and my body goes slack as the balmy night air wraps around us like a blanket. It's like no time passed, no separation happened. It's us, like it used to be. I must nod off because I jolt when she starts to pull out of my arms.

"I should go—we should . . . try to get some sleep before tomorrow." She stands and looks down at me while I scrub my hands over my face to clear the fog.

Twisting to sit on the edge of the chaise, I study my hands barely visible in the dark and decide to be honest. Heart slamming in my chest, I take a shaky breath and blurt, "God, I missed you."

Her hand touches the top of my head and fingers lace through my hair. "I know. Me too."

When she pulls it back, I reach for it. "I . . . don't want to let you go. Stay with me."

"What, like right here? Outside?"

"Or my room. Or yours?" I look up on the last word and she presses her hand to my cheek.

"We probably shouldn't. It's a big day tomorrow." Her smile says the opposite of her words.

I take a chance. "We might sleep better together." I pin her with my gaze though her eyes are hard to read in the night.

"I've no doubt. It's whether we would do any sleeping that I question."

Direct. I like that. "Fair. What if I promise to be on my best behavior?" I don't smile because I don't want her to think I'm joking. I'm not. I just want to be near her.

"I can't make that same promise."

Direct again. I stand now and touch her cheek, curl a lock of hair behind her ear and rub her satin earlobe between my thumb and forefinger. She leans into my touch instinctively, then reaches up to wind her arms around my neck. I don't hesitate. I lift her off the ground and her legs curl around my hips.

"We'll be good. Your bed or mine?"

"We're always good. That's the problem," she counters but still presses her lips to the pulse in my neck.

"Just to sleep. Pick one, Everly. Yours or mine?" She wants this, too. Her body screams it, but she shakes her head.

"I have guests."

I'm already moving toward the cottage, placing little kisses on her cheek, behind her ear, her neck.

"I'm serious, Julie. We can't." She pulls her head back from my lips but makes no attempt to unwrap her legs from my waist.

"M-hm." I lower my forehead to hers, still moving toward her cottage door. "Then talk to me. Please, Everly. I can't . . . I don't know how to walk away from you right now. I know we need sleep." I sigh and snake one hand into her silky hair, curling my fingers around her nape. "And I don't know about you, but I'm not sleeping knowing you're here within reach and not next to me." I release my grip so her legs slide down mine until her feet meet the mat at her doorstep.

Her palm lands on my cheek as her head lolls to the side.

Placing her index finger to her lips, she cracks the door and listens. Silence. She swings it wider and steps inside. I follow without a sound. The house is dark except for the dim light above the kitchen sink. She picks up a piece of paper on the bar, reads the note scribbled on it and sets it down. I peek over her shoulder.

If you need us, we're here. Just come in. ~LB

Glancing around in the muted light, I soak it all in, feeding months of curiosity. It's simple, clean, quaint. She takes my hand and moves silently down the short hallway. I stare at the closed door we pass for a couple pregnant moments. I want to ask the question but I don't. I twist my neck and look back at the empty couch. *They're all three sharing one room?*

She opens her bedroom door, pulls me inside and quietly closes the door. She slips the straps of her romper off her shoulders and lets it fall to the floor. I'm watching her, not moving. She turns and reaches for my shirt, slides it up my torso and off my head, then slips it over her head. It falls to just below her ass and nothing has ever looked sexier.

Reaching for my hand, she leads me to the adjoining bathroom and hands me a new toothbrush from the drawer. She quickly brushes her teeth and begins twisting her hair up in a knot. I brush my teeth and follow her back into her room. Peeling back the duvet cover, she slides between the sheets, holding the top sheet up invitingly. I slide in beside her. She turns her back and snuggles her ass into me like muscle memory. Sliding one arm under the pillow her head rests on, I snake the other around her body and pull her tight to my chest. My lips caress the back of her neck and, inhaling her scent deeply, I wonder how I ever slept without her the last seven months.

"God, I've missed this." She reaches up and curls her fingers around the back of my neck, pulling my lips tighter to her skin.

True to my word, I don't kiss her. I just leave my lips on her for the contact. We're touching from head to toe. Every cell in my body remembers this and exhales with me. My limbs grow heavy like my breathing. "Talk to me, Ever. Tell me about your life."

The sound of her voice pulls me back.

"You first, Julie. What have you been doing for the past seven months?" Her words are slow, heavy with drowsiness.

"The short answer? Lots of therapy." My body is drifting, letting its guard down. It's been too long.

"I'm proud of you." She yawns.

I'm going under fast. My eyelids droop.

I love you.

Chapter 23

Everly

Stretching like a cat, I yawn and blink against the light streaming in. *I forgot to close the blinds last night. LAST NIGHT!* I pitch forward, sitting up, and swing my head back and forth around my room. My empty room. I zero in on the piece of paper on my night-stand—the note Lilly left on the bar last night. Except it's Julian's handwriting on the backside of her note.

Snuck out before guests woke up. Best. Night. Sleep. Ever. J

He drew a smiley face on it. Indeed it was the best sleep I've had in . . . seven months. Before I dozed off I thought I heard him mumble "I love you", but I was so comatose I can't be sure. Maybe I imagined it. I do remember he said he'd gone to therapy. *Lots of therapy.* I place the note back on the nightstand and tap my phone screen. 8:30 a.m. I'm not sure the last time I slept so late—even on a weekend. One thing hasn't changed: we still sleep better together. My smile takes over my face as I pull my knees to my chest and rest my cheek on them. We've resolved nothing, talked about nothing. *You're going to make a helluva therapist, Everly. My slogan can be 'Do as I say, not as I do.'* I attempt to squash my thoughts and relish in the afterglow of last night. Not the most functional start but a start nonetheless. I let myself feel hopeful.

"Knock, knock." The singsong voice filters down the hall.

I jump from the sheets and yank clothes from dresser drawers. I rip Julian's shirt off my head and toss it on the bed before I spread the duvet over the mattress. I tell myself that I'm not hiding evidence. I'm an adult. I do what I want.

As I pull the tank top down over my head and squirm my arms through the armholes, my door cracks open and Tatum pokes her head through the opening. "You awake, sleeping beauty?"

"Just. What are you guys doing here so early?"

"Perfect sets rollin' in right in your backyard. Don't worry. We brought breakfast." She starts to retreat but stops and studies me for a moment.

I turn my back on her under the guise of getting my swimsuit out of my drawer. "Guess I'll need to change then."

"Okay." Her response is slow, pondering. Then she adds, "Bagel or donut hole?"

"It feels like a why choose kinda morning." I strip off the tank and my thong as she closes the door with a *hmph*. I don the swimsuit I snag off the top of the pile, blue—*like his eyes*. I snag my romper from yesterday off the floor and step into it as I step into the hall.

The guest bedroom door opens and Seth walks out shirtless, yawning and scratching his chest. His dark hair stands up in wild tufts. He turns a lazy smile on me and drops his arm on my shoulders.

"What's good, beautiful?"

"Waves are hitting apparently. Get dressed. Wake them up. Also, we've got company."

"And breakfast," Lennon calls from the kitchen.

"Sick. Okay, five minutes." Seth does an about-face and walks back into the guest room. True to his word, he's in the kitchen in five minutes, Noah and Lilly trailing behind him, sleepy but awake and dressed to surf.

"Tatum, Lennon, this is Lilly, Noah and Seth."

"Feels like we already know you," Lennon gushes. "So cool to finally meet you guys face-to-face. Ready to hit the beach? It's cookin' right now."

"Bet," Noah replies, popping another donut hole in his mouth.

"Who wants coffee?" Tatum starts passing out cardboard cups.

Everyone's hands shoot in the air.

"They're black because I didn't know what you liked, so you have to doctor them yourselves. Except yours, Ever."

"Vanilla Cold Foam?" I reach my hand out.

"Of course." She passes the drink to me.

Before we hit the beach, I text Allie to make sure she doesn't need any help.

Allie: That's what party planners are for. Have fun. Be ready by noon.

Me: Cool. Thanks.

Waiting for our set, Tatum floats next to me. I saw it on her face this morning just like I do now. My stay of execution is over. Here comes the grill. "You look different. Did you see him?"

I can't keep the smile off my face. "Yeah, last night on the beach."

"Anyone that makes you smile like that deserves a seat at the table or at least a conversation."

"That's the problem. We can't seem to keep our hands off each other long enough to have a conversation."

"Good problem to have, no? We should all be so lucky."

"Yeah, that's fair. But we do have to talk. We can't just pick up after seven months like nothing happened."

"By the look on your face, you already did that."

I fling water at her and stretch out on my board to begin paddling. "Saved by the set," I call as I paddle faster to catch the wave.

Chapter 24

JULIAN

God, she's even more beautiful now than yesterday. Standing at the top of the stairs leading to the beach, looking out over the ocean, my body reacts when I spot her on the water. She's so small from here I can't make out details, but I pick her out among the group and recognize her easily. Allie told me they went surfing, so I walked to the edge of the yard and the stairs intending to join them—to sit on the sand and watch anyway.

Seeing her with her friends laughing so casually, then catching waves and confidently riding them into the shore, I feel out of place—like I don't belong or fit into her world anymore. I opt to lean on the railing and watch from here. Their voices float up to me sporadically, combined with the constant roar of the ocean. It's evident she loves her life in Malibu. By the look of her physique, body language and overall demeanor, it agrees with her. Maybe even more than Blue Lake. *Maybe more than me?* I rub the dull ache in my chest, tap my collarbone to keep calm at the thought that maybe she's over me. She didn't seem over me last night. *Fuck, when did I become this guy? Pining for a girl like a lovesick schoolboy. She's not a girl. She's the girl.*

For six months I've been working on how to ask for what I want, to let people give it to me, love me. If I don't have the conversation, I'll never know. That's the problem. We don't seem to be able to keep our hands off each other long enough to have one. We'll never have it if I don't put myself in a place to have one, like joining her on the beach, meeting her new friends. My friends are down there, too. I deserve to see my friends, visit with them. *Right?* Only one way to find out.

Stripping off my shirt, I take off down the stairs. I still don't love cardio, but it's a necessary evil. Plus, a run might calm my nerves before I face her, them. Once I hit the sand, I strike out in the opposite direction that they're surfing. *Coward.* I could've used my earbuds and playlist right about now to drown out the voice in my head. Instead, I ask myself what Dr. Carver would say. *People want to love and be loved. That's the standard. The rarity is people like your parents. Remember that. Does Ever want to love me still? After last night, I want to believe so.*

Sweat drips into my eyes as I run out of beach. I stop in the wet sand and bend at the waist, hands braced on my knees and catch my breath. Waves swish my ankles, the cooling relief inviting me into the surf. I wade out three or four steps and plunge into the salty sea, dunking under the surface and paddling out. Instantly refreshed, I return to shore and walk back toward Ashley's stairs and the group of surfers.

As I approach the place I started from, Ever catches another wave. I stop to watch, mesmerized by her grace on the board. She always claimed she wasn't athletic but bookish. Watching her, I categorically disagree. She's incredible. I can't help the smile, the swell in my chest.

I clock the moment she notices me. It throws her off and she loses her balance. The wave takes her and the board under. The board pops up, getting tossed, but I don't see Ever. I run into the shallow water, searching for her, when she pops up and swims to her board and wades into shore with it tucked under her arm. My shoulders drop, my hand rubbing my chest in slow circles.

She approaches me, grinning. "Morning, Julie. How'd you sleep?"

"Are you okay?" I reach for her, hold her bicep and study her face.

"Yeah," she chuckles. "I don't love eating sand, but yeah, I'm good."

"You look amazing out there." My eyes comb every inch of her face for proof she's fine.

"Thanks. You look amazing wet." She drops her jaw like she shocked herself, her face crimson. "I mean . . . did you go for a swim?" She drops her board on the sand next to us.

"A run, then a swim to cool off." She dips her chin, but I'm too charmed by her words to let her duck me. "And I slept great. Best night's sleep in—"

"Months," she finishes. "Me too."

"Can we talk?" I hold my breath for her answer.

"I hope so. Maybe on a public beach in broad daylight will help." One corner of her mouth quirks and she squints up at me.

I tuck a lock of wet hair behind her ear and wink. "We'll be good. We've got an audience." I toss my head toward the group strolling in from the ocean, the five of them moving like one.

"Damn, J, go easy on the weights, brother. You lookin' huge." Noah claps me on the back.

"It's kinda my job." I hold my hands out low to my sides, palms up.

Ever speaks up, "Hey, why don't you guys get cleaned up, I'll be up in a few. Tatum, Lennon, you guys can use my shower."

"Aren't you going to introduce us?" The taller blonde speaks up.

"Oh yeah, my bad. Julian, this is Tatum and Lennon, my friends from Pepperdine."

"So nice to finally meet you, Julian." The taller twin, Lennon, tosses her head at me.

Her sister lightly backhands her arm.

"I call dibs on our shower," Lilly says to no one in particular. "See you up there. Hey, J-man." She knocks my arm with hers as she moves past us toward the stairs. That she's casual and . . . normal with me does something to my insides. It gives me courage. *'Most people aren't judging you the way you think they are. Those thoughts are mostly our thoughts about ourselves.' Thank you, Claire Carver.*

"Wanna sit?" Ever flops onto the sand, stretching out, her head on her board. With her arm slung over her eyes to block the sun, she tilts her head toward me and her gray eyes blink slow as I sit down next to her and nod in answer.

"Will you tell me about your life?" I fold my arms on my bent knees and lay my cheek on them, watching her.

"I got into Pepperdine. I start in the fall."

She's not coming back to Blue Lake.

I smile, force it to reach my eyes. "I'm so proud of you." And I am, but it feels heavy.

"Oh, and I'm Ever Tate now. Professionally. Like on my socials. They manage them. Ashley's people. I still don't like social media. And my brand is Ever Fit. It's a whole thing and goes hand in hand with my degree. Ashley's got it all figured out. I just show up. But I love it, where it's all headed. Where I'm headed."

I listen, watching the waves roll in. The sound of her voice pulls at me. I reach my hand down and rest it on the sunbaked skin of her leg. I need the contact. Proof that she's right here next to me, talking to me. "Sounds incredible. I don't do social media either. Not sure I ever will. Good thing Ashley has people for that." I smile at her, keeping it light.

"What about you? What's new? Besides your jacked physique?" She shoves my bicep and winks at me.

"Yeah, I've been going hard. It calms my nervous system, helps me sleep. That and therapy."

She sits up on that comment. "That's big, Julie. Super inspiring. You know I'm a psych major, right?"

"I do."

"Do you want to talk about it? I mean, I'd love to hear how it's going."

"Sure. If you really want to know. I'm getting better at that. Talking about stuff."

"I can't say the same. I study it. Implementing is a whole other thing."

"At least you're honest."

We stare at each other, soft smiles on our lips, eyes lingering long after the smiles fade. The electricity between us crackles, neither wanting to break the spell.

She finally does and turns her gaze back to the sea. "What happened with your parents? Can you talk about it?" She holds her breath.

"Yeah. The short answer is I mostly don't know." I follow her gaze and watch the waves crash onto the sandy shore, the foam slides back out. The air's already shifted from warm to hot. My shoulders sizzle a little with the rising sun. "The wheels of justice turn slow. Todd is locked up, waiting for trial. He pled not guilty but the evidence and witness accounts are pretty damning. What I hear is he'll be lucky if he doesn't get life."

Nodding, she faces me when she asks, "And your mom?"

I shrug because it's so much. Where do I begin? I say what I'm thinking. "I don't know where to even begin with her. She entered a court-mandated rehab facility, maybe long-term."

"Did you talk to her?"

I shake my head and watch a wave roll in and the surfer riding it. "I don't think I want to. They . . . just wanted money. An inheritance my grandfather McKay left me. It wasn't much, but to them I guess it was. I put it all in a trust for her, if she stays clean and sober—and away from him. There are stipulations in place to keep her from giving it to him or buying drugs with it. The trustee will handle it and I can wash my hands of her, him, all of it."

"And you're okay with that? Never seeing them? Her?" She's leaning back on her hands, so I twist a little to see her face.

"I really am. I never had any kind of real relationship with them anyway. According to my therapist, it's why I have such a hard time letting people in—why I shut you out." I make myself look her in the eyes when I admit that.

She nods, her eyes filling with tears. "I tried. To stay."

I cut her off. "I know. I know you did. I'm so sorry, Everly. I . . . the thought of my shit life hurting you. It wrecked me. I told myself that pushing you away was the only way to keep you safe. Part of me still feels that way—the old me. Dr. Carver says that's a lie. Those thoughts are lies. I know that now, logically. Catching up emotionally takes a little . . . a little more work. I remind myself that the old thought patterns are the lie. That the new thoughts, patterns I'm building, are the truth." I blow a long breath out through puffed cheeks and turn my head back to the horizon. "But I've done the work, Ever. I am doing the work."

Placing her hand on my shoulder blade, she rubs light circles. "I can tell. But Julian, it wasn't all you. It was a perfect storm. I watched you pull away and it reminded me of my dad when he'd return from deployment. He was there with us but he wasn't. My mom would get so sad. He was almost better when he was overseas fighting for a cause, more alive. My whole life has been one big avoidance shit show. First books, then Blue Lake, now Malibu. I'm sorry I ran, bailed on you. On us." I shake my head, cutting her off.

"No. I'm glad you did." I reach for her hand, bring it to my lips and watch her as I say, "I was a train wreck and taking you down with me. I never wanted to hurt you. I still don't. I'm so happy you're happy." I feel the pressure build behind my eyes, so I look the opposite way, stare down the beach and blink it away. "You were strong enough to walk away when I wasn't. And look what you've made for yourself. It's incredible. You're incredible."

"Thank you, Julie. I do love it here. Allie and Ashley spoil me—like the kid they never had. It's almost embarrassing, but I'd be lying if I said I didn't love the attention."

A laugh rumbles in my chest. "I get that. And your friends? The twins?"

"They're great. We met on campus. Tatum and I study the same major. They taught me how to surf. We've been inseparable since day one. How about you? Still see Taya?" She squints at me and places her free hand on her forehead to block the glare of the sun off the water.

I squeeze the hand I'm still holding. "I do. I think we feel like we're the only family we've got."

She's nodding, her lips pressed into a thin line.

"There's nothing going on. She feels like a sibling. Maybe. Not sure what that's like but it doesn't feel . . . We're just friends."

"I know. I believe you." She rolls onto her side, facing me, and props her head on one hand and draws circles in the sand with the other. "She was nothing but kind to me, even after. I just couldn't . . . It was too hard to see her, talk to her."

"I know. She knows." I feel a line of sweat run down my temple. The sun is baking. I see the fine beads on her upper lip. "Wanna go for a swim?"

"I do. It's warm. But we've gotta make it quick. Can't be late for the party." She springs off the sand and holds a hand down to me. I take it, a smile tugging my lips upward, and let her pull me off the ground. She jogs into the surf up to her waist and dives in, popping out of the surface a few feet away.

I mimic her and pop up next to her. My mouth waters at the sight of her tanned skin dripping wet. Impulsively I reach for her.

She wraps her arms and legs around me, and I pull her against me till we're nose to nose. She dips her head and kisses me, long and lingering. "Salty." She smiles against my lips.

"You too. I like it," I say against hers.

She rewards me with another kiss, this time pressing her tongue past my lips, stroking it softly. "Mmm." My body responds instantly. I break the kiss before I take her right here in the shallow surf. "We better go get ready for the party."

She nods her agreement and swims for the shore.

"Right behind you," I call. "Just need a minute here." Her giggle trails behind her as she hits the beach and scoops her board off the sand.

Standing in the sand, feet slightly apart, board tucked under her arm, with the sun glistening off her wet body she looks like a goddess. It's doing nothing to calm my raging hard-on. She cups her free hand over her eyes and squints against the sun, tracking me as I bob in the surf.

I can see her wheels turning from here. "What's going on in there, pretty girl?" I project my voice over the pulse of the tide and toss my head at her, moving my arms back and forth to keep it above the surface.

Her nose wrinkles as her lips curve. She shakes her head, sending wet locks swaying across her shoulders. Shrugging, she calls, "Are we really doing this?"

I let the waves bring me closer to shore and ground myself in the wet sand, sloshing through the tide toward her. She props the board upright next to her and leans on it as I walk to her, adjusting my clinging swim trunks. "Do *you* want to . . . do this? Be together? I didn't want to ask until I was sure I could be what you needed. What you deserve. I know we should've waited to . . . for . . ." My fingers itch to tuck her wet locks behind her ear, but I refrain from touching her.

That seems to be where we stop talking and start . . . My body wants to finish that sentence.

"That's on me. I missed you. Missed touching you. Kissing you."

I shake my head at her. "Not all you, Ever. Chemistry has never been our issue." I reach out now and touch only her hair until my fingers graze the shell of her ear as I wrap the rusty lock behind it. Her skin already feels warm again from just the few minutes out of the sea. "I want this. Us." I wag my finger between us. "But I want to always show you the best version of me. I'm doing the work."

"You already said that." She taps one fingernail on my lips and smiles. She leans in and places a light kiss on them. "I can tell, Julie. And I've been working on my shit, too. All we can do is try our best, right?" She smiles again, and I nod once, holding my breath. "Besides, we owe it to the chemistry. Don't ya think?" She looks at me under her lashes as my jaw drops on a bark of laughter.

"Yeah, sassy girl, I do." I reach for her board and tuck it under my arm, clasp her hand in my free one and we move toward the stairs in sync.

Chapter 25

Everly

As anniversary parties go this one is flawless. To be fair I don't have a frame of reference, but the twins do. Their parents are Hollywood royalty, so they know parties and even they're impressed. They float around charming everyone they talk to. The more I hang out with them, the more effortless it becomes to do the same, much to Allie and Ashley's delight.

I've drawn the line at running my social accounts but regularly agree to in-person events and promotion. It's becoming muscle memory and not as grueling as I once feared. Plus, the twins moonlight as my stylists, so that goes a long way to making me feel comfortable in my skin, less awkward.

Speaking of skin, the dress they insisted I wear is by far the prettiest I've ever worn. They call it the naked dress, which I must admit is quite accurate because it hugs every piece of my body it covers, which isn't much. Hitting just below my ass cheeks and the color of muted flesh, it makes quite a statement. That I'm not drowning in self-consciousness is a testament to my inner growth. The fitted slip dress style drapes over my torso and leaves no room for a bra. I've also never felt prettier.

Standing at one of the tall bar tables scattered around the backyard patio, the twins, Lilly, Noah and Seth and I clink our champagne glasses together on cue at Ashley's anniversary toast. He, Allie and Julian stand on the makeshift stage, rolling out future plans for the guests—mostly investors, employees and influencers.

"One more announcement before we let you eat, drink and be merry. Ever, can you join us up here?"

I smile for the crowd and set my glass down, swinging my eyes between my friends. *What was I just mentally bragging about? Self-confidence? Yeah, sure, okay.* "Uh, unexpected," I mumble to them through smiling lips. Louder, I say, "Be right back."

"Ladies and gentlemen, friends, colleagues. May I present Ever Tate, the face of our next phase—fitness psychology. At ASH, we want a complete picture of health, so this next year, we're delving deeper into the mind-body connection. A concept that was brought to us by this intelligent and innovative young mind, Ever Tate."

The heat on my cheeks tells me they're flaming, but I step onto the raised platform to the applause from our guests, smiling—hopefully—like I do this every day. I raise my hand in thanks and hopes of subduing the ovation. "Thanks, everyone. I'm not big on public speaking, so I'll just say it means the world to me that Ashley and Allie embraced my ideas. A year and a half ago, I found myself in a dark place and found solace in fitness. The thing that surprised me most was the change in my mental state. The more I exercised, the clearer and calmer my mind grew. That took me down a rabbit hole of discovery that I felt compelled to share with others. I'm excited for this next phase and so grateful to ASH for the opportunity. True transformation starts in the mind. Train your body. Rewire your mind. That's what we hope to achieve with Ever Fit. Cheers." I move across the small stage to hug Allie and Ashley. As I retreat to leave the stage, I hug Julian, too, mostly because it would look awkward not to. His hand on my hip is searing, his touch electric. It shouldn't surprise me—it's always like this with us—but still I suck in a quick, sharp breath at the contact.

His words push every ounce of air I just inhaled from my lungs. "Helluva dress, Ever. You're stunning." His lips brush my cheek in a polite formality, the words for my ears only.

"Thank you," I murmur and meet his eyes. I swallow at the hunger I see there, mirroring my own. Wet heat pools on the thin fabric of my thong as I step off the stage and walk through the tables and guests. Once back at my table, I say to the group, "I need a minute. Be right back." I make my way across the patio and around the corner to my cottage. Inwardly cringing, I slip inside to quickly don a new—dry—thong. There's no one around to witness my mortification, yet my cheeks are on fire.

Coming out of my front door, I almost collide with Taya. "Ever. Hi." She braces my shoulders from the near miss.

"Taya." A genuine smile takes over my face. "And Mitch. Hi, nice to see you." He shakes my hand formally. "I didn't realize you were coming, but I'm glad you're here." And I mean it. Seeing them gives me a warm fuzzy feeling in my chest.

"Yeah, Jay—Julian asked if we'd come."

"I'm glad he did." I hope I'm conveying more than I'm saying. I wasn't lying when I told Julian that while I study it, implementing is still a work in progress. I'm committed to navigating it, so I guess that starts with embracing the opportunities that arise. "I'm sorry I've been MIA. I just needed some time."

"No need to apologize. I get it. And time must agree with you because you look stunning." Her hands on my shoulders trail down my arms until she's holding my hands out wide at our sides, taking me in.

My cheeks flame anew at the descriptive word. *His word.*

"Thank you. Stop." I release her hands and flap them at her. "Let's go get you guys a drink."

"Yeah, sorry we're late. Traffic."

"No worries. Plenty of party left."

We stop at my table and I introduce her to the twins before Lilly, Noah and Seth greet them familiarly. We move to the bar where Julian is in an animated conversation with Auz. When he sees Taya, he pins me for a moment to gauge my reaction. I reach out and slide my hand along his forearm, where his gauzy white button-down shirt sleeve is casually rolled.

His smile looks relieved as he turns his gaze to Taya, hugs her, then shakes Mitchell's hand. "So glad you guys made it."

"Ran into some traffic. Sorry we're late," Mitchell says, then orders two champagnes from the bartender.

I want to try harder, so I add, "Taya, let me take you to say hi to Allie and Ashley." She takes her champagne flute from Mitch and walks with me to the edge of the stage.

"How is he?" She doesn't play games, and I appreciate the candor.

"He seems so good. Different. In the best way."

"Right? I think so, too. Therapy is agreeing with him."

"That you know he's going again says a lot. He's been very open about . . . everything. It's refreshing. Oh, hey, I got into Pepperdine. I start this fall."

"Oh my God, congratulations. Guess we'll be seeing each other on campus."

"I'd love that."

"Me too."

The formal party carries on for another two hours. As the guests dwindle, it morphs into a pool party. A local band sets up on the stage and begins playing popular covers. Before I can dip out and change into a swimsuit, Julian's deep baritone hits my ear from behind. "Can I get one dance with you in that dress before it's gone?"

"If I can get one with you in your . . . formalwear?" I giggle as I say it because the tan linen pants and soft white shirt are as formal as I've ever seen him. Usually clad in workout attire, he makes quite a mouthwatering picture. His skin looks tanner against the crisp white; his dark hair shines and his blue eyes rival the sky. He's still the most beautiful man I've ever seen. "Also, I didn't know you could dance."

He takes my hand and with a half twirl he whisks me onto the dance floor as the band plays "Maybe I'm Amazed." I wonder for a moment if he planned it. I decide I don't want to know. I let him sway me back and forth as he says, "I'm not sure I do." Then he admits, "I just wanted a legit reason to hold you this close in public."

"Shameless, but honest." The people, the din of conversation, everything blurs and fades around me as I stare into his face. I want to freeze time. "How long are you staying?" I don't want him to go. That realization sobers me.

"I leave tomorrow." His smile is almost a straight line and a little sad. I turn my head and rest my cheek on his pec. I breathe him in, his smell so familiar it makes me ache.

Don't go. "I wish you didn't have to leave. So soon," I amend when I realize what I implied.

"Why?" He stops swaying and leans back, his eyes bouncing back and forth between mine. "I mean . . . what do you mean?"

"I just wish we had more time." I squeeze the hand gripping mine, curled against his chest as we dance.

He nods contemplatively. "How much time?" He arches an eyebrow and begins swaying again when the song changes to something more upbeat.

I shake my head slowly, caught off guard. "I just . . ." I shake my head some more.

"What do you want, Everly? Tell me."

"More time," I repeat. "So we can talk. Without all this." I wave my hand around to indicate the party, the people.

"Okay."

"Okay, what?"

"Okay, I'll stay."

"You will?" I stop dancing now and grip his biceps. He nods, grinning widely. Forgetting our surroundings again, I throw my hands around his neck and hug him.

He must forget too because he lifts me off the ground and spins me in a circle. We realize the spectacle we're making at the same time, because he sets my feet on the ground as I cover my mouth with a giggle.

"C'mon, let's go put our suits on and go for a swim."

"I'll meet you back here in five."
"Race ya."

Chapter 26

JULIAN

Everly smacks a kiss on my cheek and walks away on pencil-thin heels in that tiny naked dress, and I shamelessly watch her go, frozen to the spot she leaves me in.

"Care to dance with me?"

I turn to see Allie beaming at me. "It would be an honor." I sweep her into my arms and twirl her to the beat of the music.

"It's so good to see you happy. It's been a minute."

"It has. And I am. Hey, you mind if I stay a little longer? Tony's been stepping up at Fit more and . . . I could use a few more days. Not sure they'll even miss me."

"Not at all. Stay as long as you want. You know you don't even have to ask. Luke would love to have you here full-time, but we agreed to you commuting as needed. Unless that changes." Allie is a subtle meddler, never pushy, but her message is clear regardless.

"Thanks," I answer vaguely. "Not sure how long, but I'll let you know when I decide. If that's okay."

"Perfectly okay. I'll tell Luke. He'll be happy to hear it."

I nod, smile and keep swaying to the beat.

My mind wanders to *her*. To what I'll do with my time here. I'm excited, like a kid on Christmas, for the first time in seven months. She's different but still as intriguing and captivating as that first day I saw her at Fit. More so. She's more confident and even more breathtaking with her sculpted surfer body. I'm in awe of her still and I want to be near her—like a planet to her sun. I scan the backyard and find her with her friends, laughing and joking, headed toward her cottage—to change into swimsuits, I assume.

When the song ends, I hug Allie for everything I want to say but don't because we're in the middle of a party. She hugs me back. I know she's barely old enough to be my mom, but she's been more nurturing to me than any woman in my life. I don't know if I have the words to tell her what that means to me—how it's shaped me. Emotion wells up to push behind my eyes. *What has Claire done to me? Unlocked some pent-up sap?* The thought makes me smile. I make a note to give her shit about it at my next appointment. "I think we're all going swimming. You and Luke joining us?"

"Maybe. I'll check with him. The last of the investors are leaving, so it'll be just friends, family." She squeezes my hand when she says family.

I lean down and kiss her on the cheek. "Okay, gonna head upstairs and change really quick."

"Sounds good."

Upstairs in my room, pulling swim trunks out of my suitcase, a female giggle draws me to the window. One of the twins leans against my Jeep and Seth has one arm resting against it beside her head. The other is twirling a lock of her hair. The conversation is giving flirty thirst. Just as I'm about to back away and drop the sheer, he leans in and pecks a soft kiss on her cheek, takes her hand and drapes it around his neck as he turns and heads toward the patio and pool. My curiosity is piqued, but it's none of my business. I strip quickly, don my swim trunks and slide a cotton muscle tank over my head.

At the pool, the chicken fights are already commencing. Lilly is on Noah's shoulders wrestling the twin on Seth's. Taya drags Mitch into the water, though he doesn't look thrilled about it. Ever is on the other twin's shoulders. Both turn as I sit on the edge of the pool, sinking my legs into the cool surface.

"I call dibs on Julian," the twin holding Ever on her shoulders calls out just before she sinks into the water, dunking Ever.

"Not fair," Ever yelps, sputtering water as she pops up and drags her hand down her face.

"That's okay, Ever, let them. We'll take them all." Taya swims over to her and adds, "Mitch is a party pooper." She waves her hand toward him where he sits opposite me on the ledge of the pool.

"I don't swim—much. How about I referee?" He takes a long drink from his solo cup; all formal festivities now morphed into a regular backyard pool party.

Lennon, I deduce from the melee of conversation, swims up to me and challenges, "Don't make me regret my choice. These fools are going down."

"I'll see what I can do." I slide into the water and dunk under the surface, popping up with Lennon on my shoulders. Ever does the same with Taya. So it's me against Everly. This just got interesting.

As we square up in the water, she moves to within an inch of my face and says for my ears only, "You're going down."

"Promise?" I arch my brow, then sweep my leg out in front of me and take hers out from under her.

As she starts to go down, she grabs my biceps and rights herself. "Oh, you thought I'd make this easy on you?" She's laughing as she tries the same move on me.

Are we talking about chicken fights? "Not even a little bit, but anything worth having is worth fighting for."

"Couldn't agree more." Her eyes spark with determination, and I almost want to let her win. Almost. Clutching her ribs in my hands, I squeeze, tickling her, and she yelps just before she loses her balance and plunges, oblivious to the two above us.

They were not oblivious to us apparently. As Lennon and Taya resurface, Taya rolls her eyes exaggeratedly and tells her, "We should've known better than to pit those two against each other. They can't stop flirting long enough to compete."

"Agreed," Lennon gripes, smiling.

The other four are still battling at the other end of the pool, bantering and shit-talking. I reach for Ever and pull her back against me, wrapping my arms around her. Leaning against the edge of the pool, we watch as they fight for dominance, laughing and enjoying the show. She rests her arms over mine, seemingly at ease in my embrace. I don't want to question it or overthink it for fear it will vaporize before me.

Hours later, we're all sprawled on the lounge chairs, talking easily, when Allie brings out a tray of snacks: mini sandwiches, fruit, vegetables, olives, cheese. Luke trails behind her with a handful of cans. "Hydrate, kids. The sun can take it out of you. Electrolyte waters." He tosses cans out to each of us.

"Thanks, Dad," Lennon replies cheekily.

The twins' parents and Ashley go way back, I learned today. She clearly feels at home enough to tease him. He and Allie seem equally delighted to cater to us like surrogate parents. The well of emotion hits me again. Dr. Carver would tell me it's tapping into something I needed, something I was missing. That I know this puts a sad smile on my face for that little kid who didn't even know what he didn't have.

Ever extends her hand and swishes the back of her index finger over my cheek. "What's going on in there?"

I capture her hand and bring the back of it to my lips. "Nothing. Just happy." I look deep into her opaque eyes and fight the pressure behind mine. I blink when I fear they're about to give me away.

"Me too." Her soft smile pops her dimples.

God, I've missed those.

"Guys," Seth announces, "Tatum and Lennon are coming back with us tomorrow to check out the surf at Pismo."

"Ooh, cool. I need to get back there and try it now that I know how," Ever exclaims.

"So come with," Tatum invites.

"Sorry. Got stuff."

Lennon, not one to mince words, says, "Is that what we're calling him? *Stuff*?"

"Shut up, Lennon," Ever barks back, smiling, her face flushing. There she is—a glimpse of the Ever I used to know.

My stomach flips watching her hide her blush. My body responds instinctively.

"Hey, everyone." Taya comes out of the pool house dressed. "Mitch and I are heading out. We have an appointment." That gets my attention and sufficiently, and thankfully, douses my reaction to Ever. She stands to hug Taya and thanks her for coming.

"I'll walk you guys out." I stand and walk to Mitch, who's standing by the back door shaking hands with Ashley. "I'll be right back," I say to Ever.

She nods, smiling, and sits back down with her friends.

Our friends, I remind myself.

Chapter 27

Everly

I'm alone on the patio when he returns. As he walks toward me, shirtless, in swim trunks that sit low on his hips, my mouth goes dry and my center goes wet. I swallow and press my knees together as he gets closer. Our eyes, locked on each other, forge an electrical current between us.

"Where'd everyone go?"

The spell is broken by his words, but the deep reverb of his tone only invites more heat to pool in my belly. His eyes are dark, like a deep sea bouncing between mine.

"Showering." I swallow again, sliding my gaze to his lips as he moistens them with the tip of his tongue. "They decided to drive back tonight to catch the morning waves." I keep my face composed, but inside I'm euphoric at having him all to myself. "Where'd Taya and Mitch have to go?"

"I think she's moving here. To Malibu. She sold her dad's ranch in South Point. She's looking for places down here since she's got a couple years of law school left. Then she can keep her horses. Mitch will continue to manage the ranch for her."

"Are they a . . ."

He's already shaking his head. "I don't think so, but I don't really know. I don't ask. She doesn't offer."

"Hmm." I hug my knees to my chest and he takes the vacant spot at the end of my lounge chair, straddling it and scooting closer to me. He rubs his palms up and down my calves and drops his chin on my knees. I can't help it. I reach up and drag my fingers through the longer hair on top of his head, brushing it off his forehead only for it to fall back where it was.

He closes his eyes, his long black lashes casting shadows on his cheeks. "Mmm." The rumbling sigh echoes in his chest. "What should we do tonight?"

Mentally shaking myself out of his trance, I blurt out the first thought in my head. "Let's go for a run down the beach before the sun sets."

His eyes blink open, but he schools his surprise. "Okay. Should I go get my shoes?"

"No, let's go barefoot. Grounding."

He looks impressed by my suggestion. He stands, still straddling the lounge chair, and pulls me up with him. Picking me up, he steps over the chair and sets me down, takes my hand and heads toward the stairs to the beach.

After our run, I want to plunge into the ocean to cool off, but I'm sticky from the sand. I'd rather shower. My legs burn from the morning surf and now the run. Standing at the bottom of the stairs that lead to Ashley's, I'm dreading the ascent. He reads me like a book, steps in front of me and reaches behind him, clasping my legs behind the knees, boosting me onto his back.

"No, Julian, you can't carry me up all those stairs." I try to wriggle out of his hold.

"Oh, but I can." He marches up the stairs, barely breathing hard. At the top he sets me on my feet, sweat dripping from his brow. "Damn, that pool looks refreshing." He swipes his hand down his face.

"C'mon. Pool house shower." I toss my head toward the outbuilding. I know what will happen. I meant for the run to distract us from our . . . tendencies. This shower is going to cement them. This man still owns me. This seemingly healed version of him melts me. Before the door closes, I drop my peach bikini bottoms and pull the tie at my back, releasing the triangle top. I swing the twin swatches over my head and drop them next to my bottoms.

His shorts land next to my little pile.

Stepping into the tiled enclosure, I twist the knob. The shower of water falls from the ceiling in a waterfall, cool and refreshing. I turn and he's there in my space. We touch palms, then lock fingers. We're breathing each other's air but still only touching hands. One step back, and my shoulder blades press against the smooth tile. He stretches our hands above my head, pinning them to the tile, too. His lips press to mine and his tongue slides into my mouth as he slides into me. When my knees start to buckle, he anchors me with his other hand under my hip. "I got you, Ever." *And he does—have me. All. Of. Me. Again. Still?* I let my mind go blank and just feel my way to that place where it's just him and me, skin to skin, and nothing else matters—the way we communicate best.

With shaky hands, I wrap a towel around me and tuck it under my arms. I blow out a breath through pursed lips as I swipe the fog from the mirror. *Hottest fucking shower ever—and not from the water temperature.* He watches me in the mirror as I brush out my hair, his hands locked on either side of the counter, pinning me in.

When I pull the locks over my shoulder, exposing one side of my neck, he swoops his head down and presses warm kisses to my pulse there. "You know . . . we should talk more." My eyes drift closed as his lips work their magic.

"M-hm." He keeps kissing me, now behind my ear, which he knows drives me crazy.

"I'm serious," I press on, trying to concentrate on my words, stop round two. "With us, it always comes down to this."

He stops and leans his chin on my shoulder and locks his calm blue eyes on mine. When I don't elaborate, he blinks and waits. "I just want . . ." I trail off because I don't know what I want. No, I do. I'm just afraid to say it. That I can admit that to myself is a huge step. I exhale and confess, "I'm scared."

He places his hands on my shoulders and turns me around to face him. "Of me?"

I'm shaking my head before he finishes asking. "No. Of course not." I curl my fingers around his neck. "No, Julian. Never you."

He still waits, saying nothing.

"I mean it. Okay?"

"Okay." He nods. "Of what then?"

I shrug. "Of not getting what I want?"

"And what do you want?" He tucks a wet strand of hair behind my ear, the ritual so familiar it tugs at me.

I lean in and press my forehead to his, close my eyes. Keeping them closed, I press my hands to his chest and gently push. "Can we do this with our clothes on?"

"I mean, we could try, but I don't recommend it." His dimples wink at me before he sobers and adds, "Kidding. Yes. I'll run up and change. Meet you at your place?"

"Let's go to sushi. Are you hungry?"

"I could eat."

"I'll drive. Ten minutes at my car?"

"Yep." He plants a quick kiss on my lips and leans into my ear and whispers, "If it's within my power, I'll always give you what you want. Whatever you want. Always." Before I can even think to respond, he pivots and leaves, the door clicking closed behind him.

Chapter 28

JULIAN

Holding her hand in the car, I ask her the little things I'm curious about. "How'd you meet Tatum and Lennon?"

"I met Tatum in Payson Library on campus. Then weirdly ran into her and her sister on the beach about a week later. Malibu gives small-town vibes, so maybe it's not that weird." Her soft giggle is giving nervous energy, so I squeeze her hand and note her dimple popping in my periphery. Another soft giggle and she continues. "They'd been surfing and were walking back to their car. I was reading on the beach. Tatum recognized me." She quickly turns to smile at me before pulling her face back to the road.

"They seem fun. I, uh, saw Lennon, I'm pretty sure, getting friendly with Seth outside the cottage earlier."

"That tracks." She laughs. "Lennon is . . . friendly. And Seth is . . . a college frat boy. But it was Tatum. I saw the way they flirted during the pool party."

"So, he and Noah and Lilly aren't like—"

She cuts me off. "The truth is I don't know. It's a don't ask, don't tell kinda thing."

"But you get what I'm asking." I study her profile now.

"Oh yeah. It's . . . let's just say I've wondered, too. But I stay out of it and don't judge."

"That's what I love about you." I freeze the moment the words leave my mouth, then rush on to cover up what I said. "I mean, you have this innate ability to meet people where they are, accept them as they are. It's incredible. And beautiful." I sober on the last part. *So beautiful—inside and out.* I'm not sure when I became a human Hallmark card, but thankfully Ever's sarcastic nature is alive and well to keep things light.

"A perfect military brat." She salutes me with a crooked smile. "I tuck it all away, ignore it. Suck it up. As a psych major, I recognize the flaws, the patterns, that it's my default setting." She shrugs, keeping her eyes on the road. "Until it becomes too much. Then I run." She slants a quick glance my way, then returns her eyes to the road and says, "Or tell the man I love to fuck off. Then run." The smile she gives me is anything but happy—more self-deprecating and maybe a little guilty.

"Like I said, I don't think I gave you much choice." I bring her hand to my lips. "I don't blame you, Ever." She smiles again, but it looks sad, even in profile. "In a way, I'm relieved you left—like it was better, safer for you to be away from me."

"I know. I came around to that—eventually. Not the safer part, but that *you thought* it was." She squeezes my hand before releasing it to claim the steering wheel with both hands, turning into a parking lot off the PCH. "Still, anger is a great motivator. I was determined to make a life for myself, by myself. One I love." Putting the car in park, she turns to smile at me—a real one this time. "We're here. Best sushi around." Through the windshield I take in the ramshackle building, weathered siding, peeling blue and green paint and a faded sign: The Salty Roll. As she follows my gaze out the windshield, maybe seeing it through my eyes, she adds, "I promise it's delicious."

With the air still warm and sticky, we opt for a table inside, near the windows so we can see the ocean. Ever asks me to trust her and orders for us. I observe quietly—in awe really—the young woman she's become. So confident and sure of herself. So at home in this life I know nothing about. I don't look at my socials, but even if I did, I don't think I'd see hers. She blocked me from her phone. I assumed that meant she blocked me from those, too. Even if she didn't, I didn't think I'd be strong enough to see the highlight reels of her life without me. Once I started therapy again, I strived to do the right thing, the healthy thing, despite how I felt. Dr. Carver and I talk a lot about how it's fine to feel our emotions, but we can't always trust that they're accurate. Spiraling about things I can't control is counterproductive.

"What's going on in there?" She points a chopstick at my forehead and smiles around a mouthful of tuna roll.

Before I can answer, she picks up another roll and stuffs it in my mouth, giggling. *So self-assured.* Mesmerizing. Smiling, I cover my mouth with my fingers as I chew. The rolls are delicious, maybe the best I've ever tasted. "I just love seeing you like this."

"Like what?" She looks genuinely confused.

I shrug and pick up another roll. "Happy? Confident." I nod once and eat the roll.

"I am. Mostly." She shrugs her shoulders, drops her eyes to her plate and pushes her food around with her chopsticks. Her voice lowers to a murmur. "Happy, that is."

"And what's lacking?" I'm glad we're in public. She's right. It always gets physical with us. Right now, my hands itch to scoop her into my arms and wrap around her until she feels like part of my skin, until she stops looking sad.

She shrugs again but doesn't answer.

"Just say it. Even if it sounds crazy. I promise I won't judge or laugh."

"You." She looks up under her lashes, her cheeks blooming.

I swallow the roll around the lump in my throat. The girl fucking owns me. I don't think she realizes how much. I know she doesn't. For all her confidence everywhere else, how can she not know what she is to me? "I'm right here."

She shakes her head. "But you'll leave. You'll go back." She shoves her plate away from her and drops the chopsticks.

"Ever, don't do that. Finish your dinner. I'm here. I'm staying . . . as long as you want me. Okay? Don't waste 'the best sushi around.'" I use finger quotes on her words.

She rewards my efforts with a little laugh and nods her head. "It is, right?" She tucks it away.

If you don't know her, you miss it. But I don't. I see all of her. And I play along, let her turn the page.

"It's pretty damn good." I pick up a roll from her plate and feed it to her.

After she swallows the bite, she sobers and says, "But you'll go back eventually."

Nope, not gonna ignore it. And I'm secretly glad she doesn't.

"I don't want to go through that again. Feel that again. Missing you. Not having you. I can't do it again. Especially now. Not after the last couple days."

"What are you saying?" My brows pinch together. "Do you . . . want to go back with me?"

She shakes her head so her hair fans around her shoulders. "I can't go back there." She looks horrified for a quick moment at the mention of Blue Lake. Then it's gone and she adds, "I've got school and I really do love my life here." She rolls her lips inward, pinching them together.

I nod because I've considered this—that Blue Lake may be tainted for her now. I sense she doesn't want to say it plainly but isn't done, so I wait. "I just want you to be in it. Too," she tacks on.

"Okay." I blink but watch her and wait. *Say it, Ever. Ask me to stay.*

"Okay? Like you'll come here? To live?" Her eyes grow saucer-like and she blinks expectantly. "Blue Lake is your home, your life."

"If you want me in your life, I will be in your life. However, wherever, whenever."

Her eyes light up, swimming with emotion. She smiles so big both dimples pop and the corners of her eyes crinkle. Then my girl tucks it all away with a few hasty blinks and snags the last roll off her plate and pops it into her mouth, smiling as she chews.

I smile, too, and swallow the lump in my throat so I can finish my rolls, thankful again we're in public or I'd lift her off her feet so that she'd wrap her legs around me and I'd kiss her until we were both panting for each other. *I'm letting her love me, Doc. I am.* "Blue Lake may have saved me once, maybe you, too, but I found out the hard way that my home isn't a place. It's you."

One tear spills from her brimming eyes unchecked, and she's never looked more beautiful.

"You're the only home I've ever known. You're my home, Ever. I wasn't sure I'd get the chance to tell you that. Show you that. It's easy to show you physically what you mean to me. I can't regret that we tend to fall back on sex because being intimate with you is the most beautiful thing I've ever experienced in my life. Therapy is helping me with the rest of it. I promised myself that if I ever got another chance with you, I'd do everything I could to show you I can be the kind of man who deserves your love. And now I'm promising you, Ever. I can be him. I *am* him. Please let me prove it to you."

Her silent tears flow unchecked as she reaches across the table and lays her palm against my cheek. My answer is her nod and then her smile that shows both dimples. Then her smile dips, just for a second, before she forces the full stretch of it back to her lips.

If I didn't know every expression she's got, I'd have missed it. I want to ask her about it, but I'm not sure I want to know—especially if it changes her mind. Or mine.

Chapter 29

Everly

Julian is leaving. Two days together flew by. I remind my heart it's not forever. Still, I spiral a little watching him throw his bags into the back of his Jeep and hug Allie and Ashley. Once they turn to go inside the main house, I push off the front fender and step into his arms.

"I don't want you to go."

"I'll be back as soon as I can, as often as I can," he vows.

I nod against his chest, the soft fabric of his shirt caressing my cheek. His biceps flex as they lock around me. I clasp my hands together behind his back, rocking from side to side, sinking my nose between his pecs. I inhale deeply. His scent is a balm to my nervous system—always has been. Sleeping so soundly next to him the last two nights has me preemptively mourning my loss of sleep until he returns.

"If you don't let go, I can't hurry and come back." He relaxes his arms and kisses the top of my head. I nod again, not trusting my voice.

We spent the whole day on the beach yesterday. The waves weren't perfect for beginners, but he let me show him a few things and even stood up and rode a few for a couple seconds before he fell. He chalked it up to his balance from kickboxing. I think he was born an athlete and just doesn't know it. We talked about our family dynamics a lot. He doesn't know where his athleticism comes from because his parents were addicts as far back as he can recall. I confessed that my urge to *run* when things get tough comes from both of mine. My dad was always happier deployed—like he needed to be over there fighting for *them* (the best friends he lost) because they no longer could. My mom can't be in our house without him for more than a couple days before you can tell she is coming out of her skin, itching to leave.

As much as I believe we are not destined to become our parents, I think some of that modeled behavior gets in and must be unlearned. A therapist would say realizing that is half the battle. I say it's the easy part. The real work is in not perpetuating the cycle—much easier said than done. Still, I'm committed. I'm done running. Now that I've had these days with Julian again, I refuse to live without him.

"Okay," I reply and let my arms slip to my sides. I step back and add, "But I'm not going to watch you drive away."

"Okay, pretty girl." He rubs my earlobe between his thumb and forefinger. "I'll see you soon, Ever. Promise." He pulls my chin to him and kisses me sweetly on the lips. "Miss me." He winks and turns to open the driver's door.

I turn and rush inside my cottage and flop on the couch, listening as the sound of the Jeep grows more distant until I can't hear it at all.

My phone dings on the coffee table with a text from Callie. She and Auz are in the studio and want me to pop in for some quick YouTube content. Perfect distraction. I reply that I'm on my way. Before I move from the couch to walk over to the building next to mine, I pull up

Julian's contact info and unblock his number, pull up his text screen and type two words.

I will.

Chapter 30

Julian

Stepping into Allie's house, *my* house, doesn't hold the same peace it used to. It's just a house now, not my home. My home has stormy gray eyes and chestnut brown hair and smells like sunshine—and now salt, sea and sand. My cheeks lift on the image swimming through my mind. I can't wait to get back to her. To give us every chance at a life together, I'm going to immerse myself in her world—even if it doesn't last. My heart plummets on that last thought, my hand flying to my chest to rub the spot that bears her name, forever inked into my skin. I'll always wonder what could've been if I don't try.

I talked to Allie and Ashley on the six-hour drive home about traveling down south more often. They teased the idea of me relocating to Malibu. Allie was right. Ashley is stoked to have me around more often. From a business standpoint, relocating would make everything easier. From a family standpoint, Allie sounds elated at the possibility. She all but begged me to move in with them—*the house has more than enough room*—but I want to prove to them I can be self-sufficient. I want to build a life separate from them, and Ever, that I can be proud of but include them in it. Not just show up and feel like I'm invading their lives.

Dr. Carver agrees. I left her a voicemail after talking to Allie and Ashley. She called me back just before I hit Blue Lake and sounds impressed with my plans. I wait for her to tell me it's too soon, too abrupt for these decisions, but she loves the idea of me getting away from Cavern County, South Point specifically.

"There's a big world out there, Julian, and moving closer to your family sounds wonderful." *My family.*

I say what I'm thinking. "My family?"

"Yes, Julian. Your family. We are not who we come from. We get to decide. I think you've chosen your family well. Being in and a part of each other's lives more regularly sounds like just what you need. I'm so happy for all of you. If there's anything I can do to help the process, just reach out."

"Of course. Thanks, Doc—Claire. Truly. Thank you."

"Julian, you did the work. I just listened."

"If you say so." I laugh to hide my discomfort.

"And you're welcome. I'm proud of you. This call made my whole day."

More awkward laughter. "Okay. Um, thanks again. Talk to you soon."

"Bye, Julian."

Walking through the rooms of my once-home, I look for personal effects—a framed photo, a phone charger, clothes, shoes and . . . not much else. Small accents here and there. This house is ready for the next chapter. Allie loves the idea. I'd only begun renting to own it from her. Now we plan to turn it into a VRBO for passive income.

I need to talk with Letty and propose she manage Fit full-time. Seeing our members step up and get certified to run classes got the wheels turning long before my recent trip down south. The idea of relocating to Southern California has been brewing for a while and not just because of Everly. SoCal is a big place. Without Everly, I'd have moved somewhere convenient, close but not exactly near Malibu, for work. With her, I want a place in the vicinity, although pricewise that's a tall order. Ashley is up to the challenge and excited to start hunting for property, real estate investment being his favorite *hobby*. Knowing him, he'll find something ridiculously expensive and offer to be my investor. I need to feel like I'm pulling my weight though. It's easy to get swept up in the idea of my *found family* as Claire calls them and reap the benefits of his affluency. There's a fine line between letting them *love* me and freeloading. Things I'm sure we'll cover in upcoming sessions as I navigate relocating. Although I don't need a therapist to tell me that sponging off someone is not something I'm willing to do, no matter how it's spun.

Entering the home gym, I look at the things that belong to me. I'll pack this whole room and move it with me. It's where I spend most of my time. It's what drowns out the noise of being alone. Not sure when I stopped being a loner. *Yes, I do.* The pressure on my chest is less, the heat in my belly not as intense. The low-level panic I feel at wanting to belong with (to?) someone is still there but not as disrupting as it used to be. Admitting that I want to belong is new, but I embrace it.

I know, Doc. We call that progress.

Stepping into the master suite, our old room, I glance around at the memories that superimpose themselves on the decor. Through the sliding doors, the sun is starting its descent into the lake. *One last Blue Lake sunset.* I sit on the lounge chair beyond the glass and watch until the last streak of light dissolves into the glass surface. It's still beautiful, but tonight it seems sad. Tonight the orb melting into the water reminds me of a match singed out in a puddle. Later, lying in bed—not our bed, my old bed in my old room—I pick up my phone and tap our text conversation and stare at her words. *I will.* I didn't reply when she sent it. I just let those two words settle over me like a weighted blanket. Now though, I want to respond.

Me: Promise?

Bubbles pop up like she's responding, then go away. Seconds later, the phone rings and her smiling face lights up the screen in the dusk of my room. I swipe to answer and tap the speaker button. Before I can say hello, she says, "I already do."

"Me too."

"What are you doing?"

"Lying in bed."

"It's like 9:00 p.m."

"I know. I was bored and . . ."

"And?"

"Lonely, I guess." I pause, but when she doesn't respond, I add, "It feels weird to say because I used to like being alone. Figured I'd just try to go to sleep early."

"I wish you were here," we say at the same time.

"No, I wish I was there," I amend. "This doesn't feel like . . . my home anymore."

"So . . . if you were here, what would we be doing?" Whether she changes the tone of our conversation on purpose to avoid the seriousness or she's just feeling playful, I'm grateful and play along.

"Oh, baby girl, we'd be . . ." I laugh at my own joke before I speak it. "Doing each other, I'm pretty sure." Her lilting giggle comes through the phone and fills the room like she's here. "God, I miss you. Your smell, your skin, your touch, your kiss."

"If you were here, I'd kiss you."

"Tell me where you are right now. I wanna picture it—you."

"I'm in my room, on my bed."

"What are you wearing?"

"Your muscle shirt."

"What else?"

"That's it."

"Ugh, Ever, you're killin' me."

"It smells like you. I don't think I'll wash it till you come back."

"If I were there, I'd pull it off you and kiss every inch of your body." I shove my boxers down one-handed and kick them the rest of the way off with my feet. I wrap my hand around my hardened length and pretend it's her hand touching me, stroking me. "Ugh," I muffle my groan with the back of my other hand. I'm not sure when we decided to take our call here, but we're in obvious agreement, fully on the same page.

"I'd tangle my fingers in your hair while you kiss me. I know you like it when I do that." Her voice goes breathless on the last two words before her moan pierces the darkness. "Mmm, Julie."

Fuck, she is so hot. This is soo hot.

My dick swells in my hand, telling me I'm close. This might be the quickest I've ever come in my life—even quicker than that first night by the pool after seven months without her. Her moans send me over the edge. "Ungh, mmm, yes."

Panting through my own orgasm, I swipe my boxers from the foot of the bed for clean-up and lie there spent. Neither of us makes a sound except to regulate our breathing. Once mine goes back to normal, my eyelids begin to droop. "I don't want to let you go."

"Same." Her reply sounds heavy, like she's almost asleep. "I wish your arms were around me right now."

"Pretend. Leave the phone by your pillow so I can hear you breathe."

"M-kay. You too."

Sunlight assaults my eyelids and I squint against the already sweltering rays coming through the sliding door. My phone still rests against my pillow but the screen is black. I blink against the daylight and tap the screen. She's gone but there's a text from her. It's barely 7:00 a.m., but still way later than I ever sleep.

Ever: Went for a beach run and coffee. Best separate night's sleep ever.

Rolling onto my back, holding the phone above my head, I stare at the screen and grin like a fool. I can't wait. I spring from the sheets, shower and dress in record time and drive to Fit.

Two hours later, I'm back at the house with a solid plan in place. Tapping my chest, I turn in slow circles, taking in my surroundings. My mind is made up. Taking the stairs two at a time, I charge into my room and drag my duffel out of the closet and toss it on the bed. I empty drawers and stuff it to the hilt. I take another bag from the top of the closet and begin filling it, too. Details don't matter—for once. They'll welcome me with open arms. I know it. My heart races at *not* having a solid plan in place, but I've never been more certain of anything.

My mind replays our conversation on my last night in Malibu as we watched the sunset on the beach. We sat on a blanket, her between my legs, back against my chest, and listened to the waves crash while the glowing orb disappeared before us. The air was thick with salty moisture, waving her hair. The breeze chilled our skin the lower the sun sank.

"This is perfect." She reaches her hand to my cheek, trapping our faces together. Her fingernails scrape along the rough shadow of hair on my jaw.

"*You're* perfect." I squeeze her in my arms and revel in the gift of this girl.

She drops her hand and sighs, her energy doing a one-eighty.

"What just happened?" Her answer is a shaky exhale. "Everly, talk to me." I lean sideways to look in her eyes. Hers are downcast. It reminds me of her shift at the sushi restaurant. I brave the question this time. "Baby, tell me what's going on in there."

Blowing air through pursed lips, she meets my eyes, her voice a hoarse whisper. "I'm not perfect." Her eyes fill and two glowing tracks race down her cheeks, on fire in the waning sun.

I don't want to tell her she's never looked more beautiful because she's clearly upset. I open my mouth to say something to erase the sadness.

She stops me with a shake of her head. "Don't, Julie. I'm not. I kissed Seth. In Pismo last year. When Taya came back."

Now it's my turn to blow air through pursed lips. "Okay. Not what I expected to come out of your mouth."

"I know." She sucks in a shaky breath to stop the sob trying to escape. "I didn't mean to. I drank a lot—that's not an excuse. I didn't . . . it didn't . . . I threw up after. I swear that's all that happened. And I . . . It was only for a second. And it was all wrong because it wasn't you and—"

"Shhh, Ever. Sweet girl. Stop." I kiss her temple as she buries her face in my chest, shaking her head and sucking in gulps of air. "None of that matters. But now I get why you were so weird around him at Christmas."

"You could tell?"

"I could tell."

"I'm so sorry, Julie. I had to tell you. I couldn't hear you say I'm perfect one more time, because I can't take it when you say things like that. I feel like a fraud." Another shaky exhale and she's gripping my chest like a lifeline. "I probably shouldn't have told you. It's selfish to confess just to absolve my guilt. Because it meant nothing. It never did. I was just spiraling at the time. But I don't want to keep secrets or lie to you by omission. I'm so sorry, Julie. You deserve better than that."

Compared to all the shit we've been through, this is not even making my radar. I couldn't care less about some random almost nothing kiss. And that surprises me a little. Maybe therapy is working better than I thought. That she is so upset is a testament to her pure heart and makes me love her even more. It also makes me want to turn her mood around. "So you threw up, huh? On him? Please tell me it was on him." My answer is her watery giggle.

"No. But . . . next to him." She sniffs and tucks her cheek against my chest.

"Close enough for me."

"You're not mad?" She tilts her head back to gauge my expression.

I kiss her upturned nose. "No, pretty girl, I'm not. But poor Seth should be if his kisses make girls want to vomit." I chuckle at my own joke, still marveling at how truly not pissed I am or even put out at all. Some drunken half kiss compared to what we have is a non-issue. She opens her mouth to clarify but I stop her. "I know it was the alcohol. Just let me have that one. Okay?"

"Okay, Julie." She sniffs again and whispers, "I love you."

"I know, Ever. I love you too. So. Much." I squeeze her again. Then I add, "That was . . . Taya coming back was . . . a lot. Under the circumstances, I'm not sure I could blame you. And I don't."

"I just ran because that's what I do. What I did," she corrects. She traces my tattoo again as she talks. "It was like I didn't have my own life, only yours. And then your life wasn't what I thought it was. So I dipped, took off."

"You don't have to explain. I kinda came around to all that over the last seven months. Had plenty of time to think."

"It's why I was so hell-bent on making a new life that was all mine. Like if I built a life that was mine, I wouldn't run anymore." She snuggles her back into my chest again and tucks her hands over mine across her ribcage, locking our fingers.

"I get that, too. And you killed it. It's a pretty solid life you've built." I dip my nose behind her ear and stare out over the darkening waves. "I'm so damn proud of you, Ever."

"I know. You already said that."

"Yeah, I did, sassy girl. And I mean it. You're magic."

"I don't want you to leave tomorrow."

"I know. Me either." She shivers in my arms. "C'mon. Let's go up and get you warm." I stand and pull her with me, spinning and lifting her off the ground. She wraps her limbs around me and kisses my neck, her hair spilling over my face, tangling in the stubble on my jaw.

I walk all the way up the steps and into her cottage like that, just breathing her in. My sunshine girl.

I can almost smell her now, even though she's not here. I can almost feel her arms around me, her body against mine. Nope, I can't wait. I'm going to be with her, with my family, with the people I love, who love me too. I'm going home.

Chapter 31

EVERLY

Two-ish years later

"Everly Tate Davis, Bachelor of Arts in Psychology, *summa cum laude.*"

Applause roars in my ears. I beam at the faces of my family and friends. Even Jessica Davis got the whole day off to fly in for the ceremony. The last time I saw my mom face-to-face was almost a year ago at Allie and Luke's wedding. She got *two* days off for that event. Whatever makes her happy. She is happy—or seems to be—so I'm happy for her. It's easy to be happy for others when you're genuinely happy yourself. And I am. So incredibly happy.

Gathering at Alumni Park for pictures, I still can't wrap my head around my life. Although I'm getting better at allowing and trusting that good things happen for me—for all of us. Julian moved down south less than two years ago with every intention of buying his own home. While property investment became a main interest of his, thanks to Ashley, he soon realized anything in his current price range would've placed him too far away for any of our liking. Ashley needed him more available for their business expansion plans and he and I needed to be—wanted to be—with each other every day.

Overseeing the project firsthand, he and Ashley ultimately decided to let him expand the cottage into a full single-story home. He got to use his innate ability to design and renovate spaces and invest his money in a more sensible way. Ashley considers it a win-win because it increases the value of his Malibu estate. I'm just grateful Julian and I get to be together every day and every night. I'm not sure I'll ever take waking up next to him for granted again.

Tonight the Ashleys are hosting my graduation party. They insisted on pulling out all the stops. After almost three years of being absolutely spoiled by them and catered to at every turn, you'd think I'd be used to it. It continues to overwhelm and even embarrass me at times—the sheer privilege I experience at their hands. Still, I'm beyond grateful for their love and support and never miss an opportunity to tell or show them. I work my ass off for the ASH empire and take on any new endeavor they throw my way. So does Julian. That we both come from meager beginnings might be why, but Ashley is such a giving soul despite his advantaged lot in life it makes it easy to work hard for him.

The spring weather is perfect and the backyard glows with celebration. The sun is beginning its descent but still high enough to keep the air a little too warm. Every breeze off the coast is a refreshing kiss to our toasty skin.

Julian brings a chilled glass of champagne to me and takes a sip from his own. "I like your dress." He dips his head and kisses my lips. His taste like crisp bubbly.

"Thanks. Tatum and Lennon call it my naked dress."

"I remember it from the anniversary party two years ago."

"You do?" I look down at it and brush my palm down my torso to the bottom hem that hits just below the top of my thighs. "They roasted me a little for wearing a two-year-old dress, but I love it."

"It's a helluva dress, so yeah. I do, too." His eyes darken to deep indigo as he tucks a strand of hair behind my ear. Touching his nose to mine, his voice rasps, "I, uh, wanna . . . can I say something?"

Tapping my index finger on his bottom lip, I smile and whisper, "Of course, babe."

He kisses me sweetly, then taps a butter knife I didn't see him holding to the flute in his other hand. Projecting his voice, he steps back and calls out, "Can I have your attention for a minute?"

Everyone falls silent.

"Thank you." He chuckles and sets the knife down on the table. *He's nervous.* My heart skips and thuds double time. He looks back at me and smiles, wipes his palm on his pant leg, exhales a breath and winks at me. "Four years ago, this girl walked into my life—or crashed—and I had no idea what was about to happen. I didn't know someone would see straight through the walls I'd built or make me want to take them down. I didn't know I could feel . . . wanted, needed.

"Everly, you opened me up to love, to being loved. You healed a part of me I didn't even realize was broken. You showed me happiness I didn't think I'd ever find—or even thought I deserved. You loved me when it wasn't easy. You believed in me when I didn't believe in myself. And somehow, through it all, you made me laugh. You made me live.

"So, today—while we celebrate you graduating and proving to the world just how unstoppable you are—I just have one question." He exhales and sucks in another deep inhale. "As my best friend and favorite person, will you do me the honor of becoming my wife for the rest of our lives?"

Gasps abound as he sets the flute down, pulls a velvet square box out of his pants pocket and kneels before me. Opening it, the stone inside catching the rays and sparkling, he continues, "Everly Tate Davis, will you marry me?"

I'm nodding. My hand covers my mouth as tears roll down my cheeks unchecked and I keep nodding.

He stands and removes the ring and sets the box next to the glass. He takes my hand and slides the ring onto my finger. It fits perfectly. "Yes?" he asks because I still haven't uttered a word.

"Yes. Yes. Absolutely, yes."

On the last *yes*, he picks me up and swings me around, kissing me soundly on the lips to the cheers, hurrahs and thunderous applause of our family and friends. I know my face is scarlet because it feels hot. Stopping the embarrassment in its tracks is seeing the track of tears on Julian's face before he buries it in the crook of my neck.

His lips find my ear. "Thank you. I love you so much, pretty girl. I'm going to spend the rest of my life trying to make you as happy as you make me."

I pull back from him and place my palms on his cheeks, swiping my thumbs across his to dry them. "You already do, beautiful boyfriend." I shriek. "I mean fiancé." I turn to the crowd and yell, "Fiancé," as I point to him with one hand and hold my other newly ringed hand up to the masses, wiggling my fingers.

Ashley yells, "Cheers to Ever and Julian."

My mom and Allie are hugging and crying. Ryan and Olivia are in a group hug with Baby Jack. Our friends are crowded around the bar, holding up shots in salute. Auz is holding a shot in each hand, standing next to Callie and her bulging baby belly, offering to take her shot as tribute. She in turn holds her glass of iced water up with a crooked smile, massaging her bump.

My heart is so full, more tears swim to my eyes and blur the scene before me. *How'd I get so lucky?*

Chapter 32

JULIAN

Six Months Later

Everly is gorgeous on a regular day. Everly on her wedding day is radiant. She walks toward me, her feather-light dress flowing behind her in the warm breeze giving ethereal grace. I hold my breath as she steps to me and takes my hand. It's a simple ceremony, just us. No groomsmen or bridesmaids. No father walking her down the aisle. No parents for either of us, but her mom is on FaceTime with Via watching. That Ever isn't bothered by that in the least is just one of the reasons I love her.

Before the newly ordained Ashley speaks, I scan the small crowd gathered on the sand, at our friends who have become family. Then I swing my gaze to the setting sun and finally back to her. *Her.* The glowing sphere sets her gray eyes on fire, luminous and shining with unshed tears. I blink several times to keep mine at bay and will myself to get through my vows without losing it. I wonder for the millionth time when I became such a marshmallow. But if that's the tradeoff for this life, *my life*, then marshmallow it is.

"Everly," I start, then exhale through puffed cheeks to the soft chuckles of the crowd. "I never thought or even dreamed this day would come for me. But it's here. You're here. And now I can't imagine living a day without you. Thank you for loving me, for showing me what it means to love and be loved—really loved. Today, I vow to love, honor and cherish you every day for the rest of my life, for better or worse, no matter what."

One tear slides down her cheek, shimmering in the sinking light. Brushing it with my thumb, I smile and keep blinking, hoping to waylay mine. She takes a deep shaky breath. "Julian, from the first day, I was drawn to you. You awakened something in me I didn't know was missing. Thank you for showing me what it feels like to be chosen, seen and protected. Today, I vow to love, honor and cherish you every day for the rest of my life, for better or worse, no matter what."

Ashley clears his throat and instructs, "Julian, repeat after me. I, Jayce Julian McKay, take you, Everly Tate Davis, to be my lawfully wedded wife, to have and to hold from this day forward until death parts us."

"I . . ." My voice comes out hoarse. I clear my throat and try again. "I, Jayce Julian McKay, take you, Everly Tate Davis, to be my lawfully wedded wife, to have and to hold from this day forward until death parts us." One tear sneaks from the corner of my eye and races down the side of my face.

"Now, Everly." Ashley chokes up and coughs to cover it up. "This is rough, guys."

The small crowd chuckles again, and a few sniffles can be heard.

I keep my eyes on her. She's solid, no tears, just the purest smile, full dimples winking at me.

Ashley begins again. "Ever, repeat after me. I, Everly Tate Davis, take you, Jayce Julian McKay, to be my lawfully wedded husband, to have and to hold from this day forward until death parts us."

Her voice is soft, shy, angelic. "I, Everly Tate Davis, take you, Jayce Julian McKay, to be my lawfully wedded husband, to have and to hold from this day forward until death parts us."

"Julian, place the ring on Everly's finger."

My hand trembles as I slide the band onto her third finger.

"Now, Everly, place the ring on Julian's finger." She's steady. Ashley is not. Through gruff emotion, he proclaims, "By the power vested in me by the state of California, I now pronounce you husband and wife. Julian, you may kiss your bride."

Cradling her face in my hands, I pull her lips to mine. Before I kiss her, I whisper, "I love you, my sweet wife, so much." I press my lips into hers and linger, breathing her in.

Cheers and applause erupt behind us, and I can't help the smile that breaks the contact. Even over the din I hear her whisper and I watch her lips move.

"I love you, husband."

Chapter 33

Everly

Five weeks later

"Tell me what's bugging you." His arms snake around me as he drops his chin on my shoulder and meets my eyes in the mirror.

I shrug because I don't have an answer. But something *is* bugging me—maybe literally. I've been feeling off since we got back from our honeymoon. Achy, sluggish, foggy brained. Maybe I caught some airplane cooties. "Maybe I'm coming down with something." He presses his lips to my temple, and I shoo him. "Maybe you shouldn't do that in case I'm contagious."

He doesn't *shoo* and instead grips me tighter, trailing kisses along my ear and neck. "I'd catch germs from you anytime, baby." He turns me in his arms and kisses me sweetly.

My head throbs and spins when I tilt it to deepen the kiss. I plant my hands on his chest and shove him back nicely but firmly. "I'm really off. Gonna try the ocean, catch a couple waves, see if that snaps me out of it."

It's November, so the water will be cold, colder than normal. California oceans are always cold, but nothing a wetsuit can't cure. I already miss the climate of Costa Rica. After ten days of nonstop honeymooning in the most beautiful place I've ever seen in person, I'm dreading the icy waves but craving the salt. And hoping the negative ions of the sea will cure what ails me.

"Want me to go with?" He tucks a strand of hair behind my ear and cups his hand around my neck, searching my eyes. Before I can answer, he amends his question to a statement. "I'll go with you."

But I'm already shaking my head. "No, they want you in the studio. You go. Tell them I'm not feeling that well and ask if I can make it up to them tomorrow."

"Babe, we're the talent. We can take a day off if we need it." One side of his mouth crooks as he winks at me.

"Ew, let's not be *those* people. And we just had ten days off." I grab a handful of the longer hair on top of his head and pull his lips to mine again, then grimace as my stomach coils. "Okay, I need air. I'll be at the beach if you need me."

The waves are mostly closed out today, but I find a couple I can ride. Mostly I float with my cheek resting on my board, dragging my hands through the water, trying to ground myself and shake the malaise. A perfect set looks to be rolling in, so I stretch out and begin to paddle. On top of the wave, I swing the board to stay there and coast, but a blinding pain stabs my abdomen. I double over, throwing off my balance. I almost recover when a rush of dizziness blurs my vision and sends me tumbling under the surface. Twisting and turning at the whim of the sea, I finally resurface to be slammed in the ribs by my board. Hooking my arms over it, I kick my feet till I can stand up and scoop the board under my arm and scramble onto the shore.

Flopping the board down first, I fall to my knees in the wet sand and collapse next to it. I roll onto my back and catch my breath. Before I can, another stabbing pain folds me in two.

Something is seriously wrong. I need help.

I look around. The beach is all but deserted. My cinch sack with my phone is farther up on the beach in the dry sand. I try to stand but double over with another pain so searing, my vision closes in on me. I drop back to my knees and crawl to my bag, rummage for my phone. I unlock it and tap Julian's name to call him.

It rings three times before he answers, breathless. "Hey, babe. Feel—"

"Something's wrong. Help me." Another pain stabs my right side, and the phone slips out of my hand right before everything goes black.

Chapter 34

JULIAN

Not knowing is the worst. My imagination is all over the place. It doesn't help that the waiting room is giving caged animal vibes. I'm trying not to pace and freak out the other people, but I'm crawling out of my skin. Ever's limp body, passed out on the beach, is superimposed on my brain and threatens to empty the contents of my stomach. When she called me for help, she uttered four words and then became unresponsive. After shouting her name to no avail, I dropped my phone and yelled at Auz to call 911 at a dead run.

Finding her on the beach collapsed, sheet-white face, clammy skin and rag doll limbs gutted me. I scooped her into my arms and ran for the stairs. The ambulance pulled up as I reached the front of the house. She was incoherent and mostly out but moaning in pain. The EMTs wouldn't let me ride with her. I had to follow them. I've never wanted to scream at traffic so much in my life. The siren helped to marginally clear the path, but LA is crowded and everyone has someplace to be.

Now in this stale lobby waiting room, I still have no idea what happened to her. Did she wipe out on a wave? Is she sick, like she said this morning? I'm on my way to the desk to harass someone—anyone—for answers when Allie and Ashley rush in.

Allie takes one look at my face and throws her arms around me. She murmurs things to me like "it'll be okay" and "she's gonna be okay."

When she finally releases me, Ashley clasps my shoulder and asks, "What do we know?"

"Nothing. They didn't tell me anything when they took her. They wouldn't let me go with her. And they"—I wave an angry hand at the desk—"don't know anything. Yet." I use quotes on the last word, then heave in a deep breath that sounds like a sob even to my own ears. I'm losing it. I throw my hand over my mouth to stop myself from breaking down.

"It's okay, Julian. It's gonna be okay. I'll see what I can find out." Ashley stalks to the desk and begins muttering to the nurse seated there.

"How long have you been waiting?" Allie puts her arm around my waist and steers me toward a chair. I don't answer or sit, just shake my head. She sits but holds my hand so that I stand in front of her.

Ashley rejoins us and motions for us to move out of the waiting room and away from others. "They're working on her. That's all she'd tell me."

"Working on what? What the fuck happened? She was out cold, so pale, but didn't look hurt beyond that. No signs of injury that I could see."

"They'll figure it out. They'll help her, Julian."

I nod again because I don't know what else to do or say. I tug the hair on top of my head and begin pacing again. "She wasn't feeling well this morning. Said she felt off, wanted to go surfing, get some fresh air. I should've gone with her."

"Don't do that to yourself," Allie scolds. "You couldn't have known what would happen."

"I still don't. Why won't they tell us what the fuck is happening?" Yanking on my hair, I turn to resume pacing. I'll be lucky if I have any hair left by the time they update us.

Help me. That's the last thing she said to me. It's playing on a loop, haunting me.

She needs to be okay. I can't take it if she's not. I won't make it if she's not. I'm trying not to let my brain go there after all the work I've done, but the whisper under all the panic says this is what Jayce Keller deserves. I know it's a lie. Old patterns rearing their ugly heads. A spike of anger has me silently yelling back, *But what does* she *deserve? She doesn't deserve this. Let her be okay. Please, God, let her be okay.* I'm not sure when I started praying or who I might be praying to, but if it saves her, allows me to keep her, I'll pray.

Dropping into a chair, elbows on my knees, I cradle my forehead in my hands and fist my fingers in my hair—*like she does. Fuck, baby, please be okay.*

Ashley's shoes step into my line of vision just before his hand lands lightly on my shoulder. He doesn't say anything, just stands there.

I'm grateful he stays silent. I don't want more noise in my head—inane platitudes. I want answers. I want Ever.

"Mr. McKay?"

I twist my neck and look up at the petite woman in scrubs, dark curly hair under a blue scrub cap. I stand, but it feels like I'm in slow motion. I track her features, posture, my eyes bouncing between hers as I approach her.

She holds out her hand. "I'm Attending Physician Michele Laine. I took care of your wife."

I shake her hand but again like I'm in slow motion. *Did she just use past tense?*

Allie and Ashley flank my sides.

"How is she?" I think I'm gripping her hand too tight. I force myself to release it, but I don't know what to do with mine now that I have.

"Let's step over here, into the hall." She sidesteps out of the waiting room a few paces, never turning her back on me. She places her hand on my forearm and meets my eyes. "Your wife suffered a ruptured ectopic pregnancy. Sometimes called a tubal pregnancy. We had to surgically remove her fallopian tube, but she should make a full recovery. We'll keep her overnight to monitor her, make sure the bleeding is stabilized."

I hear the words and mostly understand them, but I can't form any of my own. My head is buzzing like it sustained a close-range blast. *Pregnancy? Surgery?* Should *make a full recovery?*

"Can we see her?" Allie grips my other forearm.

"She's still asleep in recovery, so immediate family only. I can take you to her, Mr. McKay."

I follow her in a trance.

The room is dimly lit despite it being the middle of the day. She's lying there while tubes connect her to machines that beep. She looks so pale. I reach out and tuck a strand of hair behind her ear as the first tear spills. "She's . . . okay?" I swipe it away. "She's going to be okay?"

"Yes. She should make a full recovery." *She already said that.* "We removed the ruptured tube and stopped the bleeding. She has another perfectly healthy one on the other side and should be able to get pregnant again. It just means her chances are cut in half now with only one working fallopian tube."

"Why did . . . How did this happen? She's on the pill. We didn't—weren't trying to . . . make a baby."

"Sometimes these things just happen. It was early, probably five weeks. Six at the most. While a rupture is serious and can be life-threatening, we got to her in time. Your wife's going to be okay, Mr. McKay. She'll be waking up any time now but will be groggy. Press the call button if you need anything."

Coming to my senses enough to shake her hand, I respond, "Thank you, Doctor."

"Of course." The door whisks closed as she leaves.

I pace around all three sides of her bed before I scan the room and drag a lone chair to her bedside and sink into it. Gripping her hand, the one without the IV, I tuck it between my cheek and her thigh and rest my head there. I let the pulse in her wrist soothe me that she's here, alive. I watch her chest rise and fall and will her eyes to open, to look at me. I close mine to block out the tubes, the sterile bed. I concentrate on her pulse tapping against my fingertips, the warm velvet of her skin against my cheek.

"Julie," she croaks, "what happened?" She reaches out to touch my face, then frowns at the IV on the back of her hand.

"Baby. Shh, you're okay. You . . . had an accident." I don't know what to say to her, how to explain it.

"Surf . . ." She clears her throat and tries again. "Surfing?"

I shake my head that's suddenly pounding with the restraint to not break down.

"I don't know. You . . . Ever, you were pregnant. Five weeks, they said."

"Were?"

I nod, touch her cheek. "They call it a tubal pregnancy. It's—it can be dangerous if it ruptures. Yours did. But they caught it in time and you're going to be okay. You're okay." I'm not sure who I'm trying to convince more. I stand up to lean closer and kiss her cheek. "Want me to get the doctor?"

She shakes her head, her eyelids dropping like they're weighted. "I'm just tired."

"You lost a lot of blood." I keep petting her face, a reminder that she's here maybe. "Your color is better now." Her eyes flutter open and I smile at her, then kiss her forehead.

She smiles back, but her lids fall again.

"You sleep, okay? I'll be right here."

She nods once and her face goes slack. She's out.

I sit back down, sigh, lay my head on her hand and will my racing heart to settle.

Chapter 35

EVERLY

"I'm fine. It's been a week. Can you stop hovering already?"

"It's *only* been a week."

"The doctor didn't give me any restrictions. I'm good. Besides, I already missed assignments from our honeymoon. Plus, Tatum and Lennon have been doing all the heavy lifting for the new brand. We have an interview with our first potential client tomorrow."

"Can't they do it without you?"

"Julie, this is huge. It's a minor league baseball team. The coach is a retired major league player. I don't *want* them to do it without me. This whole business was my idea."

"Okay, I get that. But, Ever, you haven't even talked about the accident. You just pretend like nothing happened." He'd resorted to calling it the accident or the incident because I guess he didn't know what else to call it.

"What am I supposed to say? It happened. It's over. I'm fine. We didn't want to have a baby anyway. Right?" Even as he winces at the mention of the word *baby*, I know that's the one thing I can say that will shut him up. I ignore the twinge of guilt for playing that card, but the last thing I want to do is sit around and relive it. I know Julian doesn't want kids. I hadn't really thought about it until it happened and then . . . went away—in a life-threatening way.

Julian made no secret of being afraid to pass on his genes to the next generation—claiming he got lucky escaping them himself.

Ever since the doctor told us I now only have one tube and half a chance of getting pregnant, it feels like something was taken from me. It wasn't on my radar and now it's screaming in my face. So I do what I do—tuck it away, ignore it. Points for not running. Although one could argue my self-distraction is a form of running. Sometimes I hate that I'm a psych major and know all the things. Ignorance really is bliss in situations like this. I know what I'm doing and I'm gaslighting us both that I'm not.

He nods, walks the three steps to me and envelops my face in his palms. His sigh is heavy, his lips in a tight line. He pecks a kiss on the tip of my nose. "Just take it easy, okay?"

I nod slightly, restricted by his hold on my cheeks and smile. "Promise. I haven't even gone surfing yet. But that clock is ticking, mister." I arch a brow at him.

He pulls me into a bear hug and I let him. Everything goes quiet when he does. Everything feels safe, like nothing can hurt me. I blink back the pressure behind my eyes. We're going to be fine. I have him. I don't need babies—little carbon copies of him with dark brown hair and deep blue eyes. I dig my nails into the grooves of his back and pull him tighter to me until the image fades.

***

"This is exactly what I've been looking for. Depending on how we structure it, we can make this a win-win." Jason Ross, retired Angels middle infielder and now the head coach of their minor team, the Sun Rays, leans on his desk and looks from me to Lennon, then Tatum. He plans to incorporate mental health as a major part of his coaching philosophy, especially for the rehab process of injured major league players. He cast his net wide to find grad students in need of clinical hours. The competition had to be fierce.

Sitting across from him in his office, I can't help but wonder if Ashley's glowing recommendation likely tipped the scales in our favor. It doesn't embarrass me like it probably should. Tatum, Lennon and I work our asses off, and Ashley knows that. We deserve this as much as anyone. But it does drive home that saying, "it's not what you know but who you know," and frankly breaks my romantic, idealistic heart just a little. Not enough to take us out of the running for this opportunity, I admit to myself silently.

"Since we're new at this, it would greatly benefit us to structure it as an internship. The university approves it. We get clinical hours. You get the mental health support of professionals. Tatum and I will shadow the CMPCs and Lennon will shadow your trainers."

"We will still offer a fair wage for the hours worked."

"That's very generous of you, Mr. Ross."

"Please, call me Jason."

"Okay. Jason. Thank you again for this opportunity." I shake his hand as we stand to leave and note the warm dimpled smile, kind eyes that crinkle with years of laughter, life or playing baseball in the sun. Probably all three. I'm excited to work with him.

Outside on the sidewalk of the Sun Rays' athletic complex, Lennon booms, "This calls for a celebratory toast." She immediately slaps her hand over her mouth, making an O with her lips. "Wait, can you drink?"

I roll my eyes. "Yes, Lennon. I can drink. I'm fine. No restrictions. Except . . . no sex for four weeks. Three more to go." I wiggle my eyebrows, and when they both open their mouths, I put my hand up before either can speak. "Don't you two start, too. I get enough of it at home." I keep my hand up until they both acquiesce. "Where to for drinks?"

Lennon waves her hand like a game show host toward the buildings across the street, one boasting a sign that says The Sun Deck, aptly named for its rooftop bar overlooking the minor league field and the rolling Agoura Hills. Typical Southern California weather has us choosing the rooftop for our celebratory happy hour.

Tatum orders three pineapple mimosas and a basket of fries.

"Okay, so I get you don't want to talk about it, but we're your friends and that was scary. Are you gonna tell us how you're really doing?"

Lennon chimes in, "Yeah, you went from euphoric bride back from her honeymoon to emergency surgery. We're allowed to be concerned."

"No, I know. I'm sorry, guys. Not trying to be an asshole here. Just not really wanting to relive it." I hold up one hand in surrender before they come at me. "But, yeah. It was fucking scary. Almost dying aside, I don't really remember any of it. And to be honest, it's kind of a twisted relief. Julian doesn't want kids."

"Like, ever?" Tatum sets her drink down before she takes a sip.

Lennon pauses her glass on the way to her lips.

I pinch my lips in a tight straight line and shake my head. "Can you blame him with parents like his? Doesn't exactly scream Hallmark moment."

"Fair. But we study this shit, Ever. We're not our families."

"What she said," Lennon adds.

I shrug and say nothing. I lift my glass in hopes of distracting them and permanently changing the subject. "Cheers to new opportunities and the Sun Rays' newest fans."

They clink their glasses to mine and smile, showing their unnaturally white teeth, telling me they're on board with my attempt. We all laugh, take a healthy sip of the bubbles in our glasses and talk shop for the next hour as we watch the sun set.

Chapter 36

JULIAN

Ever has been nonstop since the incident. We barely see each other unless we film content together. Yes, we're married and obviously live together, but it's different. Tonight we're attending the Sun Rays' Mind and Body Benefit, a charity event to raise money for mental health programs and counseling for athletes of all ages. Allie and Ashley are attending too as All Star Contributors. If a working date is all I can get, I'll take it, but I wish I could get my wife back. I had her for five weeks, then the incident, and she's tucked it all away—like the "good military daughter" as she's called it.

Guilt still plagues me for feeling relieved. Not relieved that she lost the baby, obviously. Relieved that we're not about to be parents. That she tucks and runs when life gets tough makes my point for me. Maybe we're not all destined to become our parents, but it sure seems like most of us do to some extent without even trying. That I've worked most of my life to avoid becoming mine might be my only saving grace. I can't guarantee my offspring would fare the same. Not making little carbon copies of my parents would become my sole purpose in life if I had kids. If I'm being honest, though, my heart aches a little at the thought of never having a couple of mini chestnut-haired, stormy-eyed little girls just like her. After the accident, I couldn't stop thinking about that—the possibility of what could've been.

Watching her fasten diamond studs to her ears in the reflection, my mouth goes dry. She's always beautiful. Every. Damn. Day. Tonight, in a formal gown of dove-gray suede that sets off her eyes and hugs every curve and sparkling jeweled stilettos on her feet, she's breathtaking. My body reacts involuntarily. It's been four weeks—doctor-ordered abstinence. Maybe that's why she's so distant, but something tells me it's more than that. I catch her eye in the mirror, and she smiles, dimples on full display, and my heart flips. I'm so goddamn lucky. She's my proof that somebody believes I deserve to be happy.

Turning to me, she plays with the collar of my shirt. "No tie?" One tawny eyebrow quirks as the corner of her mouth lifts.

"Ashley said it's black tie optional. I'm *opting* out." I chuckle at my own joke as she rolls her eyes, but I see the heat under the gesture. "You don't approve?"

"Husband, you could walk in there in sweats and still be the hottest guy in the room." She swipes invisible dust off my shoulders and pecks a kiss on my lips, transferring glossy color from hers to mine.

I press mine together and swipe my tongue between them. "Mmm, cherry. But I'm not sure it's my color."

Giggling, she drags her thumb across my lips to remove the stain.

When I suck her thumb into my mouth, her eyes go dark, hungry, but just as quickly shutter and go blank. "C'mon. The car will be waiting." Her smile is sweet, her hand on my cheek soft, caressing.

If I didn't know her so well, I'd think everything is fine. But I do and she's compartmentalizing—like the pro she is. It puts a pit in my stomach that I tuck away because we have an event and people expect us to show up smiling. Turning, I place my palm on the exposed skin of her lower back and guide her out the front door.

As charity events go, this one didn't suck. More casual than most formal events, I actually enjoyed myself. Ever's new boss is so cool, such a nice guy, and seems to genuinely care about the overall health of his players. I'm impressed with the organization—and him. I'm thrilled she's a part of the program. I hope it snaps her out of her funk. And I think it will. Head coach, Jason Ross, seems genuinely interested in her new endeavor, said that his assistant discovered her (them) on socials and thought their program would align perfectly with his plans for the ongoing mental health support of his athletes. He spent most of his free time this evening with our group, picking our brains—all of us—about ASH, the McKay Method and our lives in general. Truly one of the best nights I've spent "working" in . . . maybe ever.

Now back at home, Ever is back in the mirror, removing her earrings and slipping off her high heels. The heavy sigh that escapes her lips as her bare foot hits the fuzzy rug beneath her has me pausing my own stripping down routine. "Hey, pretty girl, how ya doin'?"

"Good, Julie. Just tired." She doesn't meet my eyes in the mirror or turn to face me when she answers. "Gonna go wash off my makeup." She briefly smiles at me as she moves past me into the bathroom, closing the door behind her. Within minutes she pads barefooted into the kitchen, sans makeup, wearing one of my T-shirts, and pulls a mug down from the cabinet. "Want some hot tea?"

"No, baby. I'm good. How about a foot massage?" She squints her eyes at me. "You, I mean. You stood in heels all night. Thought maybe . . ."

"I mean, I wouldn't say no." She smiles sweetly and proceeds to make herself some tea. With her steaming mug, she shuffles to the couch and settles into the cushions as I'm coming down the short hallway with her favorite lotion. Tucking in next to her, I lift her legs, drape them over my thighs and begin rubbing them. Turning sideways to give me better access, she drapes her elbow along the back of the couch and rests her cheek on her arm, watching me. "Mmm, that feels divine." Her eyes roll back and drift closed as another moan escapes her lips.

"Tired?"

Her mug of tea is all but forgotten, steaming on a coaster on the edge of the coffee table.

"Yeah, I guess."

"Talk to me, Ever. You know the drill. You study this. Don't stuff it all down. Tell me what's going on in there." I toss my chin toward her. She sighs heavily and opens her mouth to speak, then closes it again. "You know you can say whatever you want to me."

"Do I? Can I?" Her eyes take on that haunted saucer look I've only seen a few times.

"Absolutely. I don't want sugar-coated or watered down Ever. I want you. Whatever it is. Just say it."

"I want you, too. I miss you. Us. But I'm scared." I didn't expect that.

"I don't understand. I'm right here." I stop rubbing her feet to drag her onto my lap. She curls her legs and pushes her feet between my thighs and tucks them under one of my legs. "Break this down for me, babe. What do you mean, you miss me? Not trying to be dense here, but what are you scared of? Help me understand." I rub my hands up and down her arm while she tucks her head into my neck and draws lazy circles over my shirt where she knows my tattoo is.

"It's been four weeks," she huffs.

I wait but she doesn't elaborate.

"I'm well aware." I chuckle and so does she.

"So . . . I miss you." She nuzzles her nose into my ear, her warm breath sending mini shockwaves through my system.

"Again, I'm right here. All yours. All in. You don't even have to ask."

She stops tracing my chest. "I'm scared of . . . getting pregnant. Of it happening again."

"Ever girl." It's my turn to sigh. "Do you know only like one to two percent of pregnancies are ectopic? There's very little chance of it happening in the first place, let alone happening again, especially on the pill."

She nods her head against my neck. "You researched?" She pets my cheek.

"I did." I don't look at her, just lean into her touch.

"I guess I'm just psyching myself out." She shakes her head a little, like she's trying to shake it off—her feelings—tuck it away.

"That's fair. It was fucking scary. For me, too. Finding you on the beach out cold is one of those things that lives rent-free in my head." I squeeze my arms around her unconsciously. "But, baby, nothing is going to happen to you. I promise."

"You can't promise that." She's tracing my tattoo again.

"I *do* promise. I will it to be true. I can't lose you, Ever. I won't lose you." I lean my head back from hers enough to kiss her forehead. "C'mon. Let's go to bed. I need to feel every inch of your body against every inch of mine. I hate picturing you the way I found you that day." She opens her mouth to speak, but I cut her off. "But I'm glad we talked about it. I want you to always talk to me. Whatever it is."

"I know. Thank you, Julie. Will you . . . can we . . . She lowers her lashes.

"I'm your husband, pretty girl. Like I said, I'm all yours. You don't have to ask."

She slides off my lap, takes my hand and pulls me down the hall.

Chapter 37

EVERLY

"Can we go slow?" I feel my cheeks heat and add, "I don't know why I'm so nervous."

"We can do whatever you want. Whatever you need, Ever. Always." He holds his hands out to his sides. "Tell me what you want, what you need." He steps toward me, places his hands on my cheeks and pulls my lips to his.

The aching tenderness in his kiss undoes me. The well behind my eyes spills.

Picking me up, he spins and, in one step, sets me down softly on the edge of the mattress. He reaches for the hem of his shirt and pulls it slowly up my body and over my head. I lie back, and as I scoot more fully onto the mattress, he hooks his fingers in my thong and slides it off my legs. He begins kissing the inside of my ankle, then my calf, my thigh. At my center, he pauses and looks up at me through hooded dark lashes, his eyes deep sea blue. He presses his lips to my most sensitive spot but doesn't kiss me—just the pressure of his lips and the heat of his breath.

It's been too long. I arch off the bed with a deep moan and he hasn't even started yet. The anticipation of this man is enough to make me squirm. With fingers clenched around the comforter, I beg for what I want. "Please, Julie."

His lips wrap around the bundle of nerves in the softest pinch, the slightest flick of his tongue.

I want more. I push my body down into his face, a silent plea.

"M-hm," his murmur rumbles as he sucks harder, then swirls his tongue. His hands are on the backs of my thighs, pushing my legs up and out. The weight of his arms keeps them open for him as he makes love to me with his mouth.

I want to close them, press in as the orgasm builds, but he holds them down. I'm panting, drawing ragged breaths as my body starts to quiver. He knows I'm there. The weight disappears from my right leg and it flies against his face, drapes over his back and locks in. I'm going to come. I think I say it out loud. Then his fingers glide into me as my slick walls convulse around them. "Ughhhh," I moan long and low. This orgasm is new. It rolls over me like a perfect wave that curls endlessly along the coast before it breaks, smooth, pure, euphoric.

He doesn't remove his fingers, but he doesn't move them either. He knows I don't like the sudden vacancy after an orgasm but that everything is super sensitive. He plants little kisses up my torso, pausing to attend to each breast before he nuzzles his nose into my neck, behind my ear and delivers little sucking kisses to the pulse there.

He's always giving, thoughtful, during sex. Always starts with making me feel good, making me come for him. His heart undoes me.

His whispering breath in my ear sends shock waves down my arms as he murmurs, "I love you, sweet wife." His fingers slip out as he eases himself into me. "So." He slides farther. "Much." He buries himself, his pelvic bone pressing against mine. "Ughhh, Ever." His lips are pressed to my temple as he rocks in and out so slowly it's like sweet torture. "You okay, babe?"

Gripping his hips, I try to say yes, but it comes out, "Ughh-huh." Then it becomes, "More." Then, "Please."

"You sure?" His forehead presses to mine, sweat beads on his temples.

"Yesss, more."

He pulls almost all the way out and slides into me so slowly he shakes with the restraint. The more restraint he uses, the more it reminds me of why.

"Just fuck me, Julie. Like you always do. Don't stop." Still, he's gentle. Too gentle.

The room is almost pitch dark now so he can't see my face well, but he's searching for a sign, what's okay, what's not. "I got you. Just breathe, baby. Gonna show you how sweet it can be. Okay?" He kisses me deeply, plunging his tongue in and out of my mouth, mimicking our joined bodies. Long and slow. Our lips fused together. Then he's at my ear. "Breathe," he commands. "Long, slow. Exhale."

I obey, and on a slow exhale, he slides in so deep, the manscaped hair scrapes my nerves. "Ughh, yesss."

He laces our fingers and pins my arms to the bed on each side of my face and sets a rhythm that drives me mad and teases my clit.

Fuck, yeah. C'mon, Julie. Give it to me. Stop being so careful. My panting increases with his rhythm, but still he's gentle. *Talk to me. Fuck me like you always do.* He doesn't, but this might be better. It feels like the ocean waves, slow and rolling, building, growing until I'm on top ready to drop in.

His voice, husky with his own arousal, groans near my ear, "You gonna come for me again, baby?"

Tears prick my eyes. *There he is.*

"I love you, sweet wife. Ugh. I missed this. Feels so fucking good." His breathing hitches as he swells inside me. He's going to come and I want to join him. He squeezes my hands, his forearms trembling. "I'm going to—ugh so wet, so tight. I'm going to come, babe. Come with me." With one final thrust, he pins me tight to him and convulses inside me. He rocks back and forth, swirling his hips, teases my clit until I'm quivering around him. "Yes, Ever girl. Come for me. Mmm, yes, so good." My man knows how to get me there.

I thought maybe I wouldn't and I needed to. We both needed me to.

His body drapes over mine, his heartbeat thudding steadily in my ear pressed to his chest. I want to say so much, but I want to relish this space, this peace, this quiet. So I say nothing. Then he does and it's so beautiful the damn breaks.

"This will forever be my favorite feeling—you and me, like this." His breath in my ear is a kiss on my skin. "You wrapped around me. Me inside you. Your skin on mine." He inhales deeply. "Your scent all over me. I love you so much it hurts." His words drag a sob from my throat. "Don't cry, Ever. Shhh. I got you." He rolls to his side, taking me with him, and tangles his fingers in my hair, cradling my head, and rains kisses along my temple, my forehead, my lips. He swallows my sobs with the sweetest kisses until I'm done.

Before I fall, I whisper, "I love you so much, Julie."

His response is a shaky exhale and a kiss to my ear. "Me too, Ever." Wrapping his arms tighter around me, his breathing slows almost instantly and everything goes still.

243

Chapter 38

Julian

"Is it weird he wants to meet with me, too?" I catch Ever's eyes in the bathroom mirror as I finish shaving. I'm low-key excited to join Ever for lunch with her new boss, but I don't want to intrude either.

"I don't know. Maybe a little." My heart deflates a little at her honesty. "I think he's just a super nice guy and wants to know the people in his organization better." She drags her nails lightly up and down my back, popping goosebumps on my skin.

I swipe a towel over my face and attempt to let her off the hook again. "I agree he seems very nice, but I'm not *in* his organization."

Ever rolls her eyes, her sassy dimpled smile taking over her face as she shakes her head. "It's just lunch. If you want, I can go alone. Tell him you got held up with work."

"No, I wanna go." I surprise myself admitting that. "I like him. I was just saying—"

She kisses me and pats my cheek. "Good because I like showing off my husband." *Heart reinflated.*

The restaurant Jason Ross chose is one I haven't been to before. Ashley likes and can afford the finer things in life, but he's a simple guy, so we tend to frequent more obscure places. It's probably why I like him so much. He's not constantly throwing his success in everyone's face. We prefer small and local—like our sushi spot. This place is white tablecloths and both forks—which isn't a bad thing. It just makes me wonder if my first impression of Mr. Ross was incorrect and he really is a snooty rich guy. It makes me wish I'd looked him up, did a little research. I'm not entirely sure why I care about his background other than that he seems to be interested in Everly and the twins—but mostly Everly. Not in a creepy way. He seems genuine. I guess today's lunch will help me decide. I force myself out of my head and into the present as we approach him.

"Julian. I'm so glad you could make it, too." He stands from the table and shakes my hand, gives Ever a side hug and pulls a chair out for her. "I wanted to get to know you better. Your story intrigues me."

"My story?" The needles pricking the back of my neck make the hair on my arms stand up. *Definitely should've looked him up.* After all this time, I still fall back on wanting to be invisible.

The public persona of Julian McKay and the McKay Method is something I *put on*—like a business suit. No matter how long it's been, it still doesn't come naturally to me to be on display, put myself out there, be recognized in public, treated like *someone.* I know the content creators add some of my personal stuff to my social media, but I ask them to be as vague as possible. I get final say in anything they post, and the personal stuff is minimal at best. So what's he referring to? Is it the Todd stuff? A pit forms in my stomach. While Ashley's people did their best to distance me—both me and Everly—from the whole incident, police reports and court proceedings are public record. I look him in the eye, count my inhales and exhales and wait for his reply.

A waiter shows up to take our drink order. We all order iced tea and glance at our menus, temporarily distracted.

Ross clears his throat, drawing my eyes back to his. "I'm sorry. I didn't mean to overstep or pry. I just meant the stuff with your stepdad."

"My stepdad?" One eyebrow hairpins, but I don't correct him.

"You know"—he flaps both hands in the air—"forget I brought it up. Let's talk about something else. Anything else." His smile gives chagrin.

"No, it's fine. I know it's a matter of public record and it's a pretty crazy story. But I just meant that . . . he's not my stepdad."

"Oh. So your mom and he were never married?"

"Uhhh . . ."

"Okay, let me back up." He holds his hands up in surrender, his eyes bouncing between me and Ever, who reaches under the table to rub my thigh—an attempt to soothe me, I'm sure. "Full disclosure, I'm intrigued because I'm from that area originally. I, uh, went to school with your mom."

My eyebrows draw up into the fallen hair on my forehead as a low buzz roars in my ears.

"You knew—" I blow air out through puffed cheeks. I turn to Ever, and she smiles at me, but her eyes have taken on the deer look I rarely see. I reach for the hand on my leg and squeeze it in my own. "Did you know my . . . Todd?"

He's already shaking his head.

"No, he was older than me. Outside my teammates, I didn't really have a life or any other friends. Being a student athlete didn't leave much room for anything or anyone else. But . . ." He pauses and gasps out an exhale, lips agape.

I hold my breath. Something's coming. I can feel it. I've no idea what, but I wish he'd just say it already. I knew this invite to lunch wasn't random. Growing up with Todd and Brandi taught me to read situations, energy, body language. Even though I don't have cause to do it much anymore in order to feel secure, some things—some habits—are hard to break.

I make myself speak in his silence, attempt to steer the conversation away from me. "That worked out well for you." Realizing I sound like an asshole, I add, "A worthy tradeoff, yeah?" I force my lips up in a pleasant arc, teeth showing. I see it in his eyes. It didn't work. I hold my breath again.

"It . . . I met her at a party one night. End of senior year. We were all drinking, celebrating. I was getting a full ride to UCLA; we were all graduating. Everyone had something to celebrate."

I'm no longer smiling. I just want him to get around to saying whatever he brought me here to say. He knew my mom was a drunk, a junkie. What? Did she do something crazy that night?

"Did she ever mention it?"

My brows pinch together and I know I'm glaring. I move my head side to side a couple times before I speak. "With all due respect, Mr. Ross, my mom wasn't big on story time. She spent most of my life inebriated and fighting with my father. Both were meager excuses for parents. So whatever my mom did in high school, I'm sure it wasn't something she cared to relive or share with a son she didn't seem to want."

"Didn't seem to . . ." His eyes brim and he lowers them to stare at his hands folded on the table and clears his throat. "Uh, I don't think Mr. Keller is your . . . uh . . . father."

My vision tunnels. Ever's sharp intake of breath echoes in my ear. I understand his words perfectly, but my brain refuses to comprehend their meaning.

"You think? Or you know?"

He shakes his head firmly. "I don't know anything for sure."

"But there's something to know?" My amplified tone draws looks from nearby tables. I take in the head swivels in my periphery and try to lower my voice. "What are you saying?"

The waiter appears again, and the look on his face says he knows he's interrupting. "Shall I give you more time?"

"Please." Ross nods to dismiss him without taking his eyes off mine.

Ever gives him a timid smile as he silently retreats.

I track all this without taking my eyes off the man across the table. A man who knows my mom. And me? "You don't have his last name. I assumed he was your . . . that you knew he wasn't your real father."

"I did have his name until I changed it. To my mother's maiden name. Mr. Ross—"

"Jason, please. Call me Jason." His eyes sag at the corners—his mouth, too. The man is aging before my eyes.

The hamster wheel in my brain is twirling at warp speed, but I can't form words.

Ever speaks up. "Jason, maybe you can start at the beginning. Fill in some blanks for us. This whole conversation is causing a lot of alarms to go off in our heads." My sweet girl really is going to make a kick-ass psychologist.

"Sure. Sure. I'm sorry. I'm not trying to be cryptic and I don't want to alarm either of you. I just . . . think before I do, I should cut to the chase. I think, Julian, I think I might be your real father."

Ever tightens her grasp on my hand under the table while her other hand flies to her mouth on a sharp intake of breath. I fleetingly wonder how she's managed to inhale when the air is being sucked out of the room. Jason Ross grows tiny before me as my vision darkens at the edges.

I grip my temples between the thumb and fingers of my free hand, bowing my head over the table. "What?" It comes out barely a whisper and aimed at the table my elbow is bracing to hold my head up.

His hand reaches out, touches my forearm.

I jerk back, clanging the tableware. More heads turn. I scoot my chair back, intending to leave. Ever places the napkin from her lap on the table and scoots her chair back, lacing her fingers with mine. I turn my head and look at her face. *Ever.* She slow blinks her stormy eyes at me, just once, and nods her head. *Solidarity.* It's what I need to turn back to him, face him and say, "I'm sorry. I need to—"

"Julian, please. Don't go. I don't mean to ambush you here. I'm as shocked as you are. But I couldn't—when I learned who you were—when I thought maybe—I didn't want to waste any more time. Will you please stay? Both of you?" He turns his full gaze on Ever, pleading. *Smart.* She's the way to me and he knows it. "Please?"

She looks at me for the answer, but I can tell she wants me to agree.

I nod once and scoot my chair back up to the table.

The relief is clear on his face. He smiles at both of us alternately. "Can we order some food? Just talk?"

I'm not sure how I'll eat anything right now, but I obligingly look at the menu.

The third item down under entrées is chicken broccoli alfredo. Ever and I glance at each other and smile. It's like the universe knew we'd need comfort food for this. The waiter appears from nowhere and quietly takes our order. When Ever and I order the same dish, Jason tells the waiter to make it three with a grin he bestows on all three of us, one that trips my heart rate because now it looks so familiar.

Surprisingly, we devour our meals. It's delicious. It probably helped that we made conscious small talk while we ate. As the waiter clears our plates, I decide to go all in. "I was born Jayce Julian Keller. When I was eighteen I changed my name to Julian McKay—Brandi's maiden name. When I obtained a copy of my birth certificate to legally change my name, there was no father's name listed. I never thought twice about it."

"I've always gone by Jase. She would've known me as Jase." His eyes fill again, as they've done repeatedly throughout the conversation. "We didn't exactly know each other, though. We just . . ." He rubs the side of his index finger across his forehead. "God, I'm not proud of this. We just hooked up."

"How often?" My cheeks flame as I ask, but I can't help myself.

He's already shaking his head. "Once. That night. I never saw her again after that night. She never tried to contact me. My parents lived there for several years after I left for college. She could've tried." He shakes his head as one tear rushes down his cheek. He brushes it away. "Why didn't she try?"

The question seems rhetorical, so I don't answer.

"Mr. Ross—Jason. Maybe it's not what you think. You don't know. Yes, the timing is right, but everything else is just Lifetime movie-level coincidence." His smile looks so sad I almost feel bad for the guy. I truly don't know what I think or feel except a little numb and detached.

"Only one way to find out. Would you be willing to take a paternity test with me? But Julian?" I raise my brows in answer, so he continues. "I know. You look just like my father. We both do."

"People said I looked like her, but I don't look anything like Todd."

"And your natural athleticism? Even though you never played sports." One corner of his mouth lifts, showcasing a dimple. One just like mine.

I think back to how much I loved hanging with Hal on the Little League field. Again, a weird coincidence. Genetics don't predispose you to be drawn to locations, activities, right?

"Yeah, I'll take the test. How long does it take to get results?"

"I think we'll pay to put a rush on it." The half smile and dimple again.

Chapter 39

EVERLY

My husband is the son of a major league baseball hall of famer, not a trailer park abusive degenerate. It's wild but honestly tracks. Way more than the guy I met at gunpoint at a small-town carnival. His mom may have even tried to name him after who she thought or suspected his real father was—though we may never know. I don't know if he'll ever see her again to ask. Maybe he doesn't need to. Jason "Jase" Ross, retired Angels legend and head coach of their minor league team, the Sun Rays, is more than willing to share his family with Julian and tries to almost daily. He keeps inviting him to things, including him. Julian has yet to fully embrace his new *family*, but I can tell he's warming up to the idea.

Thanksgiving may have been the turning point. I asked all our friends to come to our house the week before for Friendsgiving, since everyone would likely have family plans for the actual holiday. Once they all left and it was just the two of us—Allie and Ashley flew back east to see some of Luke's extended family—he brought it up on his own.

"Jase wants us to come over tomorrow. Meet the whole family."

I set my pen down on the notebook I was brainstorming in and turn to face him as he sits next to me on the couch. "The whole family, huh?"

"Yep. His wife, Shanna, their three kids, maybe his parents. It's a lot." His elbows rest loosely on his knees, belying the tension I know courses through him.

"What's your gut tell you?" Even though I'm watching him closely, I yelp when he snags me off my seat and pulls me into his lap.

"To stay here with my hot wife. Naked."

I straddle his lap, curling my fingers around the nape of his neck as he presses his face between my breasts. I let his breath warm the skin through my shirt and close my eyes, scraping my fingernails along his scalp until he moans. "Mmm."

"Or"—I pull back to look at him, my eyes flickering between his—"we could stop by with a set time to leave and then come home and get naked."

"What's our excuse to leave? I'm guessing you're not suggesting we tell them we have plans to get naked."

"Yeah, what's our excuse? It's gotta be a good one and I don't want to lie."

"Me either."

"Ooh, I know. The crisis center I interned at freshman year does a meal thing every Thanksgiving. We need to help."

His eyebrows pinch together, making an eleven between them.

"No, I'm serious. They always need help. If we're having a good time, we don't have to leave."

"Okay, I'm in. I love that." He kisses me soundly, picks me up off his lap and sets me back down where he snagged me from. It's still so damn hot that my man so effortlessly lifts me. He stands, rubbing his hands along his pecs restlessly. "I'm going to dip into the studio, grab a workout."

"Want company?" I close my notebook, preparing to join him.

"No, if you have work to do, go ahead." He waves a hand at me and turns to leave.

"Husband?"

He stops, pivots and dips his chin to his chest, blinking at me slow. "Yes, my wife?"

My cheeks heat. I'll never tire of hearing that. *His wife.* "Let's work out together. I'm betting it's just the stress reliever we need."

"And by *we* you mean *me*."

I just shrug and stand, take his hand and pull him toward the door.

As workouts go, this one was scorching. Auz and Callie will be sorry they missed the opportunity for content, because this man of mine can make just about anything hot. Damn, he's fucking beautiful. My sports bra is soaked with sweat. My limbs are quivering. Julian, while slicked with sweat, doesn't look winded in the least. His muscles bulge, veins pop and the hair at his nape glistens with moisture. Yet he calmly wipes down the equipment and puts things where they go while I sit on the bench, suck air into my lungs and chug water while I wait for my heartbeat to return to normal.

"Sauna?" He's standing by the doorway of the weight room when I raise my eyes to his, lungs still heaving, water bottle dangling between my knees.

I nod, lips parted.

"Need a boost?" His eyes crinkle at the corners. He's enjoying this way too much.

I flip him off as I stand on shaky legs and move toward the door.

"Was that an invitation?"

I shrug one shoulder and crook my brow as I amble through the door he holds open for me. Just as I make my way past the exit, he snakes his arm around my ribs and snatches me off my feet, cupping his other arm under my knees. I drop mine on his shoulders, curl them around his neck and get lost in his ocean eyes. He's more relaxed now after the grueling workout, his features calm. He's playful. My heart swells in my chest with relief. This beautiful creature deserves so much good, and I wish that for him with everything inside me.

That exercising is his stress reliever proves to me he was never a product of his environment. Whether he recognizes it or not, he sought other options than self-medicating with drugs and alcohol or fits of rage. He's more like the father he didn't know than he realizes. It's what I've always seen in him—since that first day in Fit watching him be so patient with his older clients and so diplomatic with his *cougar* clients. His heart is bigger than any muscle he'll ever build.

He sets me on my feet in front of the sauna door and pulls my sports bra over my head. I glance behind me like I'm checking if we're alone, even though I know Allie, Ashley and not even one employee is on the property. Going commando in the sauna will always feel taboo, but somehow that makes it better. By the grin on Julian's face, he's thinking it too but loves our partners-in-crime ritual.

Lying in bed later, I listen to the quiet thud of his heart, tracing his tattoo with my finger while he stares at the ceiling. We don't talk. I let him mull over how everything might go tomorrow. I know it's unnerving him. I know he overthinks everything—especially when it comes to letting people in, possibly setting himself up to be hurt. I also know this family won't hurt him. I don't know them any better than he does, but sometimes you can just tell people are good to their core just by being around them. That's what Jason Ross is—good to his core. I don't say it out loud, but I'm so happy this man I love more than anything will have this kind of family in his life. To feel like he comes from a real family. I'm his family. So is Allie and Luke. Even our friends. But for him to feel like he came from something better than what he thought? I want that for him. So I say nothing and let him work it all out in his head so he can feel as calm as possible before we walk in there tomorrow. I already know it's going to be great.

Chapter 40

JULIAN

"Hi, Julian, Ever." A teenage girl, probably around sixteen, opens the door of the Spanish-style home. "Come in. I'm Shaylee." The Ross home is understated and classic, yet boasts modern upgrades, evident in the entryway alone. The neighborhood gives affluent but down-to-earth. Ever gushed about it as we drove in. *The best of both worlds.* My girl really does love the beach. If we'd never broken up, she may have never discovered just how much.

"My dad's—our—um—" Her face blooms bright red under her tan. "He's in the backyard. This way." She spins, and we follow her through a dining area with a table set for seven. Just the immediate family and us.

My shoulders relax and my stomach unclenches.

We step into a modernized kitchen full of sounds and smells, with a petite pretty brunette in full motion wearing a tank top and shorts covered by an apron with a turkey on it. Ross wasn't kidding when he told us to dress casually. Ever still insisted on wearing a sundress, but I opted for shorts and a T-shirt. Southern California weather is giving summer even though it's November, and I'm not mad about it. I love warm weather. So does Ever—mostly because it means she can surf without her feet turning blue.

The woman wipes her hands on a towel, also with a turkey on it, and bounces over to us on bare feet. "Hi, I'm Shanna, Jase's wife. You met Shaylee. Jase is out back with the boys." She shakes our hands in turn as she says all this. It's firm but soft, and she clasps the back of our hands with her other as she does. Moving to French doors that open onto a covered patio overlooking an immaculate backyard that expands to a seaside view beyond, the smell of meat on a grill hits me first. "Jase, they're here," she calls out to the empty space just as three bodies charge from around the corner of the house onto the grass.

"Dad, go long," one dark-headed body yells as the other two, Jason and a younger carbon copy of him, sprint across the lawn, arms extended. The one that yelled throws a perfect spiraled football across the expanse of green while the other two tangle to catch it. At the last minute, the younger one snakes his hand between his dad's two and slaps the football to the ground.

"Gotta be better than that, old man." Jason grabs the kid in a headlock and tackles him to the ground.

"Jamie," Shanna calls to the one who threw the football, "come meet Julian and Ever."

The young man that jogs over to us looks to be in his late teens or early twenties and looks just like his dad—kinda like me. He's my height. His hair is brown but lighter than mine and curly, but his eyes are ice blue, also lighter than mine. More like his mom's. He's grinning wide, showing straight white teeth and extends his hand to me, then Ever. "Hey, Julian. Ever. Nice to meet you. I'm James. Or Jamie."

"James is our oldest," Shanna explains, then gestures toward the yard. "That pile on the lawn is our middle, Spencer." He back somersaults and stands up, then reaches a hand down to his dad and hauls him to his feet. They make their way over to us, shoving each other back and forth. "Are you two done showing off?"

"He started it," Jason says with a last shove to Spencer's shoulder. He reaches out and hugs Ever first, then me.

Caught by surprise, we hug him back one-handed because we're holding each other's.

"Sorry about that. Sometimes I have to remind them I'm still young enough to handle them."

"Don't say them. I wasn't in that," Jamie spouts, pointing toward the lawn.

"Hi, I'm Spence." He shoves his hand toward us, grinning and unapologetic. I like him already. He's just as tall as us but leaner. He drapes his arm over Shaylee's shoulders. "I see you already met the oops."

She punches him in the ribs, and not softly if his grunt is any indication.

"Shut up, asshole. You two were the experiments. I get the professionals."

He leaves his arm around her and kisses her temple. "If you say so."

Shanna chimes in. "Maybe we could offer our guests some drinks before we horrify them with our sick banter."

"I got it. Julian, come check out the fridge and pick something." Jamie tosses his head toward the outdoor kitchen, so I start to follow.

I turn to look at Ever and ask what she wants.

"I'll have whatever you're having." She smiles and answers before I can ask the question.

It's exactly what I need to ground me—her smile, her presence, our connectedness. I smile back and follow Jamie to the fridge and pick two light beers from the plethora of drinks. I return just as Shaylee hooks her arm through Ever's and turns her toward the French doors.

"C'mon, Ever. Let me give you the tour."

Ever looks over her shoulder and finds my eyes.

I wink at her so she knows I'm good and take a seat at the outdoor dining table with the rest of the Ross family. Shanna wasn't kidding about the *sick banter.* The Ross family are hysterically sarcastic but undeniably affectionate. I've not seen many family dynamics in my life—or any, really—but theirs is one to behold. It's like a dirty Hallmark card. Warm and fuzzy, hilarious and enchanting. I find them intoxicating—like I can't get enough. Like I'm cozy at home and on an exhilarating vacation all at once.

When Ever and Shaylee return from the tour, they join us at the table and seamlessly blend into the conversation in progress. Shanna leaves to check something in the kitchen and Jason gets up to check the meat on the grill, all while the conversation flows. Turns out the Ross family doesn't like traditional Thanksgiving food. Jason is slow-cooking chicken and ribs on his grill and Shanna's preparing all the side dishes that go with it—none being common holiday fare. This, too, captivates me. They're not your traditional family, yet they are. I'm so caught up in it all, I haven't once thought to breathe or felt anything but relaxed.

Jason stands up and announces, "I've got about thirty minutes left on the meat. Julian, care to take a walk with me on the beach?"

I nod and push my chair back from the table. Before I stand I look at Ever, who squeezes my hand. I kiss her cheek and follow Jason to the gate at the back of his yard.

He calls back, "Boys, help your mom. Shay, you get to entertain Ever."

"We got you, Dad."

"Don't be late, Jase. Or I'll let these boys take the meat off the grill." Shanna is already through the doors back inside before he can respond.

"She runs a tight ship." He chuckles and holds his hand out for me to precede him on the beach path.

The expanse of sand is mostly deserted except for a group playing football. We walk barefooted near the shore, having ditched our shoes at his gate. Jason doesn't mince words and dives right in. I'm expecting it, but still his frankness impresses me. "You don't seem like one for deep talks and sharing, but I just wanted to check in. See how you're feeling about being here, meeting everyone."

"I appreciate that." My hands are tucked into the pockets of my shorts and I glance sideways into his face as we walk. "I, uh, I'm trying to be better about that. Talking about things." I give a little laugh and go for it. "Therapy helps."

"Did Ever get you to go to therapy?"

"No. I've had one I see off and on for years. Allie might've been the first to suggest it."

"She's quite the lady."

"She is." When I'd normally let that be my whole response, I add, "I'm very lucky to have met her. I guess I really owe all of this . . . my success to her."

"No, son, you don't. But I get why you'd say that."

Him calling me son puts a lump in my throat, but I don't freak out. I just swallow the golf ball and focus on his words.

"She gave you the opportunities. What you did with them is on you. You're incredible, Julian." He stops walking and faces me, so I stop and face him, too. "I hope you don't mind, and I don't mean to make you uncomfortable, but I need to . . . I want you to know something. And I hope you'll hear me out." He waits, watching me, like he wants permission to continue. So I give him a nod, look him in the eyes—eyes like mine—and try not to fidget with the seam in my pocket. He takes a deep breath and exhales it slowly.

With the waves crashing behind him and the seagull cries ringing in my ears, he begins.

"I love you. You're my son. You're part of me, part of my family. I hate that I didn't know about you all these years." His eyes fill, which has pressure building behind mine. I blink to try to relieve it. "I want to be mad at her, Brandi. I do. And in some ways I am. Some people think addiction is a choice, some a disease. I think everyone is different and the truth might be somewhere in the middle. I want to believe that she knew you were mine and that's why she named you Jayce. We may never know the real circumstances. But when I think about what your life was like compared to the one I could've given you, it breaks me. I'm so sorry, Julian. I can't change it. It's like what I said about Allie. We have this opportunity now. It's up to us what we do with it. And I hope you'll let me be your family—all of us. Because the moment I suspected, the moment I saw you and knew, I loved you."

I hang my head because the dam's gonna break if I keep looking at him.

"You're so incredibly strong. The man you've made of yourself despite what you grew up in is a testament to that. You're a Ross even if you don't realize it. We're strong, determined . . . and incredibly athletic, obviously." He chuckles on that last remark, which makes me chuckle and meet his eyes again—eyes that are swimming and spilling down his cheeks. He shrugs. "But we're sensitive, too."

I swipe at an escaped tear and try to blink the rest away.

"Would you give us a chance to be your family? Give me a chance?"

"I can do that." I smile and shove my hand back into my pocket because I don't know what else to do with it.

Jase's shoulders begin to shake with emotion, and he grips my shoulder like a lifeline before he pulls me to him in a bear hug. I don't know what to do with this kind of male attention—especially demonstrative fatherly attention. I hesitate for a moment before I wrap my arms loosely around his back and pat him awkwardly. Once I do, he squeezes me even tighter.

"I love you, son."

His words are quiet compared to the roar of the ocean, but I hear them, and more, I feel them. The dam breaks. My breath hitches and I can't stop the shaking. My fingers clench the fabric of his shirt. I try to clear my throat, but it comes out a sob.

"Thank you for giving me a chance." His voice breaks and he's clapping me on the back. Then he's easing back, captures my head in his hands and bumps his forehead lightly to mine. Gripping the sides of my neck, he repeats, "I love you, son. I'm so proud of you. So proud you're mine." He swipes his thumbs across my cheeks at the wetness that won't stop. "C'mon. Prepare to eat the best ribs you've ever tasted." Hanging his arm around my shoulders, we walk back the way we came.

I stuff my hands back in my pockets and let the cool wind dry my tears. I don't speak for fear of another dam break, but the warmth in my chest, foreign as it is, expands with every step.

The ribs *are* the best I've ever tasted. Everything is mouthwatering. They even offered donut holes for dessert especially for me. "Ever told us you don't really like sweets but you're a sucker for donuts, so we had to get some."

Shanna sets a plate of cookies, cheesecake bites and donut holes in the center of the table. Ever and I insist they let us help clear dinner and clean up, which is another comic display of how families that love each other do things. The insults alone make it a competitive sport. Ever blends right in because, as she claims, her family speaks fluent sarcasm. It quickly becomes a guys versus girls scenario, which would've escalated into a full-blown water fight if Shanna hadn't scolded everyone not to flood her kitchen.

After dinner, we play liars' dice, their family tradition—they teach me and Ever how to play and we play for hours with Ever and Shaylee ultimately winning the most games. When Ever stifles her third yawn, I politely suggest that we should call it a night. I could tell Jason didn't want it to end. I kinda didn't either but . . . baby steps.

On the drive home, before we even leave the driveway, Ever grabs my hand and announces, "I love them."

Kissing the back of her hand, I feel my smile in every muscle in my face when I reply, "Me too."

Chapter 41

EVERLY

Two Years Later

"My little brainiac, the psychologist. Congratulations, my love. I'm so proud of you." Julian kisses me so sweetly, picks me up and spins me around. The foyer is crowded with fellow graduates and their family members, but he doesn't care. I laugh and try not to kick those nearby as we twirl.

"Where is everyone?" My head swivels as my feet land on the floor.

"Rushing to the restaurant. So are we, if I can navigate this traffic." He takes my hand and leads us through the throng of people toward the door.

Jase insisted on hosting a simple graduation lunch in my honor when I refused the huge party Allie and Luke wanted to throw. Now that I'm his official team psychologist, or I will be now that I have my degree in hand, he said, as my boss, it was an order. He picked the same restaurant he took us to that first day he told Julian who he was.

It's become one of our favorites.

Walking in, cheers erupt in the private room. All my favorite people in one place—except my mom and Via and Ryan. I blink away the tears that try to fall, but one escapes. I'm not sure why butterflies have taken flight in my stomach, but they're currently trying to fly out of my chest. The excitement mimics low-level panic. I rest my hand on my stomach to calm the flutters and accept all the hugs and congratulations, take my seat next to Julian and just breathe amid the swirl of conversation. When the waiter comes around to take our order, I already know even though I haven't looked at the menu. It's gotta be the chicken broccoli alfredo.

As I tell her my order, Julian's head swivels to look at me. I know he's surprised. It's a celebration, not a stressful event. Still he knows exactly what it means. It's been our comfort dish almost since day one. Squeezing my thigh under the table, he places a kiss on my temple, then orders the Chilean sea bass—our other favorite on the menu since we started coming here two years ago.

I should feel ecstatic right now, but I'm way off. Probably over-whelmed. Despite being a semi-well-known mental performance coach, I don't love being the center of attention. I still refuse to handle my own social media. Thank God for Callie's team or I wouldn't have a social presence at all. I chalk up my anxiety to the focused attention and take some covert deep breaths. I then try to zero in on the con-versations around me, commenting and laughing appropriately.

Once our plates are placed in front of us, my stomach grumbles at the smell of my comfort dish. After everyone is served, I roll noodles onto my fork and take a healthy bite of creamy sauce, meat and veg-etable just as a whiff of Julian's sea bass hits my nose. I swallow the bite, but it immediately tries to come back up. Pushing away from the table, I make it out of the room, through the restroom door and into the stall before my stomach rejects the food. *Shit!* I rinse my mouth in the sink and stare at my wan reflection. *Shit!* I press a palm against my tender breasts and mentally calculate my last period. *Shiiiiit!*

Stepping out into the dimly lit corridor, I come face-to-face with Julian leaning against the wall across from the ladies' restroom.

With his arms folded loosely across his chest and his eyes soft on mine, he greets me calmly. "Hi, sweet girl."

"You know." I swipe the back of my hand across my lips.

"I'm guessing." He shrugs, holding his arms out to me now. "You okay?"

"I . . ." I push a breath through pursed lips. "I think so. I . . ." Bursting into tears, I cover my face with my hands just as his arms wrap around me.

"Shh. It's okay. You're okay, babe. I got you."

"You sure about that?" I try to laugh, but it comes out a sob. "The timing sucks." I sniff, burying my face between his pecs. His baritone chuckle soothes me. I press my ear tighter to his chest and let its echo vibrate my cheek.

"It's perfect. You're perfect."

"Thank you for saying that." I sniff again and swipe my fist down my cheek.

"If everyone waited for the exact right time to have a baby, there'd be . . . a lot less babies," he finishes lamely, chuckling at his awkward attempt at a pep talk. "Okay, so clearly you're the motivational speaker of the two of us. But, Ever, we're going to be fine. Great, even. And I know four people who are going to flip when they find out."

"Speaking of, how am I supposed to go back out there and pretend nothing's up?"

"I say we go give the room something else to celebrate."

"Right now? What if . . . it happens again?" My breath comes out shaky as I lean my head back to look at him, gauge his real mood beyond the comforting platitudes.

"It won't. It can't." He looks steady, calm as he tucks a strand of hair behind my ear, kisses me softly on the lips and nods once like saying it out loud makes it so. "But we can wait—say whatever you want. Just not sure what they'll believe."

His confidence permeates my worry and squashes it. I nod.

"Okay?" He grins like a little kid.

I swallow and nod again.

Stepping back into our private party room, every head turns our way as the din of conversation lulls.

Julian pulls me in closer to his side and clears his throat. "Guys, it seems Ever wants to get all the celebrating done at once. She's . . . we're"—his Adam's apple bobs in his throat—"having a baby."

Erupting applause thunders through the room just as the waiter steps around us in the doorway. Julian stops her and asks if she can take away the sea bass and bring him a cup of the soup of the day despite the Southern California heat. To me, he whispers, "It's chicken and wild rice, nice and mellow. I'll eat your alfredo."

My eyes prick with tears again at his thoughtful gesture. *Okay, pregnant hormones: check.*

Stopping her as she proceeds to check on the other guests, he adds, "Can we also get some champagne for the room and a ginger ale for my wife?"

She nods and tells the room at large that she'll be right back.

Allie cries. So does Jason. Throughout the rest of the meal, Jason and Shanna share stories of her three pregnancies as well as how twins run in his family. Ever was already pale from the bout of queasiness. That disclosure drops her color another shade.

"Jase, don't scare the girl. Geez. Ever, don't listen to him." Shanna smacks his arm.

Allie chimes in. "I was a twin, remember? I mean, there's no blood tie, but twins can be fun. A built-in best friend."

"Or twice as much of . . . everything," I reply somberly.

Julian can tell the day is overwhelming me. As soon as politely possible, he makes our excuses and takes me home, draws me a bath and happily joins me when I insist. An overwhelming day maybe, but a perfect ending with my perfect man.

Chapter 42

JULIAN

Six-ish Months Later

"I swear you're psychic," I mock whisper to Jason as he sways back and forth, cradling our daughter in his arms. His only response is a quiet chuckle. He doesn't even look up from the rosy face of Kylee Sutton McKay, not even a full day old. My arms are full of an identical rosy newborn, her brother, Davis Jayce, except my eyes are on the sleeping beauty in the bed next to where I stand. I'm more in awe and in love with her than I ever thought possible. I swipe the rogue tear that escapes my brimming eyes and return my hand to the swaddled infant.

"Maybe I manifested," he concedes, to which I chuckle.

Ever's eyes flutter open and her voice croaks, "Hi, Julie."

"Hi, pretty girl." Another tear falls as I smile at her sleepy face.

Jase steps to the edge of the bed and places Kylee in Ever's waiting arms. "I'll just go check on the crowd in the waiting room.

"Thanks, Jase. I'll come out in a minute—talk to everyone."

"Take your time. You're right where you need to be." The door whooshes closed behind him.

"You did so good, baby. They're perfect. You're perfect. How ya feeling?"

She nods before she tries her voice again. "Good. Tired. Thirsty." She brushes her fingers along Kylee's cheek and sips from the straw I put to her lips.

"Your mom was just in here. She cried when I told her you named Kylee for your dad."

Ever's eyes fill with tears as she nods again. One races down her cheek, shining in the dim light. "He'd . . ." She sniffs as more tears fall and nods in lieu of trying to talk.

"I know, babe. He would." I assume the rest of her sentence and agree. "Allie cried too about using her maiden name for Kylee's middle name."

She smiles and nods again with a little laugh.

"How's Davis?" She looks up, stretching her neck to peek as I dip down to give her a better view.

"Asleep. Wanna switch?"

"It's okay. Let him sleep."

"Babe, you did so good. They said they're probably discharging you today. All of you. The babies are perfect."

It takes another five hours before I'm settling Ever into our bed with a baby nestled in each arm. She insists on holding them both, so I agree if I can hold her. Sliding in behind her with my back against the cushioned headboard, I rest my cheek on the top of her silky head.

She just showered and dried her hair, so the scent of sunshine swirls around my nose.

"I lied. When I told you that making love to you will forever be my favorite feeling." I feel her laugh more than hear it. "This will forever be my new favorite feeling."

"It may be mine, too. But give me six weeks and I may challenge that."

Chuckling, I kiss her temple. "God, I love you, sassy girl. So much."

"I love you too, Julie. Thanks for . . . this life—our life."

"Mmm, thank you, sweet wife. We're just getting started."

"Indeed."

Epilogue

JULIAN

"Hey, Doc."

"Hi, Julian. And who's this little assistant you've got?"

"This is my son, Davis. Although he's not much of an assistant, as you can see. He sleeps on the job a lot."

Her smile is soft, like her laugh. "How's being a dad?"

"Incredible. But it's like you said. It's bringing up a lot of stuff from my childhood." The screen blurs as my mind goes reflective. "Mostly how I don't get how someone—a parent—could treat their child the way mine treated me." I look down and focus on my two-month-old son, his image growing blurry as my eyes swim with emotion. "I'd burn this world down to protect him, both of them. I thought I'd never love anyone as much as I love Ever. I can't describe . . . I . . . being their dad makes me want to be better every day." I look back up at the Zoom screen, blinking to rein in the tears. Sniffling, I add, "Ugh, sorry. Ever's supposed to be the one with all the post-pregnancy hormones, and I swear I'm the one that's turned into a waterfall."

Davis stirs in my arms, so I press my lips to his forehead and he settles back down. It's their naptime but he wouldn't stay asleep, so I took him out of the nursery so he wouldn't wake Kylee. Already it seems Davis's sleep habits mimic mine and Kylee's are more like her mom's.

"You look like a natural, Julian. I think fatherhood agrees with you."

"Thanks, Doc. I, uh, did what you suggested and wrote the letters I'll never send. Went a little extra and burned them afterwards."

"To Todd and Brandi?" When I nod at the screen, she asks, "And how did it feel to get all that off your chest?"

"Not much different than before, to be honest. But gradually over the next few weeks, I noticed a shift."

She waits quietly on the other side of the monitor, pen poised above her notepad, the soft smile in place.

"As I navigated being a new dad these past weeks, I became hyper-aware of how lucky I am to have Jason as an example, which brought me around to how they must not have had good examples in their lives." I shrug my shoulders, gently so I don't wake Davis.

Claire's voice drops an octave, probably given the swaddled bundle in my arms. "Wow, Julian. That's huge. Incredible insight. Really. Proud of you."

My lips slant to the side as my brows inch up on my forehead. "Well, I can't say I totally forgive them, but I can find small amounts of grace when I think of them as little kids that maybe didn't get any better than what they gave me."

"Baby steps. And remember, forgiveness isn't even about them. It's for you."

"I'm aware. 'It's like drinking poison and expecting the other person to die.' I was listening."

"Unforgiveness, yes. Forgiving them just sets you free from the anger and bitterness. It helps us move on."

"I'm getting there. For them." I lift my son toward the display. "I'm committed to the work." I nod at her image. "I don't want to pass that on—the anger—to them. I only want them to know love."

"Julian, you know you can't protect them from every negative life experience. I don't want you to set yourself up for unrealistic parenting goals here. Every parent—most parents—want to protect their children from the ugliness of the world, but that's not how it works."

I snuggle him closer to me and count my breaths. "I'm well aware, Doc." I hear the front door close and keys settle on the entryway table. *Ever.* My heart thuds a little harder, a little louder in my chest. My pulse quickens.

Davis tunes into the change in my energy and squirms.

I exhale a long slow breath through pursed lips and raise my eyes back to Claire, bounce my arms a little until he settles again. "It's why I'm doing the work, so I can be the best dad and husband I possibly can. They deserve that."

"Julian, so do you."

I look back down at my son, my eyes swimming again. *Is this going to be my new normal?* I blink them away and nod. "I do." I press my lips to his forehead again, inhale his scent and rub my lips against his fuzzy head.

"Let's leave it here and pick this up at our next session. You're doing great, Julian."

"Thanks, Claire. For everything."

"You did the work. I just—"

"Listened. I know. Thanks for listening."

"Of course. See you next time. Bye, Davis." She whispers the last part, then the screen goes blank.

Rising out of the chair, I move toward the door and freeze. Ever leans on the jamb.

"Hi, husband." My mouth goes dry looking at her.

"Hi, wife. How'd the appointment go?"

"Clean bill of health. 'Everything is healing well, and you're good to resume all normal activities, including exercise and sexual intercourse, as you feel ready.' So really the question is, do I feel ready?" She takes the baby out of my arms, pads to the nursery and lays him down in his crib. Tiptoeing back out, she pulls the door almost closed, turns, snakes her arms around my waist and tilts her head back to meet my eyes. Hers flash with unmistakable playfulness.

"Do tell, sweet wife, are you ready?" With one arm curled around her lower back, I pull her to me. With the other, I tuck a strand of loose hair behind her ear, rubbing the smooth lobe between my thumb and finger.

She closes her eyes and leans into my touch. "So ready." She presses her lips to mine and I inhale deeply.

My sunshine girl, but now she smells like sunshine and sea and baby, and it's a scent that wants to bring me to my knees to worship this creature I'm lucky enough to call mine.

"Gonna test your favorite feeling, Julie, right now. Are you ready?" She quirks one tawny brow at me.

I lift her off the ground, her legs wrapping around me. "I am," I say against her lips as I carry her to our bedroom and lay her on the bed, following her down, stretching out beside her.

Fussing squawks from the baby monitor on the nightstand as my hand grasps one full breast. As the sound fills the room, moisture soaks her shirt. "Ugh, welcome to the new age of cock blocking." She throws an arm over her eyes and huffs out a breath, giggling.

I drop my forehead on her chest and join her mirth.

"Is it both or just one?" I glance up at the monitor and see both squirming. "I'll get a bottle."

"Okay, I've got the boob." We roll off the bed and head back the way we came. "You think we'll ever have sex again?" She throws the question over her shoulder as she precedes me down the hall.

"God, I hope so. I mean they must find a way or there'd be a lot of only children, right?"

"Fair point."

"Ever?"

She stops on her way into the nursery, hand on the door handle. "Julie." She blinks her smoky eyes at me, waiting, hair mussed, face sans makeup and shirt sporting a circle of wetness over each breast.

"You've never looked more beautiful."

Thanks and Blame

First and foremost, my real-life green flag husband.

The man who makes this full-time writing dream possible and, despite not being bookish in the least, finds a thousand ways to support me anyway. From pulling the car over for "the lighting is good here" content shots, to liking my bazillion social posts, to shamelessly promoting my books to coworkers and friends — you are the steady behind every page. I love you more than fictional men. (Most days.)

To my inner circle — the hype team I did not earn but somehow get to keep. Thanks for letting me ramble on about shit that probably makes no sense but you listen anyway, and even ask questions like it does. So thanks. I love you.

Lara, who enthusiastically pimps me out to the famous authors she meets at signings. My beta readers and my Bookstagram and BookTok besties who read, share, review, scream, and hype me like it's your full-time job. Ava, Keelie, Carina, Shalon, Jenn, Amilia — you are the real MVPs. Not sure what I did to deserve you. But I hope I figure it out so I can keep doing it.

To the editing team at Motif, thank you for turning rough drafts into something that looks intentional. You make me better every single time.

Dakota, my cover designer — respectfully, damn. You're good.

To every single ARC reader who took a chance on an indie debut series — and especially those of you who stayed through book three — you are magic. I love your feral asses more than you know.

If I forgot anyone, blame the deadlines. The gratitude is real even when my brain is chaos.

Thank you for helping me build this forever.

— Carol

ps: If this book wrecked you in any way, **please consider leaving a review**. Emotional restitution is appreciated. If Ever and Julie stayed with you, a review helps them stay with someone else.

About the Author

C.M. Wyllie is a retired stay-at-home mom and breast cancer survivor who turned her lifelong dream of writing into a full-time career—fueled by iced coffee, stubborn determination, and a love of storytelling. She's jumped from two raw, laugh-out-loud nonfiction books on her cancer journey to a mischievous children's book series about a grumpy dog and his found family, and now writes new adult romance—where heartbreak meets healing and love always gets another shot.

Her stories have just enough spice to heat things up and keep you wanting more. She writes for hopeless romantics who root for love to stumble, fall, get back up, and find their happily ever after.

Readers can subscribe to her newsletter for early access to new releases, cover reveals, character art, ARC signups, and bonus content — sometimes including freebies like stickers and behind-the-scenes chaos. Go to https://www.wylliegirl.com/subscribe for a bonus chapter and prequel.

When C.M. isn't writing, she's with her husband or adult kids—ideally both—obsessing over their pets and chasing sunsets to warm places, preferably near a beach.

286

9 781959 583110